THE MIRRORED PALACE

The Mirrored Palace

A historical novel
by

DAVID RICH

Adelaide Books
New York / Lisbon
2020

THE MIRRORED PALACE

A historical novel

By David Rich

Published by Adelaide Books, New York / Lisbon
adelaidebooks.org

Editor-in-Chief
Stevan V. Nikolic

For any information, please address Adelaide Books

at info@adelaidebooks.org

or write to:

Adelaide Books
244 Fifth Ave. Suite D27
New York, NY, 10001

ISBN: 978-1-953510-77-8

Printed in the United States of America

In memory of Mitchell Rubens and Barry O'Rourke

"Words are easy, like the wind;

Faithful friends are hard to find."

“As palace mirror’d in the stream,
as vapour mingled with the skies,
So weaves the brain of mortal man
the tangled web of Truth and Lies.”

From Burton’s “The Kasidah of Haji Abu el-Yezdi”

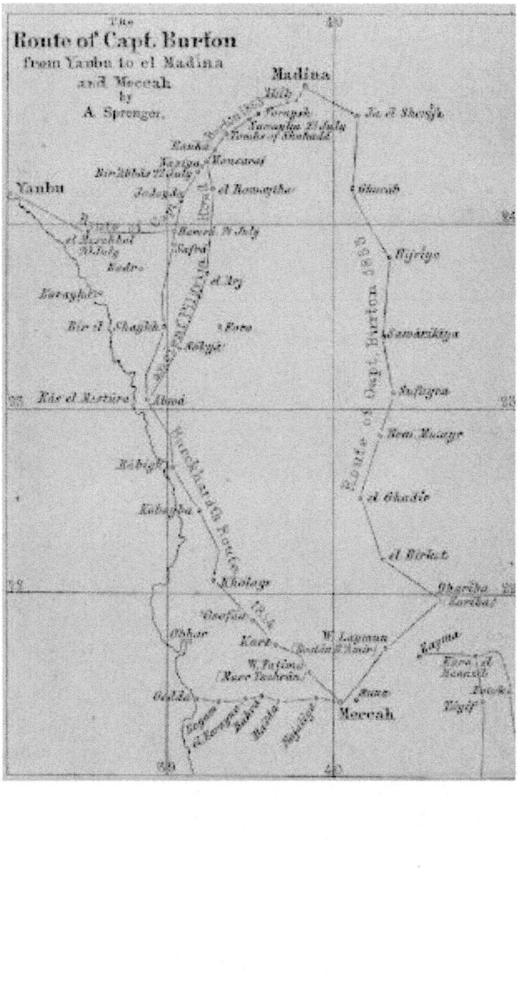

The
Route of Capt. Burton
from Yanbu to el Madina
and Meccah
by
A. Sprenger.

Madina

Yanbu

Meccah

1.

My respectable parents noticed early on that my talents ran counter to the precepts of law and order, and so decided I should be deposited into the strong and stern hands of the military.

The Civil War was twenty years gone when I graduated West Point in 1885 and the country was flexing its muscles, chasing glittering horizons at home and beyond our borders. But the Army, having deemed those same talents of mine irrepressible, sent me as far from excitement, adventure, and danger as they could, and far from my ambition and dreams, too.

Over the course of the next five years, I'd spent dreary stretches leading engineers from lighthouse to lighthouse along the eastern coast; I'd guarded warehouses of old uniforms, old saddles and old cannons; I'd guided old horses to their demise; I'd been caught organizing poker games and faro deep inside those warehouses; I'd been blamed or suspected in more pranks and audacious schemes than one man could connive in a lifetime. And all of it culminating in the moment when I was summoned to our illustrious capital city and presented to the great Brigadier General Drum, Army Adjutant General. This time I had no idea what I'd done wrong.

Sitting in a leather armchair to the side of General Drum's desk was a Captain Hayward, of the Navy, a trim young man who was already losing his hair. He took his time making his assessment of me while Drum read a file at his massive desk.

Without looking up, Drum said, "You graduated fourth from the bottom of your class at West Point, Lieutenant. How do you account for that?" His voice was soft and his Pennsylvania accent took away the threat I had come to expect from powerful Generals.

"Luck, sir."

"The story I heard was that you got the other three drunk before the final examinations."

"How do you make somebody drunk, sir?"

Drum stared at me and for a moment I thought he actually might answer before stripping me of my commission. Instead, he shrugged and said, "You're right. Every man is responsible for himself. We've formed a new section of the Adjutant General's office called Military Information Division. Have you heard of it?"

"No, sir."

Silence again as he considered whether to call out my lie. "That's correct. No one should have heard of it. And I expect you to keep that information to yourself. We've selected an array of the best young officers in the Army and assigned them to foreign embassies as attaches.... What are grinning at, Lieutenant?"

"I'm sorry, sir. I'm honored. Thrilled..."

"I said we're taking the best young officers. Not you." He smoothed his moustache and took a deep breath and then glanced at the Captain Hayward as if it were all his fault. "You might have noticed by now that the army has no real place for you and no need for you. Four years and you're still a Lieutenant and with no prospect of promotion. Yet, Major Westlake, whom I respect, thinks you have potential and has recommended you to me. Why do you think that is?"

I had a good idea of why but couldn't mention it. Westlake's wife and I had spent some lovely afternoons together at the Hotel Monaco and only stopped when his suspicions punctured his arrogance. I'd been waiting for his accusations and whatever punishment might accompany them. But Westlake's wife made him realize that to expose me would be to expose her, and him. He must have decided the best policy was to simply get me out of town.

"Major Westlake is a fine officer," I said.

"And he has a shrewd and beautiful wife." Drum seemed to have to fight to control himself while he let that sink in. He won and went on. "As I was saying, we've assigned these fine officers to foreign embassies as attaches with the true purpose of gathering information about those governments and their intentions toward us and rest of the world. Those positions are all filled. But there is another… opportunity for someone…. someone like you. Someone who – for want of a better way to put it – can get another man drunk. Captain Hayward will fill you in, Lieutenant. I hope you're the man for the job."

Hayward stood, still silent. He nodded to General Drum and went to the door.

I saluted General Drum. "Thank you, sir."

Drum shrugged. "Succeed and your past won't matter. Fail and you won't be able to tell your future from your past."

Captain Harrison Hayward walked down the steps to the first floor and down the steps outside without ever looking back to see if I was following. He knew a hungry dog when he saw one. Fort MacNair was bustling. Offices were under construction and a new barracks. Three carriages, each carrying six civilians, stopped in front of the main offices. Every man who alighted carried a briefcase and they tripped over themselves in their eagerness to get inside the administration building where the biggest buyer in the country waited for them. Hayward led me far from the structures to a picnic table alongside the Potomac. We were alone there. He sat facing east and gestured for me to sit across from him where the sun would be shining in my eyes.

He wasted no time. "We've agreed with the English, informally, to trade information. Espionage. Help each other. Share. Cooperate. Give and take. In principle. Good for both sides. Shared interests. In principle. And they are willing to begin, as a sort of trial, by allowing us to attach someone – you – to a Colonel Hodgson. They're done with him. Long time English spy. He's old now. Maybe eighty. They tried to retire him but he threw a fit. Apparently, his fits are quite fearsome. Made threats. They decided it best to allow him to continue gathering information from his sources around Europe and North Africa."

"You want me to get information out of him." I tried to sound skeptical and calm but my heart was racing.

"The Navy is growing. We're passing the Spanish and the French. The British are next." He spoke carefully, without pride or enthusiasm, measuring each word, as if any of this much discussed topic was secret. "First in the Pacific, but then… Hodgson knows the deployments, knows the priorities, knows where the Brits are strong, where they're weak. He knows the defenses at ports around the world. Knows where the Germans are concentrating, where the Russians are… But, ach… what's the use? That's all just a plan. A dream. There's little hope of getting any of it."

I ignored his sudden dive into despair. "Tell me more about him. Where was he stationed early in his career? Is he married? Who are his enemies?"

"The less said about him the better." He must have noticed my grimace at that bit of wisdom, so he carried on with more.

"Have you ever been around a spy, a lifetime veteran of it? They're impossible. And they say Hodgson is the worst of all. That's why the English are allowing this. They take credit for cooperating with us and it's a way to for them to get back at him for his behavior when they put forward the notion of him retiring. He hates Americans. You can be sure they wouldn't have gone for this plan if they thought there was any danger of Hodgson turning on them."

"Why did Hodgson agree?"

"I'm told he wants an errand boy and someone to be there in case his health fails."

I waited for more but the outburst seemed to have exhausted his supply of words. That too familiar feeling – that same feeling led me into so much trouble, knowing I should say no, but being unable to do so – overtook me. I looked at Hayward, grateful for his blunt attempt to warn me off.

"You can reject the assignment, Lieutenant. Perhaps something better will come along. But I can see you're not going to reject it, are you."

I shook my head. It occurred that perhaps I wasn't selected for my talents, but rather for my impulsiveness. I wasn't someone. I was anyone.

He said, "There is one thing… Do you know of Richard Francis Burton?"

"The explorer, author?"

He leaned forward and blocked the sun and held my eyes. "And spy. The same. You must never ask Hodgson about him. About their relationship. In any way. I'm told, no, warned, that you must never even let on that you're aware they knew each other. If you do, Hodgson will cut you off, mercilessly. And you'll never regain his company. He'll send you back and refuse all cooperation."

"I thought you said it was better for me to know less."

"I know what I said..."

"But that must be the key, the relationship with Burton."

For the first time he grinned. It was an evil, triumphant contortion. "Yes, it might be the key to success, but it's certainly the key to failure. You must never hint at it, never so much as acknowledge its existence. You're on the inside of Chinese puzzle box, Reynolds. Good luck." The glee in voice blossomed with delight as he spoke. I'd been completely wrong: he hated me.

"By chance, do you count Major Westlake among your friends?" I said.

"His wife." He stood up. "You sail for England tomorrow."

2.

There are no impatient spies, none who last. Over eight months I traveled Europe and Northern Africa with Hodgson, sometimes on eggshells, more often ignoring the thousand unnatural lacerations he bestowed. And never licking my wounds for fear that would direct him where to pour the salt. Then, while waiting in Rabat, two telegrams arrived, more activity than we had enjoyed in a week.

My telegram said that time had run out for me. I had failed in my mission. I was to return from Morocco immediately to Washington. So I wasn't to last either, despite my patience.

Hodgson hadn't revealed his telegram, which was unusual. He liked to parcel out information as a means of misdirection, as a way of forcing others into quick conclusions and dead-end decisions. Now he sat next to me whistling in the courtyard, the fat Moroccan moon low over the tiled walls, our elongated shadows blurred by the bulky, flickering tapers in each corner. It was the same tune as last night.

When he took a breath, I asked what the title was.

"*She Took a Tumble on Primrose Hill*," he said and began coughing.

"Last night you called it something different," I said. "*She Met Me When My Ship Came In*, something like that."

"Different tune, Reynolds. I'm sure of it. Subtleties..." Hodgson stifled his cough and went on. "This business – not a business at all – depends entirely on subtleties. I shouldn't have to point out what they are. Pay attention. Life and death at stake. Possibly even yours. It went like this."

We had been waiting in Rabat for one of Hodgson's sources, a water clerk at the docks, to report on German shipping in the area. The source was cagey, started with lies, wanted more money, hedged, made excuses. Hodgson was patient, of course. I got another lesson in spying.

Hodgson whistled the same tune again. I got up to leave. Even if he didn't know about my recall, I would hear gloating in his voice, no matter the topic. My thoughts focused on how to sneak away tomorrow without having to face the humiliation of goodbye.

"Where are you going, Reynolds? Sit down."

"I'll see you in the morning."

"Richard Francis Burton is dying..." He knew that would grab my attention and held his gaze on me as if to challenge me to resist. "Do sit down."

How cruel hallucinations can be. How often over these months had I fantasized hearing Burton's name spoken, though never like this, clear and ringing as the call to prayer. I puffed my cigar to lock my expression in place though my back was to Hodgson. The smoke drifted up, draping the moon like a veil. And by then there was no way to be certain the sounds ever existed at all. I turned to him, expecting to confront his impish grin reveling in my pain. That would be a sign I'd imagined everything. He surprised me – again. He was straight-backed and sharp, in pain himself and defying it. Reality can be cruel, as well.

"Your cigar smells like it was cut with hair of a skunked dog," he said.

He wasn't far off. That's how it tasted. But Hodgson was forbidden to smoke, or rather, smoking tickled something that made his insides want to come outside for a rest. I liked to remind him of his predicament whenever I could, even if it meant enduring a bad stogie.

"Would you like me to put it out?"

He breathed deeply. "Certainly not." He paused long enough to cough and recover. "You've heard of Burton, I suppose."

This was the time to pretend I hadn't looked at my cards. "I read his account of the search for the source of the Nile."

"Not his Arabian Nights? Kama Sutra?"

"Haven't gotten to the Kama Sutra yet."

"His Pilgrimage to Mecca?"

I didn't want to admit that I'd only gotten about halfway through before leaving it on the train from New York to Philadelphia, so I told him I hadn't read it. He paused long enough to make me think he didn't believe me. His eyes stayed fixed on mine and I dared not look away, though I couldn't read him at all in the irregular, pulsing light.

"Were you told that I knew him?" I didn't answer. He understood. "Yes, but not the circumstances. And you have no idea that I betrayed him. No, of course not. If you'd known that you never could have resisted asking about it. No one knows that."

His eyes drifted off and he seemed to get lost in our shadows

"It was the time of the Bab, 1852' he said. "Ever hear of him? Sufi Iman, he was. Preached love and equality, oneness with the universe, that sort of thing. Scared the authorities, though he had no outside ties and whatever ambitions he had seemed to be limited to adoration. Had an aunt like that when

I was a boy. Bring her a gift and listen to a few complaints and I could have the run of the place for weeks. Horses. Shooting. Shot those birds but hated eating them. Should you like to eat the things you hate? Hate to eat the things you like? Well, I leave all that to you to contemplate, Reynolds. I'm far too busy.

"The sultan at the time, Abn-Hassan, eventually got rid of the Bab. But not before he spread his gospel across the western part of the country. Women, in particular, followed him. Threw off their burkas and declared their independence. The army's standing orders were to observe and not interfere.

"Burton was fascinated by the Bab and Sufism. He couldn't resist any gathering of the Bab's followers and there he met Leda. She was the daughter of a nephew of the Shah, member of the Qajar family. Quite prosperous. She wasn't afraid of Burton. Teased him for his note taking. He spoke Farsi quite well but wanted more. That's how the romance began. To be alone they had to meet secretly, of course. Perhaps the stealth increased the passion, as I'm sure you're familiar with. Good for the spirits, stealth. Burton had been with many women and had thought himself in love before but never like this. He wasn't one to fool himself into it or fall in love with the very idea.

"Leda could match him in languages. Correct him, even. And match him in adventure. She had trained her horse so she could ride standing on its back. She could compete with him with a bow and arrow. She could recite poetry and write it. By day they were strangers. She studied with the Bab. She played the disobedient daughter. Burton was careful not to let his gaze fall on her and she, rarely alone, shunned all British soldiers. In the evenings, Burton donned a *kefiyah* and robes, disguising himself as a Persian. He would ride along an alley with an extra horse and climb into the garden of Leda's family's house and help Leda escape. They spent the hours in the hills outside the city making love. They made a spot near an ancient Zoroastrian ruin their own; Burton furnished it with rugs and pillows.

"One night he arrived at the garden wall, stood on his saddle and pulled himself up and when he heard hoofbeats he looked back to see the horses being led away. He jumped down and chased the thief. Burton pulled his dagger and pushed back the thief's hood: it was Leda.

"He told me, 'For the first time in my life I wasn't myself. That's what freedom is. I loved her completely. I was overwhelmed. More than that. I only loved her. I had no other thoughts or feelings.'

"That night as they lay together he told her that he was being sent back to England. 'Marry me,' he said. 'Come back there with me.'

"Leda laughed at him. 'How many women have you been with, Richard? Hundreds?'

"'One.'

"'I'm serious. How can I believe you love me…'

"'You know I do,' he said.

"'And only me.'

"'Because I've been with hundreds. If I'd loved only once before how would I know that the way I feel about you is special? I would just be in love with my own feeling. But, I'm past that. I have something to measure this against and that is why I can be certain. And so can you. If I had to spend the rest of my life sneaking out with you each night, then sneaking back, I would.'

"'Then I should try hundreds of men,' she said.

"'I would kill each one,' he said, and he quoted poetry to her. Traherne, it was… I remember it… Would you like to hear one?"

I wanted to hear how he knew all this. How did he know what lovers said to each other alone in the night? To ask was to accuse. I asked anyway.

Hodgson raised his eyebrows as if to give me a chance to retract the question. I asked him to go on.

"*One star is better far*
Than many precious stones;
One sun, which is by its own luster seen,
Is worth ten thousand golden thrones;
A juicy herb, or spire of grass,
In useful virtue, native green,
An em'rald doth surpass,
Hath in't more value, though less seen."

"I never expected to hear you recite real poetry," I said.

He was silent for a long while. At last he said, "Later, there's more… Later." He smiled at that, the kind of bitter, inner smile I've seen from men just caught committing a crime.

But something in him fought back, as if he were forcing himself, he went on. "He was too lost in love to fear the world's interference or sense any subtlety in her reaction. At dawn, before he helped her over the wall, as they tarried for one more kiss, he told her he'd be waiting the next evening. Leda said she had to be careful. Burton pressed her and she agreed.

"But she did not appear that night or the next. Burton bribed servants to bring her messages. The reply came three days later. Her note told him not to come to the alley, rather meet her at the Zoroastrian ruin.

"You can guess what happened there."

"Burton was ambushed? By Leda's family members, I suppose?"

"I always wondered if he knew what he was riding into. He had to have considered the possibility of an ambush. Four men attacked him. Did they consider that they stood no chance? Later I heard that two died, but Burton never mentioned that. He rode back frantically to Isfahan, crashing through the streets, past a group of his fellow officers who didn't recognize him at first."

Hodgson began to cough. His face grew darker and the veins bulged in his neck. Just then the muezzin's call echoed like a chorus. The spasm stopped, as if obeying a command and he gulped down a glass of *mahia*, the sweet local liquor, and sat back with his eyes closed until the call ended.

"He told you all this? Where were you?"

"You wonder if I was the one who betrayed him to the family." He said it softly and with delight, but it wasn't a question.

"I wonder where you came into the story."

"You've read the Arabian Nights, haven't you? Burton lived it. That's what I'm trying to tell you, but I can stop there if you prefer."

I did not want to give in to him. Did not want to ask to hear the rest. Ignoring him would hurt him and I wanted to pierce that smugness. Wanted to make him beg me to listen. But I said, "Please go on."

"Burton burst into Leda's house. First, he saw Leda's servant and he could read the shame on her face. He followed her into a large room where Leda's mother wept beside Leda's shrouded body. She shrieked when she saw him and jumped away. Burton threw back the shroud. There lay Leda, serene, lovely as a marble statue. Her perfection fixed in place. He was just bending to kiss her when her father came in cursing at Burton to leave at once.

"Burton drew his sword. He was calm. Detached, he said, floating outside himself. He studied the man as if he were from another world, a grotesque creature who had murdered his daughter to prevent her loving an infidel. Burton wondered – he remembered wondering – how the man could carry on for even one moment after such a horrendous act? How could he walk or talk after the strain of it? How could he recover? There was no hatred. He was a mere specimen to Burton.

"Burton's thoughts turned to himself. Grief was hitting him, threatening to knock him down any moment, disable him and he sensed he wouldn't be able to defend himself so he better kill the father immediately. Get that out of the way so he could give in to the feelings he knew were gathering. He laughed when he told me. 'I had to kill the man so I could live and get on with thinking of killing myself. And, at the same time I felt guilty to be thinking of my own preservation.'

"He didn't see two of his fellow officers who had followed him into the house. They knocked Burton out before he could kill Leda's father and dragged him away. The next day Burton left Isfahan."

So primed was I to hear more that the faint whoosh of the tapers felt like an interruption. Hodgson sat still, hands folded in his lap. A trace of amusement formed as his eyes narrowed. At last he said, "I'll be sailing for Trieste tomorrow."

I said, "I'll go along with you."

3.

The Sorpasso, bound for Trieste via Malta with the early tide, was one of those suspender and belt type buckets – a steamship masted for sail, as well. How do you rush the tide? If I was going to defy my orders to return home, then I was eager for the decision to become irrevocable. The bet was that Hodgson's telegram would trump mine. Perhaps I could use his remorse, vague as it was at this point, as a wedge to lift the armor of disdain and condescension that had kept me, so far, from getting him to seriously consider betraying his country for the benefit of mine.

Hodgson's reputation as a master of the subtleties of spying was well earned. He seldom told me anything that fit the truth without the help of a tight girdle and I realized early on that he had turned me into an infant: I learned more by watching than by being told. It was thrilling, frustrating, infuriating, invaluable. Hodgson was a puzzle with a thousand solutions, not a single one of them satisfying.

I had ignored the warnings about him – except the Burton warning – and thought I would have an easy path to success in this recruitment because the word seduction had been used, but I soon learned that seducing women is easier than seducing a spy. Fail with a woman and you need only move along to another. But I had only one target and I was failing with him. I would not get another chance. The pressure made me hesitant. Hodgson could smell that defect from miles away.

His personality vacillated unpredictably from stern and demanding to sympathetic and understanding to cajoling and charming – all essential traits of a master spy. But as time went along the interludes of weird ramblings became more frequent: the cold, off center, caustic remarks, the skewed reiterations, sometimes on target, sometimes aimed into a past only he saw. I slid from apprentice to audience and back. It was easy to understand why the British masters saw little risk in sentencing him to my company. Now, though, with the door cracked open I would have to use all he had taught me, especially patience, to learn what I had come for.

Hodgson remained in his cabin all the first day and into the second. Though I hungered for more of the Burton story, I dared not ask; never give Hodgson an opportunity to frustrate you. And because Hodgson couldn't escape me at sea – always a danger on land – I relaxed and allowed my attention to drift to the attractive young woman working so hard to engage it.

She wore a pale green dress with puffed out upper sleeves and wide shoulders which made a sharp V down to her waist. Two vertical white ruffles decorated the space in between those shoulders. On her first loop around the deck, she passed me without a glance. On her second loop she dropped her handkerchief then moved over to the rail to admire the waves or the horizon and to give me time to retrieve the bait.

I waited long enough for it to blow over the side. That earned a delicious glare featuring large green eyes. She passed along and I remained at the rail.

On her third loop she stopped and berated me in Italian that stank of Mississippi mud. The essence was that I was no gentleman. I pretended I didn't understand her and said, "It's lovely to meet you. You're very beautiful. May I walk with you?" She pretended not to understand English, but I offered my arm and she took it.

She introduced herself as Countess Gandolpho of Pisa. I claimed to be an American millionaire, which I thought gave me the moral upper hand because I, at least, admitted to being American. After a dinner washed down with three bottles of wine, we strolled on deck and stopped to admire the desert shoreline.

"But how can I look at that when you're nearby," I said.

"E tu non sei cosi orribile come pensavo che saresti stato," she said and smiled at me. There, beside a pretty woman, beneath the copious sky, caressed by a soft Mediterranean breeze, I regarded being told that I wasn't as awful as she thought I'd be as a most generous compliment and the clearest encouragement.

Her clumsiness was a major source of attraction to me, but she clung so closely that my suspicions muscled aside my inclinations. On the second night we docked at Malta and the Contessa longed for me to take her on shore. She'd heard of some "splendido clubs con bello musica and splendido ballerini." I said I would accompany her but I'd need a short term loan to cover my end of the excursion. When that failed to dislodge her from my side, I knew she'd been deployed by Hodgson to distract me, get me off the ship and strand me on the island.

Hodgson appeared soon after dark, took a stroll around the deck and stopped the second time at the bench where I sat with the Contessa.

"Thank you, my dear," he said. "That will be all."

She hopped up, brushed herself off and suddenly recovered her ability to speak English. "I offered everything short of a striptease and a free shave but this guy is just impervious. And he ain't no millionaire no matter what he says. A blind hog with his head stuck in a barrel could see that."

"Well, you see, I'm his father in law, so I'm quite pleased," Hodgson said. He's passed the test. Here." Hodgson handed her fifty dollars and, placated, she skipped down the plank.

Hodgson invited me into the bar. We took a table and he asked the barman for scotch. The drinkers had gone ashore and we shared the room with one elderly couple. Their presence and their silence reinforced our confidential tone. Hodgson told the barman to leave the bottle.

I expected more of Burton's story but Hodgson's eyes settled on the bottle and he seemed to leave the room. There was nothing left to animate him. All the hawls and yips of the ship came to life, filling the void like an audience at intermission, though Hodgson seemed to hear none of it. I tensed, ready to reach out to catch him. Suddenly, he came alive with a weak smile.

"You were slick with the Contessa, Reynolds. You've been around women. Have you ever been in love?"

"I thought I was."

"Indeed. In love with love. Same as intrigue. Often not really there. A ghost. All based on lies. Many of them unspoken." He stopped briefly as a thought took hold, then recited a new limerick. "*There once was a man who was vain/On his shirt he suffered a stain/He rubbed and he wiped/another man's shirt he swiped/But it was only a drop of rain*. Sums it up, I think. But Burton fell in love in a way you and I could never understand. He's dying now, Reynolds. Someone should know. Someone should know his, their story."

Sit still, sit still. Ban all expression. Erase the impatient curiosity consuming me. Give Hodgson nothing. I waited.

"I was still in the Army, but they had sent me to the Balkans, traveling as a representative of an impresario. I was supposed to be looking for acrobats and unusual talents. Bearded ladies, that sort of thing. Why does anyone want to see that? Have you considered?"

"I haven't."

"I have. At length. There's little else to consider in some of those small towns. A bowl of something with horse parts in it – I hope it wasn't dog – and beer of sorts… It's cruelty, that's all. They feel superior. Some peasant with a low brow and enormous ears can feel superior."

"Much as you feel superior to the peasant?"

"Exactly, Reynolds! Peasants and Americans. And Russians, too, I suppose. And women, of course, though I know better. In fact, we knew war was coming with Russia in Crimea and we very much wanted informants who could give us Russian military plans. I found one, but he would only cooperate on certain conditions. Burton was the only man I could think of who could help meet those conditions. It took weeks to track him down and it took me weeks more to make all arrangements and travel to Persia, to Herat. Ship to Karachi where a Lieutenant Ross joined me, and then overland.

"Ross was one of those officers who learned early on to hate the Indians and the Afghans and the Persians without discrimination. Unlike you, he made my arrogance seem like kindness. As we rode into Herat we came upon a caravan and a Darwaysh stepped out and blocked our way. His robes were red, green, blue in a swirl. He wanted money, of course. I gave him a few coins. Ross tried to shoo him away. I ordered him to pay his toll and probably saved our lives by doing so. Have you run across a Darwaysh, Reynolds?"

"First I would have to know what a Darwaysh is."

"Pay the toll when you do meet one. They're religious men, Sufis most often, a sort of spiritual Muslim sect. Best I could ever tell they beg and they pray and dance around a bit. Do tricks with knives. It's considered extreme bad form to turn them away. A Darwaysh might be a cobbler, tailor, a chef, even a lawyer, and might continue his practice even as he prays and begs. I don't know if it's good luck to give him money but it's definitely bad luck to refuse - often because the people who see you do so murder you.

"The Darwaysh looked at us both and told us to follow him. There was a small outpost in Herat but somehow he understood the particular reason we were there. He led us to a low clay building with a blue door. I tipped him again and he spoke in Dari to the fat Afghan on guard. I ordered Ross to wait outside knowing that if he joined me he wouldn't be able to resist showing off his disgust to Burton.

"Inside you wouldn't know it was day. There were no windows. Completely dark. The kind of place you should never enter, Reynolds, being afraid of the dark as you are."

"I'm not afraid of the dark."

"Aren't you? I wonder why not… The few oil lamps threw light beams that perished prematurely in the smoky air. The heat was oppressive and I was tempted to unbutton my coat but it was a place of compromises and I determined not to make even the smallest accommodation. The boy led me into a second room, a big room, and just as dark. I could make out bunks that lined two walls, three high. The boy indicated I was to sit on one of the pillows scattered near the back wall. A bubbling sound came from nearby and soon the smoke drifted over me. Slowly, as if the smoke took shape, languid bodies formed in the bunks. They were young and they were old, and every one of them looked my way and their expressions were pathetic. Pathetic. A mixture of shame and hope and a knowing sort of cynicism that said, 'another one of us, maybe he knows me, maybe I know him; it doesn't matter anymore.'

"I don't know how long I sat there looking back at these ruins. Suddenly a face was close to mine, very close. He was bearded and dark. Dark and bearded. Dark, bearded and his mouth was a gaping hole except for the few remaining teeth which hung like stalagmites. I said, "You're not Lieutenant Burton, are you?" He thrust the hookah pipe toward me like a child with his favorite toy. I pushed it away. He drifted back into the darkness. I waited. At last a door I hadn't noticed before opened and the boy reappeared. I followed him into the next room.

"Rectangles of light were spaced across the floor like stepping stones leading to a platform at the far end of the room. There sat Burton, cross-legged on a cushion, and bare-chested wearing only a white dhoti. He looked like a Swami, majestic and serene in his self possession. The first thing I noticed about him were his eyes – sharp, always sharp, not angry, as you might have read, but sharp, as if they could penetrate further, deeper. The boy brought in tea service and placed it beside Burton. It might have been a different boy. I can't say for sure.

"'Lieutenant Burton,' I said. "'I'm Major Hodgson.'

"He gestured for me to climb onto the platform and sit on a cushion across from him. Wordlessly, he picked up a cup, poured the tea and held it out to me. I took it. Burton picked up his cup and drank. I drank.

"At last he spoke, 'Might I see your watch, Major?' I was Major then. Have I said that? Not stuck as I am now. Not hopeful, either, as I am now, too, but on the train, so to speak. Steaming ahead. Not stuck at Colonel in a way station, a backwater, tossing from port to port, with an American, never to progress, never to achieve what was never my ambition, rather that which would allow me to quit doing what I so enjoy. Having nothing to look forward to by way of promotion has given me something to look forward to every day. Whereas becoming a General would leave me nothing to look forward to in every way. Where was I…?

"Your watch."

"Oh yes… I handed it over. Burton smiled at me. He said, 'I want to see how long it takes the poison to work.'

"'You drank your tea,' I said.

"'Not from the same pot. Care to taste mine?'

"He was correct. I tamped down my sense of panic. 'You have no reason to poison me, Burton.'

"'Is your mouth getting dry? If you think I haven't poisoned you, have some more tea. If you feel too weak to lift the cup, I'll help you.'

"I placed my hands on my knees to keep them from shaking. Sweat dripped from my forehead and I licked it as it hits my lips.

"Burton checked the watch again. 'You have only a few moments to live. Is there someone you're thinking of? Someone you wish were here?'

"'You'll never get away with it, Burton. The entire British Army will be after you. You'll be hanged and for what?" It was his composure that infuriated me. Anger fought with my fear. I felt helpless as an invalid. Burton lifted my tea pot and poured it into my cup. My tongue felt dry as sand and my throat was blocked. I thought he might toss the tea in my face. Instead, he drank it down. All of it.

"'Revenge. Threats. Now I know who you are. Refill?' He poured. I was shocked the liquid went down. 'This must be how they poisoned her,' he said. 'This is how I would do it. I would make sure she could see me pouring the tea. She knew her father was a beast, but she wouldn't have suspected him capable of this.'

"'Neither are you, apparently.'

"'Poisoning is for cowards,' he said. 'If I want to kill you, Major, I'll pretend that you have a chance of defending yourself. Anyway, the question isn't whether I could poison, it's whether I could kill my own child.'

"The report says you have no children, Burton. I hope there's no reason to doubt its accuracy."

"Burton chuckled and the chuckle built into a full throated laugh. It was relief the way a smokestack relieves. Pain and frustration were the fuel. But there was something more. Something I didn't understand until later. He was struck by the gap between the overflowing love he felt for Leda and his pathetic inability to save her or to gain revenge.

"'Imagine if such a report actually existed. Imagine the job of researching it,' he said. 'I last saw you in India, Major. What do you want here now?'

"I told him the reason for my presence in this opium den in the middle of the desert. The daughter of a Moldavian army officer had been kidnapped and sold into the harem of an Arabian prince in Medina. Her father wanted her back.

"'So he can kill her?'

"'If we help him, he will help us. War is coming between us and Russia. This man can hand over the exact placement of Russian armaments and troops in the region. We want you to rescue his daughter.'

"'What can be bought once can be bought twice. Pay the prince a fair profit and you'll have the girl.'

"'The currency, in this case, is information. As you did in India, you will disguise yourself. You will pose as a Muslim, attend the Hajj, then journey from Mecca to Medina to a celebration at the Prince's palace. There you'll find the girl. She's a blonde, by the way.'

"'No.'

"I threw down my cup, shattering it. The boy rushed in but we both ignored him. 'Damn, man, stop this pathetic, self pitying charade. You're an officer in the Queen's forces and you're being called to duty. Don't you dare say no.'

"Burton spoke calmly, ignoring my tone. 'Aren't you going to flatter me and tell me I'm the greatest spy in the empire and the only man who could possibly succeed at this?'

"'Do you need that?'

"'No, but I expected it. You're an interesting man, Major Hodgson. But I'm going to Africa. I'm going to find the source of the Nile.'

"It was my turn to laugh, knowing it would irritate him. Knowing the cynicism of it would be infuriating. I mocked him. 'The source of the Nile? Is that all? And I suppose you plan to get your backing from the Geographical Society? Well, Lieutenant Burton, let me assure you that they will back you if I tell them to and they won't if I tell them not to. In fact, they are the ostensible backers of your journey to Arabia, your cover story, so to speak.'

"Burton was stubborn. He was not going to Arabia and nothing I said would change that. His mind was made up. The Nile was his quest. It would be his life's work. All this posing was a distraction, an exhausting one. I listened. It was fascinating to hear a man who could be so cold and calculating, so ruthless in the face of danger, talk like a boy dreaming under the stars.

"When he stopped, I said, 'After you complete this mission and return with the girl I promise you the Geographical

Society will indeed back you in Africa.' I told him he could find me at the army outpost near the Citadel in the center of the town.

Hodgson stopped abruptly and I expected another coughing fit. His eyes closed for a moment. When they opened they were round and still with fear. I was certain of it because that look had never appeared before. He began to speak, stopped, closed his eyes again and said softly, "I would like to rest now, Reynolds."

I helped him back to his cabin.

4.

Trieste presented itself as a pleasant crescent of houses tiered against gentle hills. The harbor was busy. A frigate and a clipper with most of her sails down played chicken with each other and a fisherman slid past them expertly. I had to keep reminding myself that Hodgson was known to fabricate at times and I shouldn't get too excited about his Burton story until I heard more. I wanted to hear more.

Hodgson arrived beside me at the rail, fully dressed and ready to debark.

"Have you been here before, Reynolds? I forget if I asked you that last night."

"Have not," I said, knowing that he remembered asking and my answer; he remembered what the elephant forgot.

He turned toward me. "I've avoided Trieste for eighteen years," he said. The regret in his voice was more honest than his words had ever been, except for the time he told me hated to eat roasted pheasant.

Still, my uncle Henry had taught me never to ask the devil his plan so all I did was admire the view, comparing it favorably to San Francisco's.

"Burton was a liar right from the start," he said with a matter of fact bitterness. "Out of the gate. All lies. Filling the story with rocks and camels and gods. The Hajj I'm talking about. Oh, they were all there, but that wasn't the real story. No. I'm surprised you fell for it, Reynolds, being the liar you are, claiming you haven't read it. Everyone read it. Even Americans. I wouldn't be surprised to find him out shooting or riding, not dying at all."

"I hope that's true."

"Don't get your hopes up. He won't see you. Doesn't want to waste time on would be spies. You'll be left on the street. Peering in windows. Imagine it won't be your first time for that." He wanted that to hurt and I admit that it did despite the many months of punches that should have hardened me. And I made the biggest mistake anyone can make in Hodgson's presence: I allowed him to read my feelings. His watery eyes were gleeful and I imagined them sliding out of their sockets and onto the deck in their exuberance. I almost raised a foot to squash one of the slimy gobs.

"This ship carries on to Piraeus, Reynolds. Then Constantinople. Then Tripoli. Stay on board. Leave me, Reynolds." He forced a smile, but sincerity was so foreign to him that the gesture could only disown his words. "I say this as someone who has come to care for you. Nevertheless, I urge you to follow my advice." He raised his telescope and scanned the wharf, shook his head in a matter of seconds and turned again to me. Rather, he turned on me. "You think he embellished his story, don't you. Admit it! Don't lie. Not when it's useless and obvious, surely you've learned that much by now. Save the lies. You think he embellished his story…."

"Doesn't every spy embellish his story? Colonel, I've been traveling with you for just about nine months and even my dull brain has been able to absorb a thing or two about this spy business and its related fields. I've seen men and women in more extreme circumstances than I dreamed possible, living lies piled on lies so tangled a cat wouldn't touch them, men who posed as women and women who posed as men and that one in Hamburg – the man who posed as a woman posing as a man. I've seen men with three wives and three families all unbeknownst to one another. I've seen men who lived in tunnels, listening, for months and learning nothing. I've met kindhearted and generous murderers. And I've watched you treat them all with imperiousness which they accept for reasons I barely fathom. And every one of these people, fine or not, felt the need to choose one aspect, at least one – the danger, the hardship, the sacrifice, the hatred or the love – to exaggerate, no matter how stellar the reality was. So yes, when the wonder wore off on the Burton books, which was some time ago, I wondered – in a different way – if maybe the remarkable Richard Francis Burton might not have gilded the lily just a bit."

Halfway through that speech I was regretting the direction and each word started to feel like a burning match for the enemy to sight. By the end I was considering finding another line of business. Hodgson remained unmoved.

"Good job, Reynolds. You so rarely disappoint. Once again, you're exactly wrong! Burton did the opposite of what you guess. He hid the truth, played it down, buried it in mounds of detail, and all because he couldn't bear to relive the agony he'd endured while others admired him. Imagine a scientist who withheld the results of his experiments, not because they failed, but because in conducting them he had been wounded and could not bear to see the results discussed around the world. Burton didn't embellish his adventure, he censored it."

I wanted to stop the ship right there. Turn it around. Head for the open sea. Wanted Hodgson alone, uninterrupted. I wanted to know what was censored.

He raised his telescope and scanned the wharf again.

A short man with light brown skin waved at us. Hodgson shocked me by waving back. He didn't actually convey enthusiasm but it showed he knew what enthusiasm looked like.

"That's Ali, Burton's… his friend."

Ali lowered his hand and shook his head slowly from side to side. Hodgson lowered the telescope. His eyes closed. The telescope slipped out of his hand and into the bay.

He watched the telescope sink then turned his back to the rail. He placed his hand on my arm. This time he could not twist his face enough to alter the sadness and regret washing over him.

"Don't leave me, Reynolds, please. Stay here. Come with me."

For the first time I believed the sudden reversal was not a manipulation, not a ploy. Not driven by malice. It was as if his spirit had escaped. Hodgson was devastated.

5.

"We'll have to hurry," Ali said. But neither he nor Hodgson moved. Passengers and porters flowed around them. Ali was about fifty I guessed. Slim. His large, child like brown eyes contrasted with the viciousness of the scar that ran from just under his left eye down to jaw. The words the two men didn't speak felt like giant anchors. Hodgson's eyes went soft – I'd never seen that before – and lost focus and Ali seemed to share the same pain that Hodgson felt. They might have stood there forever, glued by unspoken emotions, so I introduced myself to Ali to break the spell.

Before Ali could reply, a young man, eager as a hungry dog but less sensitive, pushed his way forward with the purpose of greeting Hodgson, introducing himself, fawning and endearing himself with effusive compliments.

"Jenkins, sir, from the consulate. How was your voyage, sir? I must say this is the greatest honor. The greatest honor. I must say..."

Hodgson took Ali's arm and started away. I hadn't noticed Ali's limp until then, as he walked in step with Hodgson. Jenkins kept up his patter, though he only seemed to know a few words. At last Hodgson stopped. He aimed his eyes at Jenkins and said,

"Why are you here?"

The open disdain slapped Jenkins and he seemed to lose his breath for a moment. I knew the feeling.

"To help with your arrangements, sir. I..."

Hodgson flicked a finger toward me. Jenkins offered an envelope with information on the accommodations he had found for us. I took it and we left him behind, found a carriage and wound into the hills.

We got out before a three story amber colored villa with a stone façade and four thick columns rising above it, which, by blocking the windows, made the upper floors appear to be a fancy jail. Smoke rose above the house.

"Hot day for a fire," I said.

Hodgson looked at me as if I'd set the fire. Ali rang the bell twice, but when no one answered, he pulled a key and opened the door.

The floor of the reception area was a dark glazed terra cotta, punctuated by four columns on each side and even more columnsseparating the next room, a sort of rotunda. We went forward, up a few steps and there, in the center of the rotunda, on a sheeted plank, lay Richard Francis Burton dressed in a black woolen knee length coat and not much caring about the heat.

He was dead.

A cat sat on his chest, its tail swishing the corpse's neck.

The shoes and socks had been removed from the corpse and both feet were in encased in plaster. The right hand was also incased in plaster.

I watched Hodgson. Ali watched Hodgson. Hodgson stared at Burton's body but his critical, cynical eyes were turned inward. He shrugged, just a slight, involuntary move of the head and shoulders, as if to say, 'what's done is done.' At least that's how I took it. His eyes were watery, as always, but he didn't cry. I didn't know until much later what he was seeing.

I saw a stout old man, with grey skin to match his thinning hair and beard. There was little to connect with the fearsome, fierce Burton I'd seen in photos and portraits.

"He's the last man I would have expected to die at home," Hodgson said. "Perhaps that's what killed him." He attempted to counter the emotion with a smile but his mouth fell so quickly it only accentuated his sadness.

A small man with oily hair that looked painted on his skull rushed in from a corridor to our right. He leapt between Hodgson and the corpse. "Don't touch. The plaster must dry." The cat hissed at him.

Hodgson surprised me by stepping back. He muttered, "At least it's not a priest."

The small man said, "Oh, the priest was already here. That's why the plaster isn't dry. Took forever. I swear he was inventing new prayers as he went." The small man rushed out through the same corridor.

Ali had wandered toward the rear windows which looked over the gardens. "Oh no," escaped from him and he charged through the garden door. I followed.

Flames lunged up at the edges of a large round pit. An austere woman all in black, holding a large sheaf of papers, hurried from a wheelbarrow and tossed the papers into the fire pit. She returned to the wheelbarrow and lifted a large leather bound book with an engraved cover. Ali sped to her side. He put his hands on the book.

He said, "Not that one… please."

The woman's fierce expression softened for a moment. She glanced briefly into Ali's eyes but quickly turned her head, as if to avoid pain. I recognized Mrs. Burton from her portraits. Thick jawed and severe, gray hair pulled back, she was more squat than in the photos. She noticed me, but that only brought on a moment's hesitation. Her gaze shifted to the door.

"You!"

Hodgson stepped into the garden. If he had any sympathy for the widow it was buried beneath disdain and contempt.

Mrs. Burton let go of the book and Ali moved away with it.

Hodgson looked at the pile of books and papers. "You would," he said. His hatred equaled hers.

"Get out! Get out! Get out!"

Hodgson didn't move. Neither did Ali. "Reynolds, meet Mrs. Richard Burton demonstrating her love for her dear departed husband by destroying his life's work."

It was as if the three of them had rehearsed their parts, and I was the only audience. They had been waiting for this chance. But so good were they that they played the parts for themselves, not for me. They could hear each other, hear the unspoken words – all vitriol, I imagined – having run through it constantly all the years they were apart.

Mrs. Burton spat a quiet "get out" once more before bending to gather an unbound stack of papers. She carried them to the fire and threw them carelessly toward the pit. Most of the papers fluttered to the ground.

"Ali," Hodgson said. It was a command.

Mrs. Burton turned toward Ali. The hatred melted into challenge. Ali's eyes were coated with pain. Mrs. Burton's lip curled but it was tough to tell if she was gloating or was just relieved that Ali didn't take Hodgson's side.

Hodgson tried again. "Reynolds, take the papers."

I didn't move. Why would I?

"Reynolds, those papers are more valuable to your education than everything I could ever teach you. Take them now, before she destroys them."

I was captivated by the sight of Hodgson thwarted by this banshee in black. I spoke softly. "Mrs. Burton, would you allow me to read your husband's papers?"

"Will you promise to return them when you've finished?"

I didn't bother to look toward Hodgson. "I can not promise."

"No."

She tossed the stack into the fire. Fewer fluttered to the ground this time. Mrs. Burton calmly stepped over to the nearest stack of books. She lifted two books from the top and moved to me. She held one out. I took it. She walked close to Hodgson. Her eyes were on fire, delight now dancing with the hatred. She held the other book out to him. Hodgson didn't move.

"Before he died, Mr. Burton told me that if you arrived here, to make sure to give you a book. He didn't think it mattered which one in your case. It's a gesture. Now get out of my house."

Hodgson stood like a statue, arms at his side. The widow dropped the book at his feet. She returned to the fire and re-commenced pitching books into the pit, one by one.

Hodgson walked to the open door to his left, the library. The widow watched him.

"If it doesn't matter which book, you'll allow me to choose for myself," he said. It wasn't a question.

Hodgson turned back to Ali, beckoning him. Ali's soft eyes shifted from Hodgson to the widow and back as if measuring which would attack him first. I didn't breathe any more than Burton did. I don't know about the others.

Mrs. Burton held her stern gaze on Ali, her lips parted slightly, her thick jaw trembling.

Hodgson said, "It's a book, Ali. Just a book. He wanted me to have one."

Ali and Hodgson exchanged an odd, conspiratorial look before Ali walked past him and into the library. I thought

Hodgson would aim a nasty, triumphant remark at Mrs. Burton, but he just said, "Watch the door, Reynolds," and closed it behind him. And so I found myself on guard against an angry widow, who returned to tend her fire.

After five minutes someone began knocking on the front door. Mrs. Burton was occupied and probably didn't hear it. I had no intention of opening the door. The knocking was persistent, but always polite, gentle. After ten minutes of that, the door opened and Jenkins, holding onto the edge, peeked inside. He saw only me.

"May I come in?"

"Try not to disturb the corpse."

He entered and shut the door carefully. He skirted the corpse and came to visit me where I was guarding the library door.

"I'm Jenkins. From the consulate. Is Mrs. Burton..." He saw her through the garden windows and shrank back so I was between him and her. "I have to see Mr. Hodgson. It's urgent."

"He's not available."

"It's urgent. There's a change in his housing."

"I'll tell him."

"Is he inside there?"

"I wouldn't disturb him if you know what's good for you."

Jenkins was very concerned with what was good for him. He spent a few minutes harrumphing and grimacing and craning around for different looks at the closed library door. He was looking away when we heard the crash from inside. He spun.

Ali flung open the door. Hodgson had collapsed. Dozens of volumes had been removed from the shelves. Hodgson lay on the floor clutching a volume of Burton's translation of the Kama Sutra.

"You can see him now," I said.

6.

On the second day of Hodgson's delirium the doctor returned with a different kind of medicine, "garantiert helfen," though his visage did not inspire confidence. He was a huge man with small dark eyes and a black beard. The white smock he wore might have been clean when he put it on a few weeks ago; I just hoped the stains were marks of his meals rather than his ministrations. Hodgson opened his eyes after the doctor force fed him some medicine with a spoon. He spoke to me, "What is he doing here? Have you sold me to the butcher? Let me assure you, I'm not ready."

The doctor spoke no English so he and Hodgson settled on German. The doctor told him that he didn't know what caused the delirium but that his pleurisy was advancing and he should make arrangements to visit a clinic in Switzerland as soon as he could travel which would probably not occur for at least two months. If ever.

Hodgson turned to me and said, "He says you're to leave me alone, Reynolds. With the help of the nurse I'll recover in a matter of a week or two."

I had neglected to inform Hodgson that I had German.

The doctor left his nurse behind, Anna – as clean and small as he was dirty and large. Hodgson let her administer more medicine, dismissed her, and coughed for a while.

"Have you anything to tell me, Reynolds? If not, I suggest you find something to do other than haunting me."

I hadn't planned the lie but it came out smoothly enough. "It seems my apprenticeship has ended," I said. "I'm to travel to Shanghai as soon as possible." I was curt and matter of fact; Hodgson would never stand for gushing, or believe it. "The education you provided me is invaluable, though I'm sure there's much more I could have learned."

He fixed his eyes on mine and didn't let go. The lids disappeared completely, accentuating the pupil like a bullseye and the bullseye didn't waver in the slightest. He held on and held on. I once encountered a cougar in the woods who took the same approach. At first I hoped he might have been focusing on something other than me, then I admitted I was definitely the object of his attention and wondered if he meant to attack or flee.

This time I wondered if Hodgson had died with his eyes open. He hadn't. "You have learned quite a bit, haven't you, Reynolds."

"I wish I could stay long enough to hear more about you and Burton."

"Learned quite a bit. Less than a lot. More or less plenty. I met a man once in Messina who claimed to know nothing and he was right. Lied about everything else. That was the proof. Yes, you've learned, Reynolds. What would you like to know before you go? A parting gift from me to you."

Could he read my lie? Did he sense what was in my telegram in Rabat? Did my failure show in my eyes, in my posture? Every day for months I had woken with the hope that I would be able to move Hodgson around, I was resolved to do so, and went to sleep each night thinking 'tomorrow, tomorrow' and now I'd drawn the right cards. Did it show?

There he was waiting with a smile of phony serenity and patience, as if he knew what was coming. Still, I had to try once more.

"My superior officers are very grateful to you for all you've given me. They'd like to honor you in return."

"How very thoughtful of them. You people don't give knighthoods, do you? What's the equivalent? A cowboy hat, I suppose. I shall hang it over my mantle."

"Actually, they have in mind an honorarium, a sort of second home for you, in the United States, in New England, for the when that day comes that you decide to retire."

"That does sound lovely, Reynolds? Why didn't you mention it sooner?"

"I've been meaning to…"

"But now that you're being sent to Rangoon…"

"Shanghai. My superior officers hope they'll be able to visit you, consult with you. Your knowledge, your experience is so valuable and should be shared, don't you think. You shouldn't be forgotten, pushed aside. Shall I tell them you accept?"

"Tell them anything you want to. Tell them I insist on a bath not a shower. I thought you might ask for more about Burton."

"I would like to know…"

"Did you ever read the story he wrote about the young lieutenant who fell in love with a nun in India and convinced her to run away with him? With an accomplice, another officer, they plotted her escape. But the accomplice got lost in the dark and went into the mother superior's room and brought her out instead. The two men stuffed rags in her mouth and tied her up and ran away. I reread it often."

I had read it. "Was Burton the lieutenant? Is it true?"

"*There once was a nun in Lahore, Who found the convent to be a bore, She fell for a Brit, A man of great wit, And… and he… but she…* oh, what do you think? True or not?"

Before I could answer, Ali arrived with a suitcase filled with papers and books which he managed to rescue from Mrs. Burton's incendiary obsession. He also managed, somehow, to lift it onto the sideboard. The distraction also managed to erase any possibility of obtaining an answer from Hodgson to my entreaty.

Hodgson needed the nurse's help to shuffle over to examine the suitcase's contents. He shrugged her off when he got there and his eyes shone with the savoring greed of a pirate regarding his long lost treasure chest. I thought he was going to scoop up papers and throw them in the air. Instead, he picked up a loose page, read it, then two more. Ali and I looked on patiently.

"Which book were you given, Reynolds?" Hodgson said.

"*The Gold-mines of Midian*."

He began reciting: "*At last! Once more it is my fate to escape the prison-life of civilized Europe, and to refresh body and mind by studying nature in her noblest and most natural form – the nude.*" Though Hodgson held my eyes as he recited the opening of the book, I'm not sure he could see me; he was searching for the words, or just lost in the pleasure of speaking them. "*Again I am to enjoy a glimpse of the glorious desert; to inhale the sweet pure breath of translucent skies that show the red stars burning upon the very edge and verge of the horizon; and to strengthen myself with a short visit to the Wild Man and his old home*."

When he finished he coughed a bit and said, "And which did I choose?"

I retrieved the "*Kama Sutra*" and handed it to him.

"What do you think of it?"

I demurred.

"Come now, Reynolds. We both know you spent the past few days drinking it in."

"I might have sipped a few chapters."

"Sex, sex, sex. Genitals and sex and sex and pleasure. Burton was interested in it all. The act and the details. The variations. The possibilities. That's the problem for the merry widow, the reason she has to incinerate whatever she gets her itchy hands on. Burton was re-translating "The Scented Garden" which describes the details, the very mechanics of men enjoying each other. She feared the notion that Burton preferred men to women, born, I suppose, by his rarely preferring her. And she fears that people will read the book and think the same thing, though they'd only be speculating about his husbandly duties."

"Did he prefer men?"

"The rumor was started by enemies. All about brothels in Karachi. Young boys kidnapped and put to work satisfying the desires of English officers and a few prosperous natives. General Napier was determined to close them down but he needed evidence and no one connected to the General's staff could get close. Burton spoke Hindi fluently. He had... countless languages. He disguised himself as a native of Sindh, a wealthy trader, and was able to witness... well, I never read the report, but it provided enough detailed evidence to close the entire operation. Named names. Unfortunately, when Napier left India a copy of the report fell into the wrong hands. Burton was exposed. The perpetrators tried to kill him, failed and plotted to try again and along the way used this convenient accusation: takes one to know one.

"We're spies, Reynolds, not window peepers. We want to know what can be known and expand what can be known and make educated guesses at what can be known. That which can not be known we'll have to leave to doctors, and priests. But I would doubt this accusation, mightily, and not just because Burton so obviously favored women. Burton lived to confront fear. He wouldn't have backed down from any accusation that was true, he would have embraced it. He ran toward fear."

The thought seemed to scare him and he stopped with a quickly drawn breath. The nurse stood close by, ready to pounce if Hodgson collapsed. Ali edged behind him. Hodgson held his attention on me.

"If you really want to know, ask Ali. He'd know. I never had to ask.... What Burton loved most was people, their flaws and foibles, their darkness, their insight and their blindness. He could stand above the rest of us and still regard us with affection and respect. That infuriates some and makes others suspicious."

Was he expecting a response? I had none. He loved the man and now the man was dead. Everyone improves once he stops breathing.

"Death improves us all," Hodgson said and his lips went up briefly in a facetious smile as if to brag that he read my mind. "I thought so too at one time, but in a twisted way, I thought Burton was expendable. In all your life as a soldier or a spy you'll never make a miscalculation as despicable as that. Never."

He paused – that is, his words paused, but the tirade was still in force in the rigidity of his posture and the narrow, slitted, hard focus of his eyes.

"Do you understand my meaning, Reynolds?" He glanced momentarily at Ali but turned back to me as if Ali would scorch him. "I plotted to kill him. Burton. Richard Francis Burton. I plotted..."

I dived forward. Too late to catch him.

7.

Ali stayed for dinner and he opened up a bit about his life. He had settled in Trieste when Burton was appointed Consul here in 1872 and began a business exporting leather goods. He kept an office in Milan, as well. He and Hodgson corresponded periodically, though, he claimed, never about Burton.

"Mr. Hodgson has great respect for you," Ali said.

"Until we arrived in Trieste I didn't think he had great respect for anyone."

Ali put down his knife and fork. He glanced toward Hodgson's room: the door was closed. "Mr. Hodgson bears a grave burden. He realized too late his admiration for Burton… but I should allow him to tell you."

"But he won't, will he? He's never told anyone that story."

Ali smiled and returned to his meal. We spoke about America. He had visited with Burton, traveling to Utah where Burton interviewed John Smith of the Mormons. He compared the West to Arabia.

"The tribes are all hostile to one another. They squabble about land and water and how to worship and who can marry. They can only agree not to trust the Indians. It's how I imagine Arabia was many hundred years ago."

"Who were the Indians there?"

"I'm not sure."

"Perhaps we won't remember someday, too."

Ali went into Hodgson's room to say goodbye. I sat outside on the balcony, lit a cigar and opened the large book – Burton's translation of the Arabian Nights. This looked like an abbreviated version, hand written and illustrated by Burton. Perhaps an original draft. Some of the illustrations were complete and some were mere sketches. I leafed ahead, stopping randomly when something caught my eye. When I came to *The Tale of the Ensorceled Prince* I was struck by the illustration of the Prince: he looked like Ali, younger, but bearing the same scar.

A moment later, Ali returned. I went inside and showed him the drawing.

"May I?" He took the book and turned to *The Tale of the Fisherman and Jinni.* Looming over the page, bald, and much younger, was Hodgson as the Jinni. There could be no mistake. Something about the drawing disturbed Ali, though. He bit his lip. Then he turned to me.

"You should leave, Mr. Reynolds. Whatever it is you want from Mr. Hodgson you won't get it and you'll pay a huge price for trying. Leave now, while you can."

"While I can? You just told me he respects me."

"He does. Do you think that will stop him?"

It seemed they were old friends bound together by their reverence for Burton. Now Ali's hesitation at entering the Burton library came back but I still couldn't give it meaning. I said, "I plan to leave. I've received new orders."

He placed his hand on my arm which I took, at first, as a gesture of warmth at parting. But he didn't let go. His wide eyes were pleading.

"So I understand. I hope for your sake…"

"What?"

He relaxed his grip and forced a smile and left without another word.

I sat down and looked through the book with fresh interest. Moments later, Hodgson hobbled in. He looked pale and weak but his expression was secure and confident.

"I heard the door. I thought you might have left."

"Tomorrow."

"Indeed. Singapore, is it?"

I was going to Shanghai and knew he knew it. "Yes," I said.

"Shanghai is a stew, I understand. I always avoided it. India without gods." He sat at the dining table and declared his hunger.

I left to notify the cook, Carmela, cousin to Anna, the nurse. When I returned I placed the book in front of Hodgson, opened to the drawing of the Jinni.

He looked it over carefully. "Ah, Herat. The blue door of the opium den. I was never bald, by the way."

I expected more. None came. "How did he answer you, answer your… order?"

Carmela served Hodgson a pasta I'd never seen before in broth. "En brodo, en brodo," she said and she hung there, waiting for his reaction, his approval, despite his gruffness. Envy slid up my spine. I wanted that ability he had to inspire devotion. I was envious, but in the dark. It wasn't devotion; it couldn't be. This woman only just met him. What was it that made her wait until he nodded his blessing, like some distracted priest, before she would leave?

He stopped eating only to say to me, "You won't have time to hear it all, Reynolds. You have more important matters to attend to."

I watched him while he leafed through the book, looking for more likenesses of himself, I assumed. But his approach was different from mine. He looked each page over from top to bottom as if checking for mistakes. There was something false in that.

It was formal and structured. It was a show and I understood suddenly that he wanted me to interrupt, he was extending the process so that I would get around to interrupting. At last I had the answer to the question that had been haunting me for the long months of my tutelage under Hodgson: why did all those agents tolerate Hodgson's haughtiness and condescension? That was the lesson he wanted me to learn, the lesson I was sent here to learn. The answer was simple: he wanted their information, but he wanted their story – their whole story – more. The only way to get that was to let them talk. And they longed to talk. The agents had to hear their own story, the whole story, out loud so they could try to find out what they felt. So they could find out what it meant to them. Snippets or complaints, dismissive explanations wouldn't do. Neither would the facts. Hodgson would trick them into telling it all, or, if he had to, just wait them out. And the more they talked, the more they needed him.

I hid my excitement at this revelation and concentrated on my job – allowing Hodgson to switch sides in the equation, allowing him to play Scheherazade doling out the information, keeping me there, staying alive another day.

I said, "You didn't betray Burton over a woman, over Leda…"

His eyes flashed at me. For a moment he looked young and I thought he might jump up. I knew I hooked him. "Well put, Reynolds. I wasn't… I didn't…" Hodgson trembled and I reacted by drawing in my breath and letting it out slowly. "Oh yes," he answered. "Only man in the world who could have done it. Only one…"

Hodgson's eyes closed and fatigue was as visible as a cloak falling over him. He tried to go on but couldn't form the words.

"Tomorrow," I said. And I meant it. With the nurse, I helped put him to bed and all the while Ali's warning played like a refrain.

8.

Hodgson was still asleep. Anna was knitting in the kitchen. Without a map or plan I set out for a quick tour of Trieste. My back turned to the sun slanting down our street, I followed my long shadow between the sleeping houses. A milk cart came toward me, the horse blinkered and strolling so slowly that each step threatened to be the last. The driver kept his hat brim low. Maybe he was the one asleep. Within a few minutes I came to a long stretch of cafes and bakeries and shops but few patrons were about at that hour. I stopped for a coffee and pastry at Café Szabo overlooking the harbor. A large ship in the far distance threw brash smoke as it rounded toward the harbor. Stevedores served three ships at the docks. The coffee was good and the pastry was better and I would soon be leaving on one of those ships unless I ran back to the apartment and shook Hodgson awake and made him see the virtue in becoming a traitor. I smiled at two matronly women walking arm in arm up the hill. They turned away emphatically.

I faced the harbor again. The big brawny ship was closing in and the bad news flew proudly from the highest mast: the American flag. The U.S.S. Bungle, or Conscience, or Demotion chugging in like a scold, reciting my failure, taunting me. 'You've placed yourself above your county. You've indulged yourself. Your self-sufferance ends now.'

I answered back, 'I will turn him, I will turn him.'

But the barrage was relentless: 'Too late, too late.'

Intending retreat, I asked the waiter for directions to Villa Gosleth.

"Signore Burton?" His smile stretched across his face.

"Si."

"Un amico speciale. Aspettare…" He hurried away and returned a moment later with a small package in brown paper and tied with a string. "I soui preferiti. Budino di pane…"

I thought the news of Burton's death might crush the man, whereas if he found out in a few days, he could console himself believing Burton received this final gift of bread pudding. I made sure not to sample it until I was out of sight. Before reaching the villa I saw two boys dueling with sticks and gave them the remainder of the package.

After the fifth or sixth time I rang the bell the door was opened by a young woman in a long black dress, her blond hair pulled back in the same severe style as Mrs. Burton but that only accentuated how pretty she was. Her blue eyes were round and innocent. Her cheeks high and smooth. Her personality was another matter.

She looked me up and down and made sure to sound like I was intruding on the most important moment in her life. "What do you want?"

I introduced myself and asked to see Mrs. Burton.

"Does she know you?"

"You may ask her if you doubt me."

She drew a deep breath and it seemed she might close the door in my face, but she stepped aside, told me I may enter and she disappeared down a long hallway.

Burton's body still lay in the rotunda. A man sat beside it, his back to me and a small dynamo beside him. Wires stretched from the machine to the neck of the corpse and the man turned a wheel with weary regularity. I moved closer. Burton's neck had been cut; the embalming pipe had been cut. Dried blood flecked the skin.

The man said, "The batteries ran out so I have to turn the damn thing."

The fire was still smoldering outside but Mrs. Burton wasn't feeding it at that moment. The doorbell rang repeatedly. The man turning the wheel made no move toward the door and the young woman hadn't returned so I answered it. The postman rushed past me, muttering in Italian about how heavy his bag was – it looked it – and the long wait outside. He paused to bow to the corpse before passing into the library. I followed him. He unloaded a huge pile of letters and cards on the desk and started away, stopped abruptly and turned on heels, picked up the outgoing mail from the desk and was gone.

I'd been perusing the shelves for a couple of minutes when the young woman returned, charm intact. "What are you doing in here? These are private papers. What business do you have going through private papers? What have you got there?"

I quickly returned the book I was holding to the shelf and moved a few steps aside so she couldn't be sure which one it was. She narrowed her eyes for a moment, then turned and told me to follow her. As we passed Burton's corpse, the man with the generator said, "The blood is drained and electricity is run to check if death is certain." It wasn't clear if he was speaking to us or thinking out loud. The young woman led me down a hallway lined with watercolors of desert scenes but we passed too quickly for me admire them or confirm Burton as the artist.

"You haven't told me your name," I said. She didn't acknowledge me. "It wouldn't be Estella, by chance?"

That drew a dirty look. She told me to wait and went into Mrs. Burton's sitting room. I heard, "Daisy, what's taking so long. Show the man in."

"Thank you, Daisy," I said. She left behind a sneer.

Mrs. Burton, her black skirts spread out like the Queen, perched beside a table, a writing pad in front of her. She spoke curtly. "If you've come representing Mr. Hodgson I..."

"I haven't. I've come to apologize for intruding so suddenly the other day and to properly offer my condolences." She regarded me with narrow, suspicious eyes. "I'd read a great deal about your husband in America. He's a hero there," I said.

"He's a hero around the world."

"Indeed. Your loss is immense and, I imagine, the responsibility must feel enormous."

Her shoulders sagged and her mouth worked up and down wordlessly. "Would you care for tea, Mr. Reynolds?"

I sat across from her and asked about Burton's last days. He had been ill but never slowed his pace, she said firmly, like a school teacher reading the praise for a favorite pupil. But as she went on, sorrow and pain pierced her strict pose. He had suffered such injuries and diseases on his many adventures that it hardly seemed anything mundane as respiratory problems could limit him.

"He never complained. Never a word. Not about anything. I never knew..." Her thoughts made her gasp much like Hodgson and her aching tone matched his when he spoke of Burton's greatness. If they ever met again I did not want to be present to see them compete in their agony.

"How is it you came to be traveling with Mr. Hodgson?" His name was medicine for her pain. Vitriol revived her.

"We met on board ship. He told me he was going to visit Mr. Burton and I asked if I might come along." It was a terrible lie, vague and meaningless, but I didn't want to associate myself too closely with her devil.

"I wish Ali had never let him inside the house. He's evil. Mr. Burton cut off all contact with him years ago and you'd do well to do the same."

She turned her attention to a piece of pastry, trying to eat it delicately. Her neck stretched and her head jutted forward and she snatched a bite. The strong lower jaw reminded me of a fish darting out from a rock to snare its prey. Had she once been beautiful? She was thick, matronly and conventional now. I tried to see what Burton had seen. Horribly, images from the Kama Sutra featuring Mrs. Burton flashed across my vision.

I said, "What's the cause of your dislike of Mr. Hodgson?"

"Mr. Hodgson betrayed my husband, used him, threw him into the direst danger never expecting my husband to survive and then lied to cover up his crimes. And he lied to embarrass Richard and to hurt me. He lied to pull us apart. He's the devil himself."

"I'm sorry for you, Mrs. Burton. I didn't know." Was I taking advantage of a widow in mourning? Of course I was. But I couldn't see how it would harm her. She was hardly feeble minded and I kept thinking there had to be some reason Burton married her and stayed with her to the end. From the little I knew of him he wasn't a man to let himself be imprisoned by manners or form.

I asked her if the enmity began in Herat.

"Herat? My husband was never in Herat. I would have known." She put down her tea cup and wrinkled her forehead, trying to understand my question. She shook her head. "Hodgson betrayed Mr. Burton in Arabia."

"I haven't read that book of his."

"The story is not recounted in the book. Richard would have been subject to the full fury of the government that supported Hodgson. He never would have been allowed to publish the truth. Hodgson would have seen to that." She picked up another piece of pastry but she was too upset to bother with it and tossed it back on the plate. She rose. "I thank you for coming Mr. Reynolds. Will you be in Trieste for long?"

"I'm waiting for word from my government in that regard." I wasn't sure why I told that lie and hoped my face didn't reveal my uncertainty.

"I'll show you out."

I followed her along the hallway toward the rotunda and the front door. But she changed course suddenly and asked me to wait. She scurried away, her long black skirt brushing the floor. A moment later she returned with two volumes.

"My husband's account of his trip to Arabia. The official account. Anything Hodgson tells you will be lies."

9.

A driver was helping Hodgson into a carriage just as I arrived at the apartment. "The doctor told me that fresh air would be helpful," he said, and though he didn't laugh or smile, he meant that as an amusing and ridiculous suggestion. "Clever man. I suppose he wants some time alone with the nurse, poor woman. Should we rescue her?"

I joined him. He looked at the books I carried. After we began winding up the hill, he said, "Did the merry widow remember all my sins for you? No, you weren't there long enough."

"She said there is no Herat in the story. That Burton was never there."

"She makes sense, that woman. The unpleasant sort of sense. The type that isn't true. To erase history you have to go back to the roots. I should have thought she would have denied Isfahan."

"I didn't mention that."

"Well, if there's no Herat, there's no Isfahan and no Leda. Her logic is solid. Always was. She could claim I recruited him in Europe. I think it was her logic that finally persuaded Burton to marry her. Wasn't her beauty, was it. And you probably haven't smelled her breath. I haven't either, but I'm sure it's awful." He sighed and farted and that seemed to bring him back to the point. "She offered him a safe haven. A place for him to return to after his adventures. A place to write and rest and to prepare. Otherwise, she reasoned, he would begin to feel that he had nowhere to return to and so lose his desire to return at all."

"It worked."

"Her logic was fine. But she left out one important aspect. Her nature. Perhaps she ignored it intentionally. Perhaps she intended to change. Perhaps she even believed she could change. That would have left logic behind and required faith. Because no one can change his or her nature."

"Burton would have known that. He understood women well enough from what you've said."

"When you reach Shanghai, Reynolds, and begin to search for informants and agents never woo them with calls to adventure. Adventure is dangerous and painful and those who aren't naturally inclined will falter every time. Look for those who are naturally adventurous and woo them with logic. Even if the logic is porous. They'll believe you because they want to believe you. They're looking for an excuse to indulge their yearning. By the time the holes appear, they're too drunk on dreams to care."

The cold logic of Hodgson's life suited his nature, as did the coldness of Mrs. Burton's calculation – another point of similarity. I wondered if coldness suited me. Hodgson must have thought so or he wouldn't have explained it so nakedly.

"Burton knew her controlling nature from the start. He'd avoided the marriage for years. But after… after Arabia he was untethered from the army and wanted to concentrate all his efforts on the search for the source of the Nile. Surely, he could deal with her nature. She brought money to the bargain, as well. As time wore on and the adventures wore him down, he could spend his time writing. She might disapprove but what did he care? She wouldn't try to stop him. Burton couldn't how know how insidious her plan was. Couldn't know her intention required simply that she outlive him and then destroy whatever she did not like. And we'll never know what it was… She outfoxed him."

"You almost sound like you admire her."

"I pity her. Don't mistake the two, Reynolds."

The carriage stopped outside the Cathedral di San Giusto and the driver hopped down to help Hodgson. Hodgson left his walking stick in the carriage and stared, challenging me to insist he take it. I did not insist. The driver was also a guide, the least voluble guide I'd ever come across. He spoke in Italian captions – "mosaico originale", mosaico piu nuovo", la basilica era unita all'atra" and so on. That approach suited me as it meant fewer interruptions of my thoughts about Hodgson and Burton. Hodgson made no pretense of listening to the abbreviated narration. He seemed dazed, overwhelmed by the maze of his memories. He stumbled once on the rocky floor but caught hold of a stone pillar. A few steps later he was taken by a coughing fit, punctuated with a few curses directed at the doctor. Outside, Hodgson took my arm and pointed to a stone bench. We sat side by side watching the harbor. The U.S.S. Shameful was anchored now.

"Doesn't make you homesick, Reynolds? Always does me, though I learned to resist. Staying away from home makes it appear to be worth serving."

This time his voice betrayed no disdain, no challenge. It sounded like one of his few direct lessons: Hodgson acknowledging ambivalence.

"Tell me about the rest of Herat," I said.

"Herat… Waited three days. Sun and boredom. Made me understand the popularity of the opium den. Listened endlessly to varied tales from the storytellers in the market and endlessly repetitive complaints from Ross. Finally I spotted an Afghan shopping for a vest in the bazaar and approached him. Burton. I complimented him on his disguise but he said it was no good if I could recognize him. I said, 'The merchant didn't make you out.'

"Burton said, 'He was only looking at my purse.'

"Along with Ross we sat in the center patio of a café. Burton chatted pleasantly with us for a few minutes as if we were comrades reunited. I took that as acquiescence. I handed him a slip of paper with the information of a shop in Mecca where he would receive the invitation to the festival at the Prince's palace in Medinah. The place he would find the Moldavan woman he was to rescue. He read it and passed it back without comment.

"I said, 'How will you proceed?'

"Burton said, 'I wonder why you ask?'

"Ross said, 'Good god, man, it's a mission of the utmost importance which you are carrying out for your country.'

"Maybe it was because Burton looked so much like an Afghan, I thought he might stab Ross. But he only said, 'I'm not doing this for my country.'

"Burton ignored Ross's blustering and turned to me. I said, 'I simply thought you might need our help.'

"'And I thought you were the kind of man I could trust not to help.'

"Well, he was wrong on that count. I've never been accused of that before or after. No, I absolutely can not be trusted not to help. And, I'll confide in you, Reynolds, I do it for my country. On my own I'd be a much better person and would leave everyone alone, allow them to ruin themselves instead of helping them do it. And wouldn't I be happier.

"I said, 'I'll have someone meet you at Suez. He won't know your true identity or your mission but you might find him helpful.'"

"No."

"You might need an ally."

"No."

"You'll be killed if you're found out…"

"No. And no. Send no one. Tell no one. In fact, send Ross to the Arctic or kill him. I don't trust him. Send no one. Promise that."

"I did promise and wondered why he didn't know immediately that I was lying. My face burned with it. Just then the muezzin sang out. We were the only ones in the café and the café was the entire world. I'd ignored that feeling countless times but now I felt obligated to respond to it and didn't know how. It's the desert does that. You feel alone. Do you know? I had to admonish Ross with a harsh look to keep him from demanding Burton speak up. Burton seemed as occupied with the tea as he was in the opium house.

"At last he looked at me and said, 'Do you think I'm an arrogant man, Major?'

"What struck me was his change in tone. Gone was the challenge and the aggression. The question was meant sincerely. 'If you were arrogant, you wouldn't ask that. I would say you're confident.'

"'If I'm arrogant, it will show through, and my disguise won't work. I have to lose myself...'

"'Losing yourself won't bring her back, Burton. It wasn't arrogance. It was love...'

"He smiled. 'Are you a romantic, Major? That can't help in your job.' It seemed he wanted reassurance but I was torn between treating him as a junior officer and as an agent, an espionage agent. That would have required me to treat him sympathetically, pretending to be a friend, and I wasn't able to hold his eyes and give him that reassurance. Pretending friendship is just as hard as the real thing, I've found. I didn't understand, then, what he wanted. Do you understand? He wanted me to tell him that love wasn't a fatal weakness. That he could go on and succeed. He felt that all his successes came from looking down from above the fray, above the rest of us, and now he was stuck on the ground, tethered to an anvil made of emotion. I looked away from him as if he were diseased or worse. Doomed. I knew what I was doing to him and I couldn't face making that connection. I'm not… I wasn't then that deceitful. We couldn't know what was coming. None of us could know.'

Hodgson shivered at the memory and when it didn't stop I looked back for the driver to signal him for help but he was smoking in the shade of the church and didn't see me. Hodgson put his hand on my arm. He looked into my eyes. I dared not look away.

"It's fine. I'm fine," he said. "Yes, you know that. I know you do. The government doesn't. Put me out to pasture. Traveling around with an American. Wither subtlety? But I'll get my revenge. Do you know how? By telling you this story." He looked down toward the harbor. The planks of a steamer were being pulled up and passengers lined the rails waving goodbye. "There's a ship for Alexandria every third day and from there you can catch one bound for China." I supposed Ali had checked for him. I didn't want to talk about my trip or shipping schedules. I wanted him to go on. "Unless those Americans are here to escort you," he said and shrugged as if to say he'd deal with that when the time came.

Hodgson's hand relaxed. He coughed briefly and then, revived and calmed, he continued. "The Darwaysh, the same one with the colorful robe and vest, came onto the patio. The waiter handed over a coin and went about his business. At our table I paid him, but Ross hesitated. The Darwaysh reached across, took up Ross's cup and drank. Ross leaped out of his chair and accosted the Darwaysh, but I explained again that he could do as he pleased. Ross handed over a coin.

"All the while, Burton remained still. Finally, when the Darwaysh turned to him, Burton rose and asked for my purse. I handed over a coin. 'No,' he said. 'The whole thing.' I complied. I had to tell Ross it was an order before he would hand over his purse. Burton promptly handed them both, and his own, to the Darwaysh who couldn't hide his surprise and delight. He and Burton locked eyes for so long that I feared they might turn against each other. Instead, they locked arms. Burton said he'd meet me in Jiddah when he had the girl and they started toward the door. But he stopped and turned back and said to Ross, 'I'm doing it, Lieutenant, because I can't help myself.'

"Ross railed on after they'd gone: Burton couldn't be trusted, he's mad, gone native; I'd sent the wrong man; I must call it off.

"But I knew I'd sent the right man. The only man. And I'd sent him to his death."

10.

When the carriage drew up outside the apartment, Hodgson opened his watery eyes without prompting, drew his breath in as if about to speak, but lost the desire. He climbed down and walked through the apartment to his room. Anna, the nurse, followed him in and a little later fetched more of Carmela's broth for him.

I sat in the shade on the balcony and opened volume one of the books Mrs. Burton had given me: *Personal Narrative of a Pilgrimage to Al-Madinah & Mecca*. Hodgson's story consumed me and I read rapidly, searching for confirmation. It wasn't there. In Burton's telling he traveled from England, posing first as a Persian Darwaysh, Mirza Abdullah, before realizing that Persians were unpopular in Arabia and that he would be better off as Shaykh Abdullah, a Pathan, from the area where India met Afghanistan. Burton was practical, curious, determined, suspicious but I couldn't find the man whose grief was so overpowering that he fled his outpost and took refuge in an Afghan opium den, or the man who pretended to poison a senior officer.

He was cunning. *"After a month at Alexandria I prepared to assume the role of a wandering Darwaysh; after reforming my title from 'Mirza' to 'Shaykh' Abdullah. A Reverend man whose name I do not care to quote some time ago initiated me into his order, the Kadiriyah, under the high sounding name of Busmillah-Shah, and, after a due period of probation, he graciously elevated me to the proud position of a Murshid, or master in the mystic craft. I was therefore sufficiently well acquainted with the tenets and the practices of these Oriental Freemasons. No character in the Moslem world is so proper for disguise as that of the Darwaysh. It is assumed by all ranks, ages and creeds; by the nobleman who has been disgraced at court, and by the peasant who is too idle to till the ground; by Dives who is weary of life and by Lazarus who begs his bread from door to door. Further, the Darwaysh is allowed to ignore ceremony and politeness, as one who ceases to appear on the stage of life; he may pray or not, marry or remain single as he pleases, be respectable in cloth of frieze as in cloth of gold, and no one asks him - the chartered vagabond – Why he comes here? Or wherefore he goes there? He may wend his way on foot alone, or ride his Arab mare followed by a dozen servants; he is equally feared without weapons as swaggering through the streets armed to the teeth. The more haughty and offensive he is to the people, the more they respect him; a decided advantage to the traveler of choleric temperament. In the hour of imminent danger, he has only to become a maniac, and he is safe; a madman in the East, like a notably eccentric character in the West, is allowed to say or do whatever the spirit directs. Add to this character a little knowledge of medicine, 'a moderate skill in magic, and a reputation for caring for nothing but study and books,' together with capital sufficient to save you from the chance of starving, and you appear in the East to peculiar advantage. The only danger of the "Mystic Path" is, that the Darwaysh's ragged coat not unfrequently covers the cut-throat, and, if seized in the society of such a "brother," you may reluctantly become his companion, under the stick or stake."*

Burton spent a month in Alexandria before traveling down the Nile to Cairo. He details his possessions: a *Miswak* (a tooth stick – brushes are to be avoided because the bristles might be suspected as to be from a hog), a wooden comb; a goat skinned water bag called a *Zemzemiya*, which makes the water taste bad but you use it anyway because if you drink from a tumbler, it's possible pig-eating lips had previously touched it and you would lose reputation; a Persian rug that serves as couch, chair, table, and place of worship; a pillow and a blanket and a sheet which also serves as tent; an umbrella; a housewife (for pins and needles, thread and buttons); a dagger; an inkstand and pen-holder; a "mighty rosary, which on occasion might have been converted into a weapon of offense."

On the proper method of carrying money: *"A common cotton purse secured in a breast pocket (for Egypt now abounds in that civilised animal, the pickpocket) contained silver pieces and small change. My gold, of which I carried twenty five sovereigns, and papers, were committed to a substantial leathern belt of Maghrabi manufacture, made to be strapped round the waist under the dress... The great inconvenience of the belt is its weight, especially where dollars must be carried, as in Arabia, causing chafes and discomfort at night."*

Eventually, he procured two pistols, as well.

In Cairo he set himself up as a doctor by treating a few people and not charging them, knowing they would spread the word about his abilities. He developed a better class of clients and he details how to treat them – with a deft mix of superiority and deference. *"Then you examine his tongue, you feel his pulse, you look learned, and – he is talking all the time – after hearing a detailed list of all his ailments, you gravely discover them, taking for the same as much praise to yourself as does the practicing phrenologist for a similar simple exercise of the reasoning faculties. The disease, to be respectable, must invariably be connected with one of the four temperaments, or the four elements, or the "humors of Hippocrates." Cure is easy, but it will take time, and you, the doctor, require attention; any little rudeness it is in your power to punish by an alteration in the pill, or the powder, and, so unknown is professional honour, that none will brave your displeasure... When you administer with your own hand the remedy – half a dozen huge bread pills, dipped in a solution of aloes or cinnamon water, flavoured with assafoetida, which in the case of the dyspeptic rich often suffice, if they will but diet themselves – you are careful to say, 'In the name of Allah, the Compassionate, the Merciful.' And after the patient has been dosed, 'Praise be to Allah, the Curer, the Healer;' you then call for pen, ink, and paper, and write some such prescription as this:*

A.

'In the name of Allah, the Compassionate, the Merciful, and blessings and peace be upon our Lord the Apostle, and his family; and his companions one and all! But afterwards let him take the bees-honey and cinnamon and album graecum, of each half a part, and of ginger a whole part, which let him pound and mix with the honey, and form boluses, each bolus the weight of a Miskal, and of it let use every day a Miskal on the saliva. Verily its effects are wonderful. And let him abstain from flesh, fish, vegetables, sweetmeats, flatulent food, acids of all descriptions, as well as the major ablution, and live perfect quiet. So shall he be cured by the help of the King, the Healer. And The Peace.'

As for the multi-colored robe that Burton bought from the Darwaysh in Herat, in the book he says he traded a *jubbah* (which is plain) for a *za'abut,* which matches the description Hodgson gave. Was Hodgson lying? What for? It was impossible to imagine the meeting in Herat didn't take place. Hodgson's emotion was too strong to be a fake. He often lied but only to achieve his ends. What motive could he have to lie to me about events thirty five years in the past?

Why would Burton lie?

Burton sounded more like an anthropologist than a spy. He's cataloguing – habits, customs, fears, myths, goals – rather than discovering specific bits of information that might have hidden meanings – the nefarious, the dangerous, the weak. But he acts like a spy; anthropologists don't usually go in elaborate disguise. Still, he keeps all mention of secret missions to himself. It was best, I decided, to believe that he was blending the two roles – anthropologist and spy – using one to prepare for the other.

Ali startled me out of my musings long before I had solved the issue. My presence did not startle him. I wondered why. "I came to see if Mr. Hodgson needed me," he said.

I told him Hodgson was resting. "He told me about Herat."

"I should like to have heard it. Mr. Burton hardly talked about it."

Carmela appeared and reported that Hodgson was still asleep and peaceful, that she would be going out for a few hours, that Anna was preparing lamb and pasta for dinner.

Ali politely asked if he might stay, though he didn't mean it as a question. Something bothered him. His manner was cold, his usual politeness perfunctory. He sat down and I gave him a summary of Hodgson's account. Ali said he hadn't heard about the poisoned tea before but did not doubt that Burton played that trick.

I asked, "How did you meet Burton?"

Ali said, "Why are you here, Mr. Reynolds?"

"I missed my ship."

"Mrs. Burton sent for me today. I've just come from the villa. She asked me about you… I covered your lie to her. The one about casually meeting Mr. Hodgson. But now I would like to know about the other one – that you intend to stay in Trieste for a while."

"I'm interested to hear Hodgson's version of Burton's Hajj. I'd heard rumors."

"You'll please forgive me saying that you don't seem like a man to disobey orders only to hear a story, Mr. Reynolds."

The gentle rhythm of his speech kept him from sounding angry. It was the intense sincerity that conveyed the anger. "Mrs. Burton is suffering greatly. I don't wish to see her hurt further."

"And Hodgson…"

"I've tried to warn you."

"He won't live long, Ali. Someone should hear him out. You're the only other person who knows the true story."

"And no one will listen to me."

He was right, of course. I said, "Mrs. Burton will drown you out."

Ali rose wordlessly. He left the room and I leaned over to see him peeking in on Hodgson. On his way back, he retrieved the large Arabian Nights volume. He sat, opened the book on his lap and searched through it. Without looking up, he said, "Where have you stopped in Mr. Burton's account?"

"Burton quarreled with the drunken Albanian soldier in Cairo. People turned against him, were questioning him more, so he decided it was to time to light out for the Hajj a few days early."

Ali's eyes settled past me on the wall or curtains. He breathed deeply and when he spoke his anger was gone and the memory quelled his emotions. "Oh yes, yes. He doesn't mention the police coming for him, does he? The fight caused a commotion in the wakaleh. Mr. Burton thought he had calmed the Albanian and so he retired to his room. Not long after that he heard a crash, but Mr. Burton was drunk, too, and tired and allowed himself to ignore whatever it was. But the noise grew, a crowd formed. There was a knock on Mr. Burton's door. It was the boy with the eyepatch. Mr. Burton had seen him before around the Greek quarter where he was staying – eyepatch and long hair that hung over his other eye. Mr. Burton had once offered to treat the eye but the boy ran away from him. The boy told Mr. Burton that the Albanian had fallen to his death and the crowd was blaming Burton. The police had been summoned.

"The boy led Mr. Burton to the Muslim quarter and he stayed with the boy's relatives while the boy returned to the wakaleh and retrieved the remainder of Mr. Burton's possessions. The boy then disappeared and the next night, Burton 'lit out' as you say."

"Who was the boy? Why did he help Burton?"

Ali's eyes wandered across the ceiling moldings and the draperies as if they held the answer. When his gaze made its way back to me, he said, "It was a fortuitous escape because it led to my introduction to Mr. Burton. Of course, I did not know then his true identity."

11.

Ali leafed through the big volume on his lap. When he stopped, he turned the book around and passed it on to me. The drawing was of a boy peeking around a curtain at a woman's calf, bare to the knee, raised and held in a man's hand.

"I would like to tell you… I was born into the Muzziana tribe. Bedouins. I never met my mother or my father, at least not to my knowledge. I was passed around, a slave from the time I could remember. Even taken to Cairo once and Alexandria where I learned how to rob the travelers getting off of ships. But while I was stealing, I was stolen and sold and ended up back in the desert with a band of Muzziana led by a very bad character named Gamil.

"I was twelve at the time. We were riding toward Suez – only a day away – where there would be many Hajjis to rob. A rider charged down a hill toward us. Swords were drawn and rifles raised but the rider did not slow down. Only a crazy man would attack in this way and we saw it was a Darwaysh so we all relaxed. He rode toward Gamil, and I rode right up to the Darwaysh and asked for bakhshish, thinking he dare not refuse in the face of so many weapons, but the Darwaysh said 'Mafish.' Nothing. Gamil liked that. I think it confirmed the Darwaysh's craziness. Of course he asked the Darwaysh who he was, where he came from. I remember the reply very well because once I heard it, I vowed to become this man's servant and leave behind this bunch of brigands.

"'I am a travelling Darwaysh fulfilling my quest to visit the holy cities of Mecca and Medinah. I can lead you in prayers to heal your spirit or, as I am a doctor by training, I can heal your body from your eyeballs to the nails on your toes. I can fight and I can love and I can teach you, even you, to do either.'

"Gamil said, 'You have no servant, Darwaysh.'

"'Not at the moment, but you seem an unlikely man to want the job.'

"Gamil laughed and gave him the honor of riding with him at the front. When we camped, the Darwaysh told stories of home in Sind. Especially about the women there. I was captivated as you might imagine. Looking back, I should have known that this would only make Gamil and the others jealous of the Darwaysh.

"Suez was filled with beggars, thieves, confidence men who preyed on the Hajjis and merchants from all over who were waiting for ships to deliver them to Arabia. The caravan broke up. I snuck away and followed the Darwaysh until we were out of sight of the others. 'Darwaysh, I want to be your servant,' I said. 'I'm a poor orphan and you must rescue me from these rascals who have kidnapped me to help in their nefarious plots and evil deeds. Only a man such as you, brave as the lion, strong as the ox, wise as the hawk can answer my prayers. Allow me to serve you, Darwaysh.' I told him more of my life, of my travels, and of being sold and stolen.

"'You tell me you're a thief and spend your time in the company of conniving rascals which does not make me desire your company. Then you flatter me as if to make me a victim of my own vanity. If you desire to be my servant, give me reasons to hire you.'

"'You're going to the wrong office for your passport. You have to see the Bey first. Come, I'll show you. I can do this and much more to smooth your journey. I, myself, have been a Hajji and my experience will be useful to you. And I'm an excellent cook.'

"'I shall call you Ali Alf Aba – Ali of a Thousand Fathers. Well, then that's settled and it seems I've been sent the perfect servant.'

"So I had a new name, which I cherished, and a new master, though I didn't understand the meaning of his last statement until much later, after I'd learned his true identity. But I meant all the flattery. From the look in his eyes I could tell that I'd never met a person like the Darwaysh before. This was the beginning of life for me. I vowed to follow him and learn all I could. And my first lessons came rushing at me.

"We waited outside the Bey's office in the sun with the other pilgrims for an hour before our turn came to wait in the tiny, crowded and hotter waiting room. The Darwaysh took great interest in the other applicants, even giving medical advice and being paid for it, too, which impressed me further. Just before it was the Darwaysh's turn to see the Bey, a thin, weaselly sort of man, his hair matted with sweat and one ear disfigured by cuts, came in. He grumbled a bit about the closeness as he pushed his way onto the bench. Then he noticed the Darwaysh and his mouth fell open and a look of puzzlement came over him. The man stared as if in a trance. Just at that moment we were called inside to see the Bey. The Darwaysh never seemed to notice the little man.

"The Bey was a soft and lazy man, and mean spirited. A servant fanned him while he lay across his divan, periodically slurping something from a cup. The Darwaysh handed over his papers and the Bey took the most superficial glance and handed them back. He sipped his tea, smacked his lips and said that since the visa was issued in Alexandria it was invalid, the Darwaysh would have to return to Cairo and have it reissued. The Darwaysh said he had renewed it in Cairo. That was not good enough, though. It had to be reissued, not renewed. The Darwaysh stayed calm and asked the Bey to reissue it. By then the Bey was calling for the next applicant, but the Darwaysh did not move.

"A soldier escorted the next pilgrim in. The Darwaysh still did not move. The Bey looked away from him and gestured to the soldier to remove him. The Darwaysh said, 'How long has your stomach bothered you? I'm a doctor.' For a moment it looked like the Bey was considering whether to order the Darwaysh killed on the spot. 'You're drinking ginger tea, I can smell it, and it hasn't helped. I have pills to give you relief,' the Darwaysh said, still calm and direct.

"The Bey gestured angrily at the pilgrim and the soldier. 'Get out of here now!'

"With some effort and many sighs the Bey rose and led us beyond the curtain into his living quarters. There the Darwaysh handed over three pills and the Bey took them. The Darwaysh placed a box full of the pills on the table along with his visa. 'Take two pills a day and in one week you'll feel like a young lion, again. My visa…'

"'My wife... she has a pain in her leg.'

"The Darwaysh was firm: the visa. The Bey signed it and stamped it. Satisfied, the Darwaysh asked him to bring in his wife. She was taller than the Bey. All we could see of her behind the abaya and burka were her beautiful eyes which attached themselves to the Darwaysh. He met them and held them. She was hesitant to show her leg. The Darwaysh understood and asked the Bey to leave the room.

"'Your wife is reluctant to have me examine her pain in your presence,' the Darwaysh said.

"The Bey flashed angrily at the wife.

"'If you don't trust me, I'll leave.' The Darwaysh spoke softly, calmly, but there was challenge in his voice and I could see that the Bey expected obsequiousness.

"The Bey regained his dignity by shooing me out through the curtain. He warned the Darwaysh not to be long and retired further into the residence. The office had been cleared out. I was alone. I stood on the bench and peeked around the curtain.

"The wife sat on the divan and her eyes followed the Darwaysh closely as he drew up a chair across from her and sat. He asked her where the pain was and when it came. His eyes never left hers. It seemed that the clock ticked forever before she finally touched a spot on her calf. The Darwaysh put out his hand. The wife nodded ever so slightly. Her assent, it was. But her eyes never left his. The Darwaysh gently slid his hand behind her calf and lifted it toward him. The abaya draped back a bit revealing her ankle. The Darwaysh lifted the sandal from her foot. Their eyes stayed locked together. It was like a dance, a dance while still, so every little movement became thrilling. I was only twelve, remember!

"Gently, ever so gently and slowly, the Darwaysh slipped the abaya up, exposing her calf. He ran his finger along the soft curve of her lower leg, up to the under side of her knee. He paused there, paused his hand and his eyes never left hers. Would he go higher? Dare he? I was afraid for him, afraid the Bey would burst in. At last, the Darwaysh, moved his hand lower. Quietly, he said, 'Does it hurt here?'

"The wife gasped at the sound of his voice breaking the spell. The Darwaysh's lips curled in a smile. His hand applied a slight pressure and the wife squirmed, just a bit. Just as quickly, she looked away and the Darwaysh understood. He pulled the abaya down to cover her leg, but he held on for one long, tender moment before setting her foot down.

"'I will give you oil to rub on the spot,' he said and rose just as the Bey entered. The Darwaysh handed the oil to the Bey. 'For your wife,' he said. 'No charge.'

"What magic was it? I wanted to ask the Darwaysh but didn't know what to say. That was only the beginning of my education. We found lodging in a filthy room where goats would wander in – and out, they didn't like it much – and the flies were awful… I was never someone who liked being indoors. Still don't. But Suez was dangerous and those who stayed in the alleys were robbed, or worse. I hardly slept for fear Gamil's men would come to kill the Darwaysh and take me away again. At night I saw the Darwaysh writing in a book he kept hidden inside his robes. I warned him to be careful. If he was found out, people would suspect him for a spy. He thanked me for my concern, but he kept on writing. We spent two nights there waiting for the ship to Yenbo.

"We were on our way to the market square when Gamil and two of his comrades, very mean men they were, came out of an alley and fell in behind us. The Darwaysh put his hand on my shoulder which is all that kept me from fleeing. A moment later we heard the cries, 'Stop them! Stop them, I've been robbed!' A young man ran from the alley begging anyone for help. The Darwaysh turned to face Gamil and his men. I wanted to run and wanted the Darwaysh to run because I knew what Gamil could do if someone opposed him. But as he approached, the Darwaysh held out his cup. 'A portion for the poor,' he said.

"Gamil said, "Move aside. I should charge you for riding with us.'

"'It's bad luck to refuse.'

"'It's bad luck to refuse a Darwaysh, but how do I know you are one? You say you're a Pathan, but how do I know. How do I know you're a doctor?'

"'I think your bad luck is about to begin,' the Darwaysh said.

"Gamil turned his attention to me. 'Ali, I have always treated you well. It is I who freed you. I who let you ride with us and fed you and even gave you a share of our booty. You would be wise to abandon this stranger now. It will not go well for him or for anyone who is with him. Come over here, Ali.'

"A crowd formed. I was very scared. I had seen many times how vicious and cruel Gamil could be. Certainly, when he was done with the Darwaysh he would kill me. But I understood, too, that he was going to punish me cruelly if I came over to him. He only wanted that to weaken the Darwaysh. Gamil did not care for me. He could steal other boys. Even by that age, I had taken many gambles and been lucky most of the times, but this was the most dangerous gamble of all. The Darwaysh smiled at me. It was as if he knew my mind and was careful not influence me one way or another. I stayed put.

The two thieves moved close behind the Darwaysh and then everything happened in a blur. The Darwaysh spun and snatched the sword from the scabbard of one of the thieves and pulled his own dagger with his other hand – all in one motion. He hit the thief on the head with the face of the sword and the thief lost his balance and fell to his knees. The Darwaysh elbowed the other thief in his windpipe, crunching it. The sound was like a walnut being cracked. I can still hear it. Gamil had his dagger in hand, but the Darwaysh slashed and Gamil dropped it. They faced each other. Gamil still had a pistol in his belt. The Darwaysh moved sideways so he could see the two thieves.

"'I'm a religious man so I'm going to tell you the truth,' the Darwaysh said. 'You have no chance of pulling that pistol and firing it before I slash your hand, possibly cutting it off because this sword looks sharp. But then, you don't believe anything I say, so, it seems, you'll have to try it.'

One of the thieves began to get up. The Darwaysh kicked him in the head and quickly turned on Gamil and slashed his hand as he was attempting to pull his pistol. Gamil screamed at the pain. The Darwaysh put the sword at his throat.

"'Is it still attached? You are a fortunate man. Now, to prove that I'm a doctor, I'll cut you open and as I remove each organ I'll explain its function. Ready?'

"Gamil was sweating with fear. He swore to Allah that he believed the Darwaysh was a holy man and a Pathan and a doctor. The Darwaysh told him to return the purse to the young man with glasses and Gamil did so immediately. The Darwaysh removed the sword from Gamil's neck. Gamil jumped up and ran away. I knew then the Darwaysh was the greatest man I had ever met or would meet and I knew that this was the greatest day of my life. The crowd seemed paralyzed in awe. I guided the Darwaysh through them toward the ticketing office. The young man who was robbed caught up with us.

"'Thank you, Darwaysh,' he said. 'You saved me and I will pay you back forever, however I can. Omar Barzouki is my name. From Cairo.' I got my first good look at him. He was short and soft, puffy. His hair was cut short and oiled neatly. I understood why Gamil and his men chose him. He offered up a handful of coins and the Darwaysh accepted them.

"'You would have been safer staying in Cairo, it seems.'

"'Life is adventure, they say. Have you booked passage on the Golden Thread?'

"'We are on our way to do that right now.'

"'Marvelous! Then we shall travel together and become close friends. From dire circumstances come great opportunities. But I must ask you first – do you know that little man who is following us?'

"It was the weaselly man from the Bey's office. The Darwaysh and Barzouki said *Alhamdulillah* and they would meet again on board the Golden Thread. I followed the Darwaysh down a narrow lane and into a stall selling leather goods. First he checked to make sure Barzouki wasn't lurking about and when the weaselly man came along, the Darwaysh intercepted him.

"'Are you sick, friend?" he said. The man said he wasn't ill. 'Perhaps it's spiritual comfort you seek,' the Darwaysh said. The weaselly man was relaxed and smiling. He was going on the Hajj for that purpose. 'I'm asking why you're following me,' the Darwaysh said.

"The weaselly man seemed pleased by the question. 'Oh, that's because I knew you before... In Persia... You were English then. My name is Faris, by the way.'

The Darwaysh moved closer to Faris, towering over him. He took hold of the front of Faris's shirt but not so roughly as to draw attention. 'You saw what I did to the thief who doubted me?'

"'I meant no offense.'

"Faris seemed sincere. He wasn't like Gamil. There was no challenge in him. And the Darwaysh understood that. He spoke softly but in a way that was very firm. 'You're mistaken. Do not bother me again or you'll face the consequences.'

"Faris just shrugged as if nothing had happened and walked away. I waited to see where we would go next. I was overwhelmed with joy at all the adventure and mystery of my new life. I told the Darwaysh that as part of my wages he must teach me all he knows.

"'You may learn all you can,' he said.'

"'Including how to fight.'

"'Including how to pray.'

And we proceeded to the mosque.

12.

"There must have been well over a hundred pilgrims – Mughrabis, Persians, Indians, Bedouins – jostling to get on board the ship and fifty more who didn't have tickets thinking they could just push on. Many did. Some recognized the Darwaysh from his confrontation with Gamil and so paid proper respect and moved aside. The rest the Darwaysh cut through and I held onto his robe and once we made it on board he fought our way to the poop deck, wanting to secure a spot up where there were some corners unoccupied and it might give us relief from the stench below. But the way was blocked by a huge black man with a bald head and enormous muscles. He was stronger than even the Darwaysh. He said, 'No one may pass until I, Sa'ad al Jinna, called by my friends the Demon, allow it. What say you to that?'

"The Darwaysh replied, 'I say I would be honored to be able to address Sa'ad as the Demon.'

"'I have fought all across the known world, excepting the Americas, and one such as you will be short work for Sa'ad al Jinna. I will not admit anyone without the word of my master, Omar...'

"Sa'ad pointed towards a cot at the far end of the poop deck. Barzouki lay there like a prince. When he saw the Darwaysh, he bounded up and told Sa'ad that the Darwaysh was their friend who had saved his purse. Sa'ad hugged the Darwaysh and lifted him up onto the poop deck and I came along. Sa'ad was filled with praise for the Darwaysh and with many promises to repay the good deed. We had only just begun to settle our provisions in a spot we could defend when two Mughrabis tried to take advantage of Sa'ad's distraction and to climb up. Sa'ad turned on them with a quarterstaff and beat them back into the arms of their friends.

While I arranged our space, Barzouki complained to the Darwaysh. 'Ample space! That's what they said at the shipping office. Ample space for a flea.'

"'I expect the fleas are crowded in, too,' the Darwaysh said.

"'Well, smooth seas don't make skillful sailors.' Then Barzouki and the Darwaysh noticed the Mughrabis massing for a full on attack on the poop deck. They were yelling and shaking their knives and sticks. A few poor crew members attempted to push them back but they were quickly overwhelmed. The Mugharbis were being pushed from behind, too, by the other passengers – and why not! They looked like they thought it was all fun.

"Sa'ad lifted up one of the sailors and put him to guard the stairway. He called Barzouki, 'Come, my little Omar, and show you are a man to be reckoned with.' Barzouki took a quarterstaff and Sa'ad handed another one to the Darwaysh.

"The Darwaysh handed the stick to me and said, 'Use two hands and try to whack them where it hurts. The shoulders and arms. Their heads are too hard.'

"And while Barzouki and Sa'ad and me and the sailor whacked away at the Mughrabis, the Darwaysh returned to our corner and he began setting out his cot. I didn't have time to wonder at this because no matter how hard we hit the Mughrabis there was always another one ready to try us more.

My arms were ready to fall off. A Mughrabi grabbed my stick and only because Sa'ad hit him did I recover. I yelled back to the Darwaysh to help us.

"He turned so casually, as if there were no commotion at all, as if someone had asked him what day it was. He strolled toward us, but detoured toward the huge water urn at the rail. Without hesitating he placed two hands against it and leaned forward and pushed it onto the Mughrabis. Water cascaded over them and the urn cracked heads. But most of all, I think, they were stunned. Sa'ad bellowed at them to go away and the sailors took over and pushed them away.

"Sa'ad embraced the Darwaysh and called him a wise man. Barzouki returned to his cot. The ship cast off and for a while at least, the sun became our biggest enemy and no water jug or quarterstaffs would protect us. We started our prayers and when we finished those and stood, Faris was coming up the stairway. The Darwaysh went over to him and it seemed he might toss Faris overboard.

"Faris said, 'I only want to speak with you for a moment, please.'

"The Darwaysh said, 'I've told you, you mistake me for someone else.'

"Barzouki was coming over to join us. Faris said, 'Meet me. Allow me to speak to you. I have information which could bring you unbearable anguish, or unending delight.'

"The Darwaysh told him to speak right there, that he had nothing to hide. Faris spoke hurriedly, 'Tonight the ship docks and we sleep ashore. Please. We'll meet here, on board, near the bow. Just after the moon rises above the hills. Unbearable anguish or unending delight.' And he turned away before Barzouki arrived. Barzouki was all bravery then, offering to deal with Faris, but the Darwaysh changed the subject.

"I forget what Mr. Burton wrote about this part of the trip. It was monotonous. Monotonous in a way that traveling on that same desert could never be. On the desert there is always danger and… wonder, but traveling alongside it removed both and made the blandness oppressive.

"Barzouki lounged in a hammock, being served by Sa'ad as if he were royalty, while he told the Darwaysh about his life in Cairo. His family had arranged for him to apprentice with a trader in Medinah when the Hajj was ended. The Darwaysh congratulated him but Barzouki cried out, 'For what? What kind of life is that for me?'

"'What would you rather be?' the Darwaysh said.

"'You'll laugh at me.'

"'What strikes the oyster does not damage the pearl.'

"'I'm a philosopher.' He almost swallowed the words and his expression sagged like a man admitting to a crime.

"Sa'ad glared at the Darwaysh as if daring him to laugh. 'He is a philosopher. He is brilliant. I've heard him explain the tides and the emotions of women.'

"'My family has money but won't allow me any until I've learned to make it on my own. I shall make it on my own but not their way.'

"'When he was just a baby I was a servant to his family,' Sa'ad said. 'I won my freedom, and set forth to see the wonders of the world as my own man. I had wives, I had medals, but I had no peace. In freedom, I learned, the greatest happiness came not from glory, but in closeness to others. I was free to choose my path. I was half a man without my little Omar to look after. He will be great and in his greatness I will share.'

"The Darwaysh said, 'I would like to hear more about the emotions of women.'

"Sa'ad said, 'I can tell by his tone that the Darwaysh is a man who has been in love. Yes, Darwaysh?'

"The Darwaysh swallowed and seemed to have to force himself to answer. Just two words, but such sadness as I had never heard. 'I have.'

"'You may learn from him, Omar,' Sa'ad said.

"What did I know? I only knew thieves like Gamil and his men. I only knew tricks and lies. Who were these men and why did a man like the Darwaysh speak with them? Why did he show them respect? Faris seemed to be a crook of some kind, though not the kind I was familiar with. And Barzouki was the kind of man thieves took advantage of – as Gamil had in Suez – but now he acted like he was important and brave and worldly. But I tried my best to walk like the Darwaysh and look at people as he did and so I was patient.

"The ship lowered anchor at Za'afarana to load more water. The passengers did not want to go ashore at first because they didn't want to lose their hard won spots, uncomfortable as they were. But we were escorted onto the beach with vociferous admonitions from the Rais and the crew about peacefulness. The groups all hung together even on shore. The Mughrabis were snarling at us and Sa'ad snarled back. There was cool, fresh water and dates and pomegranates and trees for shade and it was a much better spot than either Suez or the ship.

"After dark, the Darwaysh got up suddenly. I jumped up, too, but he told me to rest. He took along his medical box and walked over to the Mughrabis. I don't know what went on – he never told me – but I saw him doctoring them, even one who had a bump on his head from the water jug. Most of the others fell asleep and even Sa'ad closed his eyes. I only pretended.

"The Darwaysh wandered farther along and went past the Mughrabis and farther, beyond where the campfires ended into a grove of date palms. The moon was merely a scythe and he just disappeared. I had to walk calmly after him because I didn't want to be noticed and by the time I saw him he had stripped off his robe, his shirt and his sandals and was stashing them, along with his medicine box, next to a tree. The last thing he did before sneaking down to the water was to check the dagger in his belt.

"I couldn't swim so I couldn't follow. So I don't know exactly what happened on board the ship, but the Darwaysh found…

"Wait, Ali. I know exactly what happened." It was Hodgson, leaning on his cane as if he had been listening for a while.

13.

Ali and I both jumped up to help him settle into the large, leather armchair. "It's never been told before. We should tell it right," Hodgson said. He looked away from Ali when he spoke and Ali grimaced. "Tell it once, that kind of thing, did you mention it was dark, Ali? It was dark, but not stormy. The water, as you might have guessed, was wetter than it was warm, though warm enough. Warm enough to… Warm enough and dark… and…"

Whatever thoughts he had evaporated, but he didn't appear to be perturbed. He smiled and stared at Ali until Ali finally met his eyes. "Tell it right. No great men here so no lies. You did very well, Ali. I never knew you'd been to Alexandria."

Ali didn't answer. Silence stretched. I expected Hodgson to snap it but he showed no signs of starting. Finally, I said, "The ship. Burton swam out to the ship… Please go on."

"Oh, I really shouldn't, couldn't really… oh, well, if you insist," Hodgson said and started in without pause. "This time Burton expected an ambush. He snuck on deck and crouched low against the gunwale, listening. What he heard was snoring from the two sailors on guard. He started fore, passed close by the sleeping men, but heard another sound behind him and followed it slowly aft. The slash of moon and the stars were enough that Burton's silhouette would show when he climbed onto the poop deck. As he passed beside the ladder, he heard a sound from below.

Suddenly, Ali burst out, "You weren't there. You couldn't know this. I was there when he told this. He never said…"

Hodgson jolted upright and his face reddened. His eyes blazed with warning at Ali. And Ali seemed to understand. Something passed between them that made Ali close his eyes and nod in assent. Or apology. I couldn't tell which it was.

Hodgson continued. "I would rise and demonstrate but I can't right now, nevertheless I am certain that he opened the hatch. It wasn't heavy." He stopped and waited for more from Ali but Ali was done protesting. "Faris toppled forward. Burton caught him and felt the warm blood oozing from his chest and Faris's hand grasped Burton's and held it there.

"'I want to tell you something,' Faris whispered.

"Burton gazed into the darkness below. He wanted to withdraw his hand so he could extract the knife but Faris held tight, held Burton's hand against his chest. He asked Faris who attacked him.

"Faris sputtered a bit, trying to gain his breath. 'I want to tell you… I was a slave trader…'

"But that was all he could muster. Faris's heart stopped beating under Burton's hand with a suddenness that stunned him. 'The things we see now', yes? Gone today. Not exactly withering like grass, but nevertheless… Burton extracted himself from Faris's grip and wiped the blood on Faris's shirt. Though the danger waited below in the hold, Burton forced himself to turn his back on it to gaze around the ship. The sailors still snored in gulps with the regularity of the waves. The only light came from the few remaining fires on the beach and the faint pulses of the stars. Burton drew his knife and walked down into the dark cabin below.

"He kept close to the walls and waited for his eyes to adjust. Down there the creaking of the hull echoed with strange music. The hatch slammed shut. Burton bounded up the stairs and onto the deck. No one was about. Then, from behind he heard a whisper.

"'Darwaysh…'

"It was Barzouki, standing over Faris's body, and holding a quarterstaff in two hands. 'I was sleeping. I heard a noise,' he said.

Burton asked why he was on board and Barzouki said he had bribed the Rais to allow him to stay on board so he could get some sleep.

"'Where is Sa'ad?'

"'On the beach telling stories, I'm sure, to whomever will listen, even the sand flies. Sometimes I need to get away.'

"'I didn't kill him.'

"'Of course not,' Barzouki said. 'And neither did I. But there he lies and here we stand. Will we ever discover who did?'

Burton understood immediately that any suspicions he had of Barzouki were secondary to establishing his own innocence. He could fling suspicion on the other man but he was the more likely suspect. And suspicion could lead to discovery of his disguise.

"'Why should I care about finding out who killed him?' Burton said.

"'Here we stand. If the authorities make inquiries they'll detain us and end our Hajj. I suggest we throw the body overboard.'

"'You seem to miss the point,' Burton said. 'I did not kill him.'

"'Forgive me, Darwaysh, but what happened is not as important as what others will think has happened.'

"'If we do this, we'll be more than friends. We'll be partners.'

"Barzouki said, 'Even if you had killed him, I would be honored.'

"'If I had killed him, Barzouki, you'd be dead. Pick up his legs.'

"Heave ho went the body, windward side. Burton climbed up onto the gunwale intending to follow the body and anchor it to rocks so it wouldn't be discovered. Barzouki became frightened: the killer might be on board. He begged Burton not to leave him alone.

"Burton said, 'If you're going ashore, I suggest you start now, before the sharks come around."

"'I can't swim.'

"Burton dove in, leaving Barzouki behind."

14.

"The next days were spent… How does Burton tell it? Where's that book? Beautiful lies. Lovely deception. Seeking shade. Sunsets. Ragged Bedouin, unruly Mughrabis. No mentions of dead bodies. Oh, one, but don't read that. A baby… Go on, read to me, Reynolds."

"Where?"

"I've read it several times. What do I care where? Just read. I'll tell you if I want you to change. You must know that by now."

I retrieved the book. Ali said, "Try chapter eleven."

I scanned quickly, skipped the first paragraph and began to read: "*Morning – The air is mild and balmy as that of an Italian spring; thick mists roll down the valleys along the sea, and a haze like mother-o'-pearl crowns the headlands. The distant rocks show Titanic walls, lofty donjons, huge protecting bastions, and moats full of deep shade. At their base runs a sea of amethyst, and as earth receives the first touches of light, their summits, almost transparent, mingle with the jasper tints of the sky. Nothing can be more delicious than this hour. But as…*"

Hodgson interrupted. "Rocks? What story talks about rocks? We've all seen the sky. When an agent talks to me about rocks I know he is hiding something. People. Stories are about people. People alone and people together. Rocks are filler.

Rocks are places for people to hide just as the sky is for god to hide in. Or dream of hiding. Back up. Back up to Tur. Before that. The part about the Mughrabis."

He settled back into his seat and smiled, lips tight together, like a fat man being served a pie. I skipped back a few pages and skimmed quickly. I started again:

"Next morning (7th July) before the cerulean hue had vanished from the hills, we set sail. It was not long before we came to a proper sense of our position. The box containing my store of provisions, and, worse still, my opium, was at the bottom of the hold, perfectly unapproachable; we had, therefore, the pleasure of breaking our fast on 'Mare's skin', and a species of biscuit, hard as stone and quite as tasteless. During the day, whilst insufferable splendour reigned above, the dashing of the waters below kept my nest in a state of perpetual drench. At night rose a cold, bright moon, with dews falling so thick and clammy that the skin felt as though it would never be dry again. It is, also, by no means pleasant to sleep upon a broken cot about four feet long by two broad, with the certainty that a false movement would throw you overboard, and a conviction that if you do fall from a Sambuk under sail, no mortal power can save you. And as under all circumstances in the East, dozing is one's chief occupation, the reader will understand that the want of it left me in utter, utter idleness.

"The gale was light that day, and the sunbeams were fire; our crew preferred crouching in the shade of the sail to taking advantage of what wind there was." Here I made the mistake of looking up: Hodgson was rolling his hand as if gesturing to passersby to get out of his way. Move on was the command. I skimmed to a spot where the ship had docked for the night.

"Presently, the Rais joined our party, and the usual story telling began. The old man knew the name of each hill, and had a legend for every nook and corner in sight..."

"Does it say there that the Captain was just a bore? Burton is so polite. Names of hills? Go on, go on," Hodgson said. He didn't do the hand command so I picked up where I was interrupted.

"He dwelt at length upon the life of Abu Zulaymah, the patron saint of these seas, whose little tomb stands at no great distance from our bivouac place and told us how he sits watching over the safety of pious mariners in a cave among the neighboring rocks, and sipping his coffee, which is brought in a raw state from Meccah by green birds, and prepared in the usual way by the hands of ministering angels. He showed us the spot where the terrible king of Egypt, when close upon the heels of the children if Israel, was whelmed in the 'hell of waters,' and he warned us that next day our way would be through breakers, and reefs, and dangerous currents, over whose troubled depths, since that awful day, the Ifrit of the storm has never ceased his sable wing. The wincing of the hearers proved that the shaft of the old man's words was sharp; but as night was advancing, we unrolled our rugs and fell asleep upon the sand, all of us happy, for we had fed and drunk, and – the homo sapiens is a hopeful animal – we made sure that in the morrow the Ifrit would be merciful, and allow us to eat fresh dates at the harbour of Tur."

"Not Tur. Did I say Tur? Not Tur. In Tur they get stuck. Dull spot. My mistake. It's Al-Wijh that I want. Skip to Al-Wijh, please. That's where the fun begins."

"Chapter eleven," Ali said.

"The dawn of the next day saw our sail flapping in the idle air. And it was not without difficulty that in the course of the forenoon we entered Wijh Harbour, distant from Dumayghah but very few miles. Al-Wijh is also a natural anchorage, in no way differing from that where we passed the night, except in being small and shallower and less secure. From this place to Cairo the road is safe. The town is a collection of round huts meanly built of round stones,

and clustering upon a piece of elevated rock on the northern side of the creek. It is distant about six miles from the inland fort of the same name, which receives the Egyptian caravan, and which thrives, like its port, by selling water and provisions to pilgrims. The little bazaar, almost washed by every high tide, provided us with mutton, rice, baked bread, and the other necessities of life at a moderate rate. Luxuries also were to be found: a druggist sold me an ounce of opium at a Chinese price."

I stopped and looked up at Hodgson. No hand gestures this time, but expectation in his eyes. "I'll skip the description of the coffee house and the smoke, steam and flies and gnats."

"Excellent, Reynolds. Next comes a fight."

"Our happiness in this Paradise – for such it was to us after the 'Golden Wire' – was nearly sacrificed by Sa'ad the Demon, whose abominable temper led him at once into a quarrel with the master of the café. And the latter, an ill-looking, squint-eyed, low-browed, broad-shouldered fellow, showed himself nowise unwilling to meet the Demon half way. The two worthies, after a brief bandying of bad words, seized each other's throats leisurely, so as to give the spectators time and encouragement to interfere. But when friends and acquaintances were hanging on to both heroes so firmly that they could not move hand or arm, their wrath, as usual, rose, till it was terrible to see. The little village resounded with the war, and many a sturdy knave rushed in, sword or cudgel in hand, so as not to lose the sport. During the heat of the fray, a pistol which was in Omar Effendi's hand went off – accidently of course – and the ball passed so close to the tins containing the black and muddy Mocha, that it drew the attention of all parties. As if by magic, the storm was lulled. A friend recognized Sa'ad the Demon and swore that he was no black slave, but a soldier at Al-Madinah – 'no waiter but a Knight Templar.' This caused him to be looked upon as rather a distinguished man, and he proved

his right to the honor by insisting that his late enemy should feed with him, and when the other decorously hung back, by dragging him to dinner with loud cries.

"My alias that day was severely tried. Besides the Persian pilgrims, a number of nondescripts who came in the same vessel were hanging about the coffee-house; lying down, smoking, drinking water, bathing and picking their teeth with their daggers. One inquisitive man was always at my side. He called himself a Pathan (Afghan settled in India); he could speak five or six languages; he knew a number of people everywhere, and had travelled far and wide over Central Asia. These fellows are always good detectors of an incognito. I avoided answering his question about my native place, and after telling him that I had no longer name or nation, being a Darwaysh, I asked him, when he insisted upon my having been born somewhere to guess for himself. To my joy he claimed me for a brother Pathan, and in the course of conversation he declared himself to be the nephew of an old Afghan merchant, a gallant old man who had been civil to me in Cairo. We then sat smoking together with 'effusion.' Becoming confidential, he complained that he, a Sunni, or orthodox Muslim, had been abused, maltreated, and beaten by his fellow-travellers, the heretical Persian pilgrims. I naturally offered to arm my party, to take up our cudgels, and to revenge my compatriot. This thoroughly Sulaymanian style of doing business could not fail to make him sure of his man. He declined, however, wisely remembering that he had nearly a fortnight of the Persians' society still to endure. But he promised himself gratification, when he reached Meccah, of sheathing his Charay in the chief offender's heart."

"He writes fiction so well, doesn't he?" It was as if Hodgson had been given a jolt of electricity – the kind of jolt that didn't work on Burton's corpse. His voice was strong and he leaned forward with urgency. "But let's return to the truth and leave the rocks and the sky behind. There were problems, Reynolds. No movement, but plenty of activity. What problems? Burton had too little information about the relationship between Faris and Barzouki to press the issue yet. He wondered if Barzouki would claim to have done the murder out of gratitude for Burton's help in Suez. Did that mean that Barzouki knew the nature of the threat Faris posed? Did Faris pose a separate, unrelated threat to Barzouki? That would have been a nice coincidence. Since Barzouki survived the night aboard ship, it was almost certain that he was the murderer, but Burton did not understand why he had done it. And more important, what had he learned from Faris? Did Barzouki now have Faris's knowledge? That would make him doubly dangerous – he could lay blame for the murder and then reveal Burton's true identity. If Barzouki killed Faris for that knowledge then he could only have malign intent. But there was more, something bigger that blocked all the rest. What obstacle had Burton encountered? What was it, Reynolds? Come now, feel the sun and the heat and stare across at Barzouki and smile and at Sa'ad and talk to them about the Hajj, about medicine, about philosophy. What was the problem?"

As the rant went on I stopped paying attention to Ali. Now I turned to him. His brow was knitted tight and his eyes were seeing some horror beyond anything Hodgson had said. He didn't acknowledge me and I doubted he registered my presence at all. I said his name but he didn't react.

"You can't ignore the question, Reynolds. No ignoring. Ignore the question and the problem grows worse. Which is a problem in itself. Now, what was the problem?" Hodgson said.

Ali got up. "Goodbye, Mr. Reynolds."

Hodgson said, "Have I said the wrong thing, Ali? Lied? Not yet, I think, though I consider it with each sentence. Please stay, Ali."

"The Darwaysh did not kill Faris," Ali said.

"Stipulated!" Hodgson clapped his hands together. "Now, please, as you have established I might need you."

Ali sat down as if nothing bothered him anymore. Their enigmatic charade having paused, it was my turn, again, to have the darkness focused on me. I was ready.

"You're here at the creation, Reynolds. Gape in awe, then tell me the problem Burton faced."

"When I came to London you followed me."

"Followed you? Followed you? Is that your answer?"

"Why did you follow me?"

Hodgson sighed. His lips pulled back in a grimace of defeat. Slowly they drew upward to form a reluctant smile. "You're absolutely right, Reynolds. Congratulations. I followed you because I'd been put out to pasture, retired, passed over, ignored, sent before my time into this hellish void, attached to an American, relegated. Relegated, but no dogs barking at me. At least none that I heard. I followed you, cane and all, because the Home Office would not allocate the manpower required to do so."

"You followed me because you wanted to verify my identity. That was Burton's problem. He'd spent all his energy and thought on establishing and embellishing his own identity and that led him to taking the word of others at face value. He didn't know who Barzouki really was or Sa'ad or Ali. Anyone, even Gamil. And he was helpless to find out. He had spent his time wondering what they thought about him."

"Keep it in mind, Reynolds." His eyes closed and his head bent forward. I waited. He didn't move. I listened. His breathing was heavy and thick, but the intervals were regular. I waited. I was about to summon the nurse when Hodgson's head snapped up and his eyes popped open. Sadness coated those eyes again and he lifted his brows to offset it like a thief asking for sympathy.

"Burton could only brazen it out," he said. "Too late to know who Faris was and each question would sound like an accusation to Barzouki. The sun and Sa'ad made any action out of the question.

"Burton had booked his passage to Yenbo rather than Jiddah, planning on going first to Medina along with most of the pilgrims. He thought it would give him more time to blend in, and a chance to scout out the Prince's palace. There were camels to be procured and supplies purchased. Ali can tell you more about that. He debarked first to beat the rush for the best animals. As Burton was leaving he saw the Rais with three Bedouins who hadn't been on board the ship. The Rais looked around and seeing Burton, pointed toward him.

"The three Bedouins followed Burton to the market corral where he purchased three camels, one extra for his gear. To the stalls where he purchased saddles, a *shugduf,* and food and medical supplies. They followed him to the lodging he found for Ali and himself; the caravan for Medina was set to leave in two days. They followed him to the mosque and prayed behind him. They stepped up after the darkness deepened. Burton and Ali had dinner with friends they had made on board ship and were returning to their lodging.

"The three Bedouins didn't surround Burton as Gamil had done. Didn't draw their weapons. Burton proffered his cup and each placed a coin in it. Very respectable fellows, they were. Abdullah, the eldest, did the talking. What were the names of the others, Ali?"

"Hossein and Danesh. Danesh was only slightly older than me."

"Abdullah explained that they were Faris's brothers, there to join him on the Hajj. 'The Rais told us you spoke with Faris on the ship. When was the last time you saw him?'

"'I did meet Faris. But it's been days since I saw him last,' Burton said. He didn't sense danger, not at that moment; he wanted information and he worried that they might know about his true identity as Faris did. "He came to me, said he wanted to speak further about something private. I assumed it was a spiritual matter. Would you know anything about that?'

"The middle brother, Hossein, shouted angrily, 'He's lying.' And his hand hit his scabbard, but Abdullah held him back.

"Abdullah said, 'Darwaysh, you know more and would be wise to tell us now. Where is my brother?'

"'Perhaps it was an illness he suffered from?'

"Hossein added another threat from behind Abdullah.

"'I did not harm your brother,' Burton said. 'But if you doubt me, you have three choices: You may fight me, you may tell the authorities, or you may walk away.'

"'We have another choice,' Abdullah said. 'We can wait and watch.'

"Abdullah and Hossein walked away. Danesh, the youngest brother, waited behind, studying Burton. But when Burton spoke to him, asking if he needed a doctor, Danesh ran away."

Hodgson stopped. His eyelids slid down for a long moment, though his head didn't bow. When he opened them, he lifted his eyebrows again, but this time it seemed as if that were all he had the strength for. "Couldn't trust them. Couldn't fight them. Couldn't eliminate them. Couldn't get help. Stuck together they were. Traveling companions. Barzouki and Sa'ad and the brothers with Burton day and night. Know what that's like, don't you. Traveling with the enemy. Toting along your own danger? Better to stay still or keep moving? Back to the wall or room to run? There would be bandits on the way, too. Burton needed eyes all around his head. He was exhilarated."

15.

I sent a note to Mrs. Burton, asking her to lunch at Café Orientale, expecting her to refuse to appear in public so early in her mourning and hoping I would be invited back to the villa. Instead, she accepted but preferred Café Stella Polare at noon.

Mrs. Burton's appearance brought on a stuttering, bumbling, fawning conniption in the maître d' and that alerted the other patrons – mostly elderly – who stared openly. The maître d' kept up his yammering and scraping and bowing all the way to the table, like a dog after the scraps. He wasn't getting any, not from Mrs. Burton. She held her severe face tight, but in the sureness of her gait and her assiduous inattention to his manic ministrations I could tell she enjoyed the tribute. The stares from the others didn't scold her, they buoyed her. She wore all black and an abundance of it. Much more than mourning attire, it was a declaration of inviolability, a weapon. It was impossible to imagine her wearing anything else.

Somehow the maître d' managed to pour a glass of wine without sprinkling it around the premises. As soon as he scampered away, Mrs. Burton said, "I suppose Mr. Hodgson has been refuting my husband's account of his Hajj."

"I was hoping you could clear that up."

She didn't answer. Hatred twisted her features and her thin lips became thinner and tightened into a snarl. The waiter appeared with menus and the maître d' hovered not far behind, ready to pounce. Mrs. Burton waved off the card and said, "I will have my usual meal. And Mr. Reynolds will have... the other meal."

The waiter bowed quickly and departed. Mrs. Burton said, "Mr. Burton always prefers the mutton chop here. They cook it in the Hungarian style. I have the petrale." She couldn't keep the challenge from her voice: I dare you to change a thing.

I retreated in order to advance, asking how she'd been coping with her loss. The snarl abated. The words poured out. News of her husband's death was spreading and letters of condolence and remembrance were in flowing in a widening stream. She was determined to answer all and that activity helped console her and focus her thoughts. The funeral, a proper Catholic funeral, would take place in two days. A British war vessel was in port and the sailors would attend in dress uniforms. She decided Burton would be buried in England. She would erect a memorial there to him. Its form still under consideration. Something to celebrate all the facets of the man – adventurer, writer and husband.

"And spy?"

"He was never a spy, Mr. Reynolds. Despite what lies Mr. Hodgson might be telling you."

"I wonder why he lies about it."

"To assuage his guilt."

I waited. She sipped her wine. She glanced toward a table of women to her left. Three of them nodded but Mrs. Burton might have been staring at specks of dust. My only job was to not interrupt with even the slightest show of impatience as she prepared her answer.

Not knowing what his job was, the maître d' swooped in and skidded to a stop just inches from disaster and plucked the wine bottle. "Mrs. Burton... Madame Burton, how is everything today. Gemutlich? Simpatico? You honor us on this special occasion. You..."

"Put that down and go away."

He bowed so low that he bumped his head on the table. The wine tilted and spilled into the bucket and he scooted away.

Mrs. Burton's urge to speak of Hodgson's betrayal had vaporized. Did I know her husband was a master swordsman, that he defeated – humiliated! – the famous Monsieur Constantine. She was there. She witnessed the match. Seven touches. Seven consecutive touches! She witnessed his expertise. She witnessed the affection the others had for him and the respect he earned that day. Men feared him, were awed by him. And women! They fawned and paraded and plotted.

"Did you know that before I met Burton I'd visited a gypsy whose name also was Burton, and who foresaw that I, Isabel, was destined to marry a man named Burton? I rejected numerous offers, many offers, from dreadfully dull men, and I resolved that if Richard Francis Burton didn't marry me, I would remain alone throughout my life. I even thought I would join a convent. It was a simple decision really. Having known him, any other man would fall short and it would be unfair to whomever I should marry. Many of the girls were afraid of him. You never met Richard but the portraits are accurate – his eyes were fierce. And his conversation was equally intense and if someone bored him he simply turned away. The mothers hated him because they knew they could never control him. But that wildness made me wait for him.

"It was in Boulogne, you know, where we met, where he courted me. We had to sneak around. He was so inventive, even disguised himself. Though, as I said... those eyes! He proposed to me and I, my soul, flew, and he begged me to wait for him to return from Arabia and swore he would return… We were married not long after he returned from the Hajj. I never returned to earth."

She hardly drew breath, left no gaps where I could insert a question that might alter her course. The delivery was intentional. It wasn't the gushing of a woman in love. It was a discourse on the nature of reality. She intended to paint a picture with such exhaustive zeal that it would overwhelm all contradiction, blot out any hint of inconsistency. Though I've often had doubts about masterpieces I never threw paint on any and I managed not to question her version of the world.

"His dream – he had so many dreams – so many dreams and he lived them all, as no man before him – his dream when we fell in love was to make the pilgrimage to Mecca and Medinah. He had a plan. He spoke Arabic and Farsi and Pashto. He petitioned the Royal Geographical Society for backing and they pledged it. Of course they did. And when he returned we would marry. I'll confess, Mr. Reynolds, that I would have rather married Richard before the Hajj despite the risk of becoming an instant widow. I cared not the least that he had no prospects and little income. He had plans, and faith in himself and I knew, we knew, that he would return and we would marry because our love was that strong. That's the story, Mr. Reynolds. That's the truth. I'm the living proof of it. Richard endured a barbaric ordeal, survived the most underhanded betrayal and returned and married me. It was his love for me that sustained and fortified him throughout his odyssey. Here are some of the memorial plans…"

She thrust a folded sheet of paper at me so suddenly that I never saw her remove it from her purse. Maybe it had been taped underneath the table. I unfolded it and examined the drawing of something resembling a tent or hut.

"A Bedouin tent. Richard always said that was where he was most comfortable. Outside of our home."

I admired the drawing and the sentiment and asked more about the plans. Where would she erect the monument? She hadn't decided. She hadn't settled on the construction material. Would there be a library attached? Surely, the British government would fund this for one of their bravest, most intrepid heroes. I agreed, doing my best to gently rush her through this part, fearful that the maître d', like some rotating cuckoo clock, would pop up without warning and end the meeting in a cascade of stains and broken glass.

When she paused at last, I tried a wild guess, hoping to be corrected. "I suppose Hodgson didn't arrive to transport Mr. Burton out of Arabia when the Hajj was over. Left him hanging there in disguise."

Her eyes narrowed into small coals of suspicion and her mouth pulled back. I thought of signaling the maître d' to rescue me. "You're impatient, Mr. Reynolds. Impatient people end up with bad information. I've told you the important things. My love for Richard and his for me was true and lasting. His fortitude was unmatched. His scholarship historic. Mr. Hodgson's trickery and disgusting machinations failed. Richard survived. And so Mr. Hodgson made up lies to distract from his own duplicitous misdeeds."

With that she rose, creating a whirlpool that sucked attention from all corners of the room. I joined her on the way out, though she didn't need me to make it a procession.

It was easy to understand her motive for telling the story the way she did – Burton as a great hero and their love as illustrious and unshakeable – and just as difficult to understand Hodgson's motive for telling it his way – with himself as the villain. That riddle made me tend to lean toward Hodgson's version. I wished more than ever I could have met Burton so I could assess his version which seemed like it was going to leave all intrigue and treachery out altogether. Maybe he thought the truth would make him look bad.

16.

The apartment was different. Quiet. No chattering from the kitchen and no smell of food preparation.

Hodgson's door was open. The bed was stripped of sheets and blankets, pillows stacked in the middle. The closets were empty.

It was easy to find a rig but no amount of urging, whether in Italian or German, could induce the carriage driver to bother his horse to anything more vigorous than an indifferent amble. Cursing in English didn't help either. The slow, methodical clip-clop taunted like a metronome all the way downhill and along the quay. A ship from Marseilles had just dumped a horde of passengers and I had to fight the surge to reach the harbormaster's hut.

That gave me time to watch as a tender delivered three American sailors – two petty officers in blue jackets and a seaman – to the dock. There to corral me, no doubt. I slithered away as fast as possible.

On the roof of the hut, two tall men sent semaphore signals to the ships entering the bay. Beside them, four men looked through telescopes to read the signals from the ships. Each man had a cigar plugged into his mouth. Boys with sheaves of papers ran into and out of the hut, dodging around me and anyone else in the vicinity. The hut stunk of cigars. Four men, each with a lit stub, bent over their shipping logs. The harbormaster himself sat on a tall stool and puffed energetically on a newly lit cigar.

"English ships? Is that what you want? Plenty of English ships. Never a shortage of those. Got English ships to spare. Now, maybe you mean ships bound for England? No ships for England today. But I don't know where a ship might end up after it leaves here. Had one bound for America once, ended up in India. Only heard about it because the mother of a sailor on board received a silk cloak and tried to sell it to my wife. No, that was another ship – went on to China. The one that went to India… well, he sent back something. You can check the sheets. Posted outside. All the shipping times and ports of call are listed there," he said, the cigar rolling in teeth.

"Are those the passenger lists?"

I pointed to a stack of papers at the edge of a long counter. He started to speak again, "Well, it's difficult to say, though, yes, every passenger is…"

A boy scrambled in and dropped two sheets on top of the pile. I spoke quickly and hopped over to the pile and said, "Thank you. I'll just check these."

The harbormaster sent out a cloud of smoke and he half smiled before turning back to his window. On the third sheet – the list of passengers for a ship bound for Lisbon – was Hodgson's name with an x beside it and the fare he paid.

Hodgson had sailed an hour ago. I was sunk. My prospects were iron weights plunging me deeper. I stood there dumb and still, staring at the same horizon as the spotters, but the horizon was my enemy now. The U.S. ship – the steel protected U.S.S. Atlanta, I saw it on the sheets – stared back at me and I considered desertion. Months ago Hodgson had introduced me to a

British deserter who had set himself up in Turkey as a tutor to the children of government officials, thinking he could prosper but avoid the attention of foreigners. Hodgson discovered him and then owned him and worked him mercilessly, forcing him to steal from every employer whether Hodgson needed the information or not. Desertion was the deepest grave.

I checked the sheets again. Same result. The harbor master looked at me with something resembling sympathy. "What does the X beside a name mean?" I said.

"Well, it might mean a few things. It might mean the person's name has an X in it and the typist just put it in the wrong place. Happens now and then. No time to correct it. Everyone is busy nowadays. Could mean there's a special issue with that passenger though the typist is supposed to put a Z in that case. Hardly matters…"

"Does it usually mean that the passenger didn't board?"

I was out of there before he started his second sentence.

Jenkins would know where Hodgson was and I rushed up toward the consulate, but just yards away I stopped and ducked into an alley: the three American sailors came out. Once they had turned a corner, I went in. Jenkins was at his desk reading a book. The office was tiny, windowless. He closed the book and laid it on his desk when he saw me: *The Inner House*, by Walter Besant.

"Those men, Jenkins, were they asking for me?"

He was wary of me and quickly stuffed the book in a drawer. "No. They didn't mention you. Why should they? This is the British consulate you know. Not the American consulate."

That was a relief. Now I could get down to business. "You didn't tell them where to find Mr. Hodgson, did you?"

"What? No! I didn't say anything. They didn't ask." He jumped up. His chair hit the back wall. We faced each other across the desk

"They're German agents. They intend to seize him. They're clever."

"No, they're Americans."

"No need to be insulting, Jenkins. Anyway, what would Americans be doing here? They're Germans I tell you."

"They said they're here for Mr. Burton's funeral." Further relief.

"We must warn Hodgson immediately."

"I'll send a cable."

"No! It's not secure. I must go there. How long will it take?"

"About two hours, but you won't get a driver at this time of day."

"Why not?"

"There's no night time traffic coming back. Everyone checks out of the resort in the morning. So they can walk in the mountains."

"No train?"

Jenkins stopped suddenly and stared at me. A grin formed revealing a horrible jumble of yellow and brown stubs. "You don't know where he is, do you?"

"Of course I do."

"No you don't. He told me not to tell anyone. He stressed anyone. He meant you."

"But you've just told me, Jenkins. Goodbye."

His protestations followed me down the stairs and out the door. I found a carriage driver and asked him to take me to the resort about a two hour ride away, near the mountains. "Opcina? Not tonight. Tomorrow."

I arranged to be picked up at the apartment.

17.

The Café Taksim serves Turkish food and, apparently, women, young and old, craving those delicacies flock there in the evenings. Hodgson had mentioned the place in his discourse on my reading of the Kama Sutra, and careful eavesdropping on Carmela and Anna, whose niece is one of those women, confirmed its reputation. I sensed this would be my last opportunity to experience this wonder for myself.

The place was decorated with red velvet, smoke and mirrors. But the magic was the oldest secret in the world. A fifty lira tip secured a precarious path to a table for two. Music and conversation battled for dominance. Laughter struck without warning. The waiter, a fat, sweating, greasy man, asked if I knew where I wanted to send drinks before he asked what I wanted for myself.

Conversation snuck over, under, around the music. None in English. Five business men each spoke incessantly, no one ever stopping to listen to another. They seemed happy with everything they heard, though. Two young men entertained four young women wearing enough makeup for ten. The men spoke German and the women did not speak at all, or even pretend to understand what the men said.

What did they know of the Kama Sutra, those women and those young men? Chapters full, I guessed, but none of it written and none expressed with Burton's subtle detail and elegance. The room presented a different kind of storytelling: experience over intellect. This was instinct elevated to compulsion.

'When a man enjoys many women altogether, it is called the congress of a herd of cow.'

'Though a woman is reserved, and keeps her feelings concealed; yet when she gets on the top of a man, she then shows all her love and desire. A man should gather from the actions of the woman of what disposition she is, and in what way she likes to be enjoyed. A woman during her monthly courses, a woman who has been lately confined, and a fat woman should not be made to act the part of a man.'

'When the woman places one of her legs on her lover's shoulder, and stretches the other out, and then places the latter on his shoulder, and stretches out the other, and continues to do so alternately, it is called the 'splitting of a bamboo'.

'When one of her legs is placed on the head, and the other is stretched out, it is called the 'fixing of a nail'. This is learnt by practice only.'

Those were just a few of the passages I had sipped and now they ran as narration for the scene in front of me, which developed into an orgy, patiently, methodically, relentlessly, like storm clouds swelling together. Two women kissed. One sat on the other's lap facing her, and put her legs up and leaned back and a third woman leaned down and kissed her passionately. A man and woman tangoed and dramatically removed a piece of clothing at each change. Farther from me, in the corners, the people were already naked and making love. Changing partners. Clothes weren't removed – they disappeared, melted, were thrown aloft. Women lifted men. Men did flips. The positions were impossible, exaggerations of the drawings and descriptions in Burton's Kama Sutra.

The waiter appeared before me, blocking the beautiful view. I opened my mouth to order. "A mixture of sesamum seed with rice," I said. I heard myself but couldn't correct the gaffe; it was a position Burton named in the book. For a moment, it seemed the waiter understood me. I looked around me; the orgy continued and I was immeasurably relieved. Even the arrival of a plate of grilled octopus over eggplant and tomatoes couldn't shake me out of my delightful trance.

The food meant nothing. I wanted to watch the orgy and I sighed to see it re-forming like a company coming on stage for the second act, when a cackle pierced the air and shattered the view. The Countess Gandolpho strutted through the haze, heading toward me, towing a small, older man in a fez. She bumped a table and a woman grabbed at her skirt. "Lay off, tootsie," the Countess said. The other woman understood the tone, if not the words, and hopped up, but a man pulled her onto his lap and she whispered to him and they laughed.

The Countess dragged her beau to my table. "Meester Reynolds. You founda me at last. I can not escape you, yes. You came here to finda me, no?"

"No."

"You teeease me so. This, your rival, is Mustafa Bey. Have you met?" She swayed and his grip tightened to keep her from falling into the next table.

"Yes, we're old friends." I doubt the old guy understood English but he raised his eyebrows in a greeting of complicity and supplication. We understood each other. An orgy of sorts was dancing behind his eyes, too. The Countess mussed my hair and insisted I join them at Club Vendemia. I told her I was waiting for someone.

She smiled and fought to keep her eyes open. "Mr. Hodgson, I suppose?"

"His daughter."

And with that, the lovely fantasia was lost. The Countess's cackle faded, leaving Hodgson's voice repeating his sharp comments and leading me back to Burton and his Hajj. And my effort to decipher it all.

18.

"The population of Yanbu – one of the most bigoted and quarrelsome races in Al-Hijaz – strikes the eye after arriving from Egypt, as decidedly a new feature. The Shaykh or gentleman is over-armed and over-dressed, as Fashion, the Tyrant of the Desert as well as of the court, dictates to a person of his consequence. The civilized traveller from Al-Madinah sticks in his waist-shawl a loaded pistol, garnished with crimson silk cord, but he partially conceals the butt-end under the flap of his jacket. The Irregular soldier struts down the street a small armoury of weapons: one look at the man's countenance suffices to tell you what he is. Here and there stalk grim Badawin, wild as their native wastes, and in all the dignity of pride and dirt; they are also armed to the teeth, and even the presence of the policeman's quarterstaff cannot keep their swords in their scabbards. What we should call the peaceful part of the population never leave the house without the 'Nabbut' over the right shoulder, and the larger, longer, and the heavier the weapon is, the more gallantry does the bearer claim. The people of Yanbu practice the use of this implement diligently; they become expert in delivering a head-blow so violent as to break through any guard, and with it they always decide their trivial quarrels. The dress of the women differs but little from that of the Egyptians, except in the face veil, which is generally white.

Burton was a fan of the face veil, *"the most coquettish article of women's attire… It conceals coarse skins, fleshy noses, wide mouths, and vanishing chins whilst it sets off to best advantage what in these lands is almost always lustrous and liquid – the eye. Who has not remarked on this at a masquerade ball?"*

The talk around town told of bandits on the road to Medinah. The Hazimi tribe was on patrol. Daghastanis reported that they gave the *Salam*, but got no reply which meant the Hazimi meant to fight. But the Daghastanis claimed they weren't going far and that, they thought, made the Hazimi not bother with them. Travelers at the end of their journeys were usually out of money.

Burton bought a *shugduf,* which consists of two cots bound together by rope and wood and slung over the camels back; a person rode on each side, the weight balanced by jugs of water. A *shugduf* was considered effeminate, but Burton had cut his foot while wading before arriving in Yanbu; it was painful and it wasn't healing. His servant rode on the other side. Quite comfortable, Burton said. They spent an evening on the terrace of the wakaleh, Sa'ad the Demon telling tales, everyone feasting on mutton and rice, pipes and coffee, then they prayed the *Isha,* the evening prayer, and went to sleep to prepare for their departure the next day. They packed up the camels – always a troublesome process – and were off for Medinah, with stops along the way.

Medinah first, not Mecca as Hodgson claimed. Medinah.

No mention of Faris's brothers. A friend warns him to speak only Arabic along the way as speakers of Farsi and other languages are looked down on, but the warning has nothing to do with his supposed mission.

I read on, wanting to get ahead of Hodgson, wanting to be able to catch him out in his telling.

Slowly my suspicion turned and shone on Burton. If you wanted to disguise a spy mission this was the way to do it. Bury it under a mountain of detail. Footnotes. Drawings. Anecdotes. Bury it all under precision. He paid two dollars for the *shugduf.* The water here is sweet, there brackish. The houses are "*roughly built of limestone and coralline, and their walls full of fossils crumble like almond cake.*" The suk, the cafes, the custom house. In detail. An Arab Shaykh…

I must now take the liberty of presenting to the reader an Arab Shaykh fully equipped for travelling. Nothing can be more picturesque than the costume, and it is with regret that we see it exchanged in the towns and more civilised parts for any other. The long locks or shaven scalps are surmounted by a white cotton skull-cap, over which is a Kufiyah – a large square kerchief of silk and cotton mixed, and generally of a dark red colour with a bright yellow border, from which depend crimson silk twists ending in little tassels that reach the wearer's waist. Doubled into a triangle, and bound with an Aakal or fillet of rope, a skein of yarn or a twist of wool, the kerchief fits the head close behind: it projects over the forehead, shading the eyes, and giving a fierce look to the countenance. On certain occasions one end is brought round the lower part of the face, and is fastened behind the head. This veiling of features is technically called Lisam: the chiefs generally fight so, and it is the usual disguise when a man fears the avenger of blood, or a woman starts to take her Sar. In hot weather it is supposed to keep the Samun, in cold weather the cartarrh, from the lungs.

And footnotes for all of it. *Aakal* – great men bind a twisted shawl to keep the kerchief in place. And, there are regional and class variations. *Sar* – blood revenge.

The body dress is simply a Kamis or cotton shirt: tight sleeved, opening in front and adorned around the waist and collar, and down the breast, with an embroidery like net-work; it extends from neck to foot. Some wear wide trousers, but the Bedawin consider such things effeminate, and they have not yet fallen into the folly of socks and stockings. Over the Kamis is thrown a long skirted and short sleeved cloak of camel's hair, called an Aba. It is made in many patterns, and of all materials from pure silk to coarse sheep's wool; some prefer it brown, others white others striped; in Al-Hijaz the favourite hue is white, embroidered with gold, tinsel or yellow thread in two large triangles, capped with broad bands and other figures running down the shoulders and sides of the back. It is lined inside the shoulders and breast with handsome stuffs of silk and cotton mixed, and is tied in front by elaborate strings, and tassels or acrons of silk and gold. A sash confines the Kamis at the waist, and supports the silver hilted Jambiyah or crooked dagger; the picturesque Arab sandal completes the costume. Finally, the Shaykh's arms are a sword and a matchlock slung behind his back; in his right hand he carries a short javelin or a light crooked stick, about two feet and a half long, called a Mas'hab, used for guiding camels.

The poorer class of Arabs twist round their waist, next to the skin, a long plait of greasy leather, to support the back; and they gird the shirt at the middle with a cord, or with a coarse sash. The dagger is stuck in this scarf, and a bandolier slung over the shoulder carries the cartridge-case, powder-flask, flint and steel, priming-horn, and other necessaries. With the traveller, the waist is an elaborate affair. Next to the skin is worn the money pouch, concealed by the Kamis; the latter is girt with a waist shawl, over which is trapped a leathern belt. The latter article should always be well garnished with a pair of long-barrelled and silver mounted flint pistols, a large and a small dagger, and an iron ramrod with pincers inside; a little leathern pouch fastened to the waist-strap on the right side contains cartridge, wadding, and flask of priming powder. The sword hangs over the shoulder by crimson silk cords and huge tassels; well-dressed men apply the same showy ornaments to their pistols. In the hand may be born a bell mouthed blunderbuss or better still, a long single-barrel gun with an ounce bore. All these weapons must shine like silver, if you wish to be respected; for the knightly care of arms is here a sign of manliness.

There was more, much more. And fascinating footnotes: *Some men wear a little dagger strapped round the leg below the knee. Its use is this: when the enemy gets you under, he can prevent you bringing your hand up to the weapon in your waist-belt; but before he cuts your throat, you may slip your fingers down to the knee, and persuade him to stop by a stab in the perineum. The article I chiefly accused myself of forgetting was a stout English clasp-knife with a large handle, a blade like an 'Arkansas tooth-pick,' and possessing the other useful appliance of picker, fleam, tweezers, lancet and punch.*

He wrote it all down on the spot. When to use the pencil, when to switch to the pen, the correct ink – English – the ink stand, the notebook hidden in a breast pocket. Even the shift from Arabic to English once he decided no one would discover this bit of guile. The caravan launches at last for Medinah, just twelve camels in their group, joining many others, single file, one woman, dirty clothing to disguise their prosperity, two miles an hour, left at 6pm, stopped at 3am, rose at 9am. Pipes and meals, biscuits, rice, milkless tea, *kahk* – a bread – and how it's made, vile tasting *Akit* – dried sour milk dissolved in water – sour milk and sweet milk when they could get it from a local Bedawin with a flock of sheep or goats.

The towns with their fluid names, different to different tribes. The scorching sun, the dry rain, the wadis and granite hills and boulders and dark caves – Hodgson's rocks! – and lack of anything living at all except those in the caravan.

I read until dawn. Past dawn, until the street below was loud enough to remind me that a carriage would be arriving to take me to Opcina.

19.

We wound up the steep roads past Sottomonte and when we reached the plain the driver stopped and told me get down. I didn't have to ask why: the view. To the left, villas and churches in the main part of Trieste were stacked, without roots, and threatening to slide down into the Adriatic, a deep, heavy blue from here. Higher up, in the villages, outlying churches and houses showed like mushroom caps amongst the clumps of forest.

The driver insisted I sit beside him so he could narrate the brief remainder of the trip. A large white obelisk, just a tall white dart, came into view first. It marked the beginning of *Strada Napoleonica,* cut by the General's troops when they came to Trieste in 1797. Soon we were on that road and heading toward the obelisk and the resort called Daneu's Inn. The main building was three stories with a gabled, pantile roof. Attached to the left was a matching two story addition.

The town was decked out, but I didn't think it was in my honor. "Fete, fete," the driver said. Flags and flowers and colored draperies hung from every window. But no citizens in sight. Even the dogs and cats seem have deserted the place. We drifted into faint music and around a curve the road was blocked by the progression of women in white lace and red, green and brown cotton dresses, and men, some of them in lederhosen. Leading the way were the priests. The obelisk lay ahead and I was thrilled to think they might kneel there and set their wreaths – a pagan ceremony. But they stopped at the church a quarter mile short of the obelisk, and we carried on.

The lobby was quiet. An elderly woman sat watching the weather, her hands folded in her lap and knuckles white with tension as if she were expecting something horrible to come out of the sky. A somewhat younger couple sipped beers in silence. Sweat coated the man's forehead. He wiped it off when he saw me looking at him. Hikers. The clerk spoke only Slovenian but I managed to register. When he read my name, he perked up and learned to speak German: "Herr Hodgson erwartet dich. Sol ich ihm mitteilen Sie angekommen sind?" Before I could answer, the whistling began – the same song I'd last heard in Rabat. I turned. Ali was escorting Hodgson into the lobby. "I've heard that before. What's that tune called?" I said.

Hodgson said, "It's called, Her Heart Was Pure As My Mind."

Ali's big eyes looked me up and down, taking my measure, and for the first time I could see the boy thief he claimed he had been. The scar on his cheek looked sinister now but his voice was still soft and pleasing. "Please join us on the terrace, Mr. Reynolds. You must be thirsty after your journey."

I tipped the bellman and followed Hodgson and Ali out there. Hodgson sat with his back to the distant white peaked mountains, the Carnaline Alps, I later learned. I forced myself to admire the view while he spoke, a pleasantness to deflect the sneering that was coming my way. He started in with gusto.

"Still around, Reynolds? Haven't left for Djakarta, or Rangoon, or Hong Kong? If you want to go nowhere you've come to the right place, Reynolds. We're not in Italy, really, are we. Not in Hungary, either. Not Slovenia. Not Austria. Not

Croatia. Not China for the matter. Sit down, sit down. We've hardly talked, have we. Not really. Not really conversed. I've done the talking. Most of it. Most of it, as you pleased. But it hasn't been satisfactory, not at all. Has it?"

It took me a moment to realize he meant to stop for a reply. "It's been fascinating," I said. "But not satisfactory. You saw to that."

He drew in a long breath and smiled. "I wonder if that could be remedied. Now you're being sent home, aren't you? No more stories about Shanghai. Recalled. No promotion in the works. You'll be assigned to some battleship – the U.S.S. Boring – patrolling… where do you think? Off the coast of Chile? Guarding one end or the other of the Panama Canal? Quite a list of diseases there. Malaria foremost, though I prefer dengue fever. The name is as awful sounding as the disease. Dungy fever."

His eyes had been glowing with triumph but they suddenly sagged and I realized he meant that to indicate sympathy. If I wasn't so inured to his machinations I might have been grateful for the feelings. The transition was slick and all it once it struck me how much practice he had at these shifts and how he used them when recruiting his agents and…

I was being recruited! It came as an epiphany: obvious, inevitable and shocking. I was delighted. Hodgson intended me to be his salvation, just as I intended for him to be mine. It didn't matter how long he'd planned it, didn't matter what past manipulations and ill treatment were designed to edge me toward this moment. All that mattered was that now both ends of the line had hooks attached. I looked from Hodgson to Ali and back trying my best to indicate that I was nibbling the bait, without actually moving my lips.

"Been courting the dreary widow, Reynolds? How is she? Determined, I'd bet. Fierce. Insistent. Gratified at the tributes poring in. Think the powers that be in Trieste will conspire to keep her here? Find a new husband for her? Be careful, Reynolds, they might try to recruit you. Prisoner of Trieste. Happened to a better man than you. No American Consul here yet. I'll vouch for your diplomatic skills. I warn you, though, when last I saw her, almost twenty years ago, her skirts were far less ample. Consider that going forward. The villa might not be vast enough for the two of you. Crowd you out."

"She's planning a funeral for day after tomorrow. Will you go?"

"A Catholic funeral with all the flummery. It would have killed Burton. The honors she wanted him to have in life and the god he had no business with."

"Should he have a Muslim funeral?"

"You should know better by now. He posed as a Muslim and participated in every prayer and ritual, and all that didn't make him a Muslim and they would have killed him the moment he was unmasked. Here, in Trieste, he participated in every Catholic prayer and ritual, but why should we assume it wasn't also a pose? Or assume that Mrs. Burton wouldn't have killed him if he were unmasked."

He was right and he managed to make me feel foolish, again. "You left Burton at Yanbu," I said. "Catching a caravan to Medinah. Please go on with the story. The true story."

He ignored me. The waiter delivered tea for Hodgson and Ali and beer for me. "There are ways to put a shine on you, Reynolds… I might be able to help you with your senior officers, might be able to smooth your return. Make them see your value."

I knew the pitch. He would offer information about British plans, or, more probably, information the British had garnered about Spain or Mexico or China. He would tell me to claim that I stole it. Tell me how to present it, when to present it for maximum impact. He would become the mentor I hoped he'd be when I started out. And then the requests for favors would come. Small at first. Which battleships are accompanying the merchant fleet through Suez? Who is commanding the fleet in Hawaii? Questions soaked in complicity. More to follow. Bigger items. Secrets. Stolen documents. Then the targeting of other possible recruits. Maybe in the Army, or the War Office or the State Department. I knew the pitch and I was eager for the chance to parry it. And I knew eagerness would make him step back.

"How? How can you help? I doubt anyone can help me now." I shrugged as if my destiny were sealed.

Hodgson drew a deep breath and made an unsuccessful effort to turn and look at the mountains. He sipped his tea. "You should understand the political situation…"

And I, foolishly, thought he was he was talking about the United States, thought he was still reeling me in. He had shifted, though; easing the line.

20.

"The Turks ruled Arabia – al-Hijaz, as Burton called it. They ruled ineptly, cruelly, corruptly and reluctantly. They would have preferred, by this time, to leave Arabia to the Egyptians, who would have been equally lousy overlords of that realm and equally confused and lazy in their governing, but they, at least, knew enough to suppress that natural desire governments have for expansion. The reluctance of the Turks was matched by the fervor of various tribes to rule the land, but so numerous were the factions and so corrupt themselves that their most strenuous efforts were directed against each other and victories were measured in what was stolen, rather than any larger, territorial gains. The Turks understood bribery and they understood murder and so kept the groups, if not under control, under their pudgy thumbs.

"All this meant that the Hajjis were in constant danger and the paltry escorts of Turkish troops – Albanians, actually – did not scare the bandits one bit. The bandits sat in the hills and fired at caravans, raided encampments while travelers slept and sometimes attacked directly and openly. The main culprit along the road to Medina was also named Sa'ad – the Bandit, chief of the *Sumaydah* and the *Mahamid*, which are sub-families of the *Hamidah*, which, in turn, is the main faction of the *Beni-Harb*. Thus Sa'ad hoped to rule over all the *Beni-Harb*. And thus would he be ruler of all the holy land.

"Sa'ad the Demon liked to expound on his namesake and travelers gathered eagerly round him.

"'See that mountain? The blue one? Just beyond the peak lies Sa'ad's aerie, a soft valley of untold beauty and bounty. Orchards and forests and bubbling springs and pomegranates and dates. A garden paradise equal to Iram. There lives Sa'ad the Bandit, tall and handsome as a king and wise as a vizier, and no one can enter who is not of his coterie. From there, they swoop down on travelers and thence they disappear. Chests they have, filled with gold and jewels – pearls and emeralds – stolen from unlucky travelers like us. And, women, too. Only the most beautiful of those to pass on this road to Medinah, or back to the sea. No need for your mother to worry there Walid…'

"And the travelers chuckled, even Walid's mother, but not Walid. And not Barzouki, who had other dangers on his mind. After Sa'ad had finished and his audience drifted away to sleep or to keep watch, Omar paced outside the tent, keeping his hand on his pistol. His gaze kept turning away from the mountains, to the side of the encampment where Faris's brothers rested.

"'Did I scare you, my beloved Omar, with my stories of the Bandit in his lair? Don't worry. Sa'ad the Demon will always protect you.'

"'I'm not afraid of Sa'ad the Bandit. I know your stories by now, don't I.'

"'My brave Omar, something is bothering you. I know you well, but can not read your mind every time.'

"'There are bigger threats in this camp than in those hills, Sa'ad.'

"'Who is bothering you? Whoever it is will face Sa'ad the Demon and regret even one glance in your direction.'

"Barzouki didn't answer at first…"

I interrupted. "Wait… wait. How can you know what was said between those two in private?"

Hodgson sipped his tea and then licked his lips. "Are these the exact words? I doubt it. But I know what happened and I'm telling you and you would be wise to believe me. Do you believe me?"

I had no idea whether I believed him or not, but I had to let him think he was reeling me in. "I want to believe you. In all matters. That's why I asked."

"Ask Ali."

Ali said. "The Darwaysh was too friendly with Barzouki for my taste. I spied on him. I overheard the conversation."

"Have I been accurate?" Hodgson said.

Ali nodded. "Oh yes. Barzouki knew how to manipulate Sa'ad. He kept this going for days. Working Sa'ad into a frenzy but Barzouki would never speak of the brothers and Sa'ad knew nothing of them."

Hodgson took over. "They rode east during the nights, the moon hardly more than a tease, along *wadis* and up *misyals,* stony ramps between hills, stopping at brackish wells that denoted a 'village', just a few huts and a flock of sheep. It was hot. Ali can confirm that."

Ali said, "It was hot, indeed."

Hodgson went on. "There were rocks and more rocks and you can read about them on your own. They were all hot. Some poet – Indian, I think – wrote, *Take care, do not neglect that sleeping dagger, its tale is always the gossip of death.* And that haunted Burton as he played out strategies to rid himself of his problems: the brothers, who seemed to be all around him, and Barzouki, who was always by his side. He could incite some Bedawin, or even Mughrabis, who, by then, held deep respect for Burton, against the brothers. But Burton couldn't depend on the outcome and to fall under suspicion of being the source of the clash would bring humiliation. As for Barzouki, Burton decided only that it was best to keep him close by. Still, no plan seemed satisfactory and Burton's mind bounced back haphazardly without ever coming to rest in a conclusion."

Ali said, "Barzouki kept pouting and fretting and Sa'ad became more and more agitated and by the time our caravan reached al-Hamra, Sa'ad thought of little else and his mood kept everyone else away from him. After we set up camp, it was revealed we would be there for days waiting for another caravan to join us and for enough soldiers to accompany us on the forthcoming dangerous part of the journey toward Al-Medinah. The Darwaysh purchased a sheep, had it *halaled,* and Barzouki, seeing the head laid aside, sold it to the Mughrabis for just three piastres. The head is a delicacy and the price was low and the beneficiaries were much reviled so he was teased mercilessly. Sa'ad bellowed at anyone who dared mock Barzouki and was ready to go farther. Barzouki could only calm him down by promising to divulge the source of his distraction.

"Sa'ad burst from the tent – so enraged Barzouki didn't see me – and lumbered like a giant denting the earth with each step, across the encampment to where the brothers were resting. I swear stones fell from the sides of the huts along the way. Some of the travelers jeered at Sa'ad, just to tease him as he passed them, and many followed to see what trouble he'd start.

"The brothers jumped up the moment they saw him. Hossein drew his sword. Abdullah stepped in front of him to confront Sa'ad first. Sa'ad lifted Abdullah by the kamis with one hand and threw him aside. Hossein slashed at Sa'ad, but Sa'ad leaned away and grabbed Hossein's arm as it went past, and took the sword from his hand as easily as if he were a child who'd stolen a fig. The youngest brother, Danesh, pulled his sword. Travelers behind Sa'ad cheered the boy on. Sa'ad laughed.

"'Come now, little brother, you must lay down your sword.'

"'Why should I,' said Danesh.

"'Because if you defeat me, you'll humiliate your brothers by accomplishing what they never could. Now lower your sword.'

"Danesh looked at Abdullah who was just getting up and holding onto his arm in pain. Abdullah nodded. Danesh lowered his sword.

"Abdullah moved close to Sa'ad and drew a short, curved blade. He slashed at Sa'ad so suddenly the blade cut Sa'ad's clothing. That was bad. Omar was yelling for Sa'ad to stop. 'Sa'ad, please, they haven't done anything.'

"Hossein used the distraction to sweep out Sa'ad's feet and he landed on the hard rocks. Travelers laughed. Sa'ad bounced up. The brothers spread out around him. Sa'ad quickly swept up Danesh and it looked like he would crush him. Abdullah and Hossein were paralyzed.

"'I, Sa'ad the Demon, will brook no resistance. You will leave this caravan immediately. Tonight. I will keep this boy until you go and send him to you after we reach Medinah. Do not defy the Demon, I warn you.'

"The Darwaysh pushed through the crowd and came up behind Sa'ad. He spoke softly. 'Please release the boy, Sa'ad.'

"Sa'ad spun. 'Do not interfere, Darwaysh. I warn you, too.'

"'Then go ahead and crush him to death, and you'll be remembered as a killer of little boys. Sa'ad the Baby Killer. Your fame will spread. I'll spread it.'

"Sa'ad's countenance flickered. He hadn't considered such a dire consequence. He spun back on the other brothers to keep them from encroaching.

"'Sa'ad the Demon can defeat three armed men with only one hand why are you lowering yourself? Fear? I know you could never be afraid, but will others have such faith in you? The Sa'ad I've come to know has wisdom enough to allow his foes to retreat.'

"Hossein shouted, 'We will never retreat!'

"But Abdullah held him back. 'We have meant no harm to your friend or to yourself, great Demon. We have no interest in battling you. If you will release our brother we will consider the matter closed.'

"The Darwaysh said, 'The problem, Sa'ad, is that the boy will fight to the death. You may very well kill the older ones and that would be honorable, but then you would have to kill the boy and that…' The Darwaysh broke off and gestured to the onlookers as if their opinion was the most important part for Sa'ad. And with that, the Darwaysh handed Sa'ad the boy's blade.

"Sa'ad lowered Danesh to the ground, handed him his sword and patted his behind to push him away. Abdullah grabbed him. Hossein was still armed and ready.

"Sa'ad pounded his chest proudly and faced the crowd. 'Everyone has seen Sa'ad the Demon face down three weapons and that without so much as a sweat. Long live the legend of Sa'ad.'

"The Darwaysh shouted, 'Long live the legend of Sa'ad.' And the crowd joined in and followed Sa'ad as he lumbered back to his tent.

"The Darwaysh was not finished. He put an arm around Barzouki and walked him over to face Abdullah and Hossein. 'This is Omar Barzouki. He also spoke with Faris on board the ship. Since you've been accused of bothering him, I thought you should meet.'

"Barzouki stood there wide eyed with fear and would have fled but the Darwaysh held tight to him.

"Abdullah said, 'You will not distract me. I'm watching you.'

"'In that case you should know that I'm leaving this caravan and joining the others who are traveling south, directly to Mecca. We leave tomorrow.'

21.

"The Darwaysh and I busied ourselves for the next few hours packing up. Word of our imminent departure spread and dinner became an elaborate celebration. Sa'ad told stories about the Darwaysh, some of which were true. Many spoke of how his medicine had helped them. How he counseled them on religious matters. There were many pledges to reunite in Mecca. A squad of Mughrabis offered the Darwaysh a parting gift: a dagger with a handle encrusted with amethysts the color of grapes. Many expressed their fear for the Darwaysh taking this more dangerous route. He was mysterious about the decision to change his itinerary, never mentioning that he planned to visit Medina after Mecca.

"Barzouki pouted, alone at his tent.

"When the commotion waned, the Darwaysh found Barzouki outside his tent and sat next to him. Barzouki spoke harshly. 'Darwaysh, why did you do that to me?'

"'You seem nervous about them. If you are going to talk to them, I'd rather find out now.'

"Barzouki took that as an insult. 'I will never tell them anything,' he said.

"'You baited poor Sa'ad.'

"'They're dangerous men!'

"'Perhaps you should talk to them. Tell them what you know.'

"'We have a bond, Darwaysh. Are you turning on me?'

"'Why did you come on the Hajj, Omar?'

"'It's our duty. At least once in our lifetimes. My family decided...'

"'No, I mean, why you now? Me now? Faris? Why them? Look around. If everything is written, then what happens must be part of a pattern.'

"'We experience as Allah deems...'

"'It can't just be a list. I found Faris as he was dying for a reason. I don't think Faris's brothers are my enemies. I think we're here to help each other. They need an answer and I do, too.'

"'I am not your answer!'

"'Will you join me in going directly to Mecca, Omar?'

"'It's far too dangerous. And I want to visit the prophet's tomb in Medinah.'

"The Darwaysh rose. He waited and Omar rose as well and they bowed to each other and put their hands on each others shoulders.

"'All men are dangerous, Omar. Sometimes I think that's why we don't like to be alone.'

"'I don't understand.'

"'It's the danger that attracts us.'

"The Darwaysh turned away. Before he had gone three steps, Barzouki called out to him. 'Darwaysh, promise you'll stay with me and my family in Mecca. If you live to get there.'

"The Darwaysh came close to him. Very close. 'I will,' he said. 'If you tell me why you killed Faris.'

22.

"Barzouki departed. Faris still dead. The brothers still hovered." Hodgson's liquid eyes rolled back and forth from Ali to me like marbles seeking a resting place.

I said, "Why would he let a murderer go? Why not spill to the brothers about Barzouki?"

"You've been a good listener for months, Reynolds. I've tested you. You even listened when I told that long story about the conjoined twins who stole the Macedonian jewels. Remember? They each swallowed one."

"You haven't told me that story."

"How brave you are to mention it, and well played. It will have to wait until later. But it seems you haven't been paying attention. First rule of the job, Reynolds – attention must be paid. Quite certain you know that. I suppose you want to return to the subject of you and your future. Only natural. *There was a young man in Kentucky/ Who believed himself increasingly lucky/He decided to think/His shit didn't stink/'Til he fell into something quite mucky.* It's those last lines that keep me going. Don't tell me if you think of a good one.

"Burton wasn't posing as a Sufi. He lived it. He wouldn't run toward his destiny or away from it. The opium den in Herat cemented that lesson: I found him, even there. If Barzouki was meant to come back into his life, so he would. If the brothers were going to try to kill him, Burton would resist. He could promise himself nothing more. He meant what he said about danger and liking it. Needing it."

He coughed. Ali reached out. "It's getting chilly. Shall we go inside?"

"More tea would be nice."

Ali gestured to the waiter.

Hodgson went on, "The caravan from Damascus boasted a thousand riders by the time Burton joined. There were Turks and Khazars, Lebanese, Syrians, East Indians and many of the much derided Persians. Bandits buzzed them as consistently as flies and bit, too And the new caravan meant new travel mates and that meant new interest in Burton as Darwaysh and fresh suspicions of his identity.

"They crossed a treacherous field of black lava, sharp and uneven, and faced days of the dreadful *sammun,* the dry furnace wind. Camels and horses collapsed from the heat – it was hot – and were left to the carrion birds, except those whose throats are cut according to law – they were cut for steaks by half-starved Hajjis from Africa. There were fights and deaths, horrible deaths by beast and heat – a Turk stabbed and gutted an Arab camel driver and left him in a pit for the sun and whatever impatient scavengers came along. But the caravan shrugged them off, grew and oozed forward like a fearsome creature stalking its destiny.

"As the sun rose on the third day, trumpets echoed off the hills. The caravan stopped. Another caravan, this one bigger and more diverse and more spectacular, came round a hill. The procession awed Burton. First came Africans, dressed in white, their heads shaved. Behind them a lone rider pounding on his kettle drum, followed by a single camel whose standard bearer carried a green flag with white lettering. Wahhabis, proud and fierce, followed in double file, each carrying a spear, a rifle or a dagger. Their women travel with them, also riding. Next came a small, withered old man riding a magnificent Ghazala, an enormous female camel with the stride of a giraffe. This was the Sharif of Mecca, the holiest man in Arabia. Two attendants shielded him from the sun with green umbrellas.

"The two caravans merged with considerable bickering, taunting, boasting and most of all, threatening. They had only reached an uneasy order for an hour or so and were passing through a narrow canyon when bandits appeared on the clifftops. Blue puffs followed and a moment later two pilgrims fell. Fighters leapt from their camels and snatched up their weapons. Most of the pilgrims were not fighters. They panicked, retreating in a mess of collisions, spills and trampling. Then came the boulders.

"Burton found himself on the forward side of the caravan, along with the Sharif and his guard and the majority of the Wahabis. They surrounded the Sharif and rode forward to the mouth of the canyon thinking they could escape, but Burton could see the trap. He'd encountered the same situation in Sind. Snipers would be waiting for the riders to leave the canyon. Probably waiting for the Sharif. Burton rode toward the lead Wahhabi, a man named Khaled and cut him off.

"Khaled didn't want to listen to this Darwaysh. He raised his gun and pointed it at Burton.

"'That temptation leads to death,' Burton said. 'Snipers.'

"And Khaled needed no proof. Three other riders had charged ahead and two were shot immediately. Khaled halted the Sharif's guard. Burton raced to the mouth of the passage, dismounted, and ordered others to form a blockade to keep any of the panicked Hajjis from riding into the sniper fire.

"But they were stuck and there was no reason for the bandits to quit. The Sharif's guard shifted him close to the canyon wall where the snipers would have no angle with their shots. Wahhabis began climbing toward the cliff, toward the snipers. Burton joined them. He hadn't gone more than ten feet up when he looked back on the other side of the avalanche. The bulk of caravan members were retreating into the range of the snipers. The brothers, though, did not retreat. They were watching Burton.

"Burton slid deeper into a fold in the canyon wall, hoping to reach the top ledge behind the shooters. He decided to follow the first ledge on the chance the narrow pathway led all the way to the top as it curved around the promontory. He hadn't gone far when he heard the voice behind him.

"'Lay down your pistol, Darwaysh. But don't turn around.'

"Burton laid down his pistol. And he turned around. The bandit was a small man, middle aged and scrawny with a wild beard and hair.

"'Hand over your money belt, Darwaysh, and you will live.'

"'It's bad luck for you if I'm hurt.'

"'It's bad luck for both of us. Hand it over. Come, a Darwaysh will never starve.'

"As if the bullet had already struck without sound or force, Burton knew he was dead. And at that moment, the Darwaysh robe felt like a fifty stone shackle and his assumed identity became a grotesque greasepaint caricature. He wanted out. Wanted to strip off his robe, strip off all his clothing. Wash away the entire charade. Disguise had always meant freedom but now it was a prison. He longed to speak English.

"He thought of Leda. Not in terms of going off to meet her in some mythical after life. Just the opposite: in life there were distractions but this aching moment would be eternal. The loneliness of death made him long for her. He thought, again, how she had missed this moment – the moment of knowledge that she was going to die, going to be murdered. Burton's predicament was plain for him to see. The bandit was an open book, no matter what lies he told. But Leda had trusted her killers, never had time or reason to look for second meanings. Again, his guilt sickened him.

"The bandit stepped cautiously forward, repeating his demands.

"Burton spoke English. 'Come closer and I'll take you with me. Come along. Try to take the belt. We'll go to hell together, brothers that we are.'

"Burton's tone was enough for the bandit to understand his intentions. He ordered Burton to remove the belt. 'If I have to shoot you, I'll take your belt at the bottom of the canyon.'

"Burton began quoting insults, just for the sounds. He just wanted to hear the words. 'Thou elvish-marked, abortive, rooting hog, Thou that wast sealed in thy nativity, The slave of nature and the son of hell, Thou slander of thy heavy mother's womb, Thou loathèd issue of thy father's loins, Thou rag of honor.' He smiled as he spoke, refreshed, and the bandit smiled back.

"The bandit came closer. He pointed at the ridge above them. 'All of my brothers are up there. You're helpless. The prophet wants us to share and not to waste. Give me the belt.'

"Again, Burton chose English. 'Sblood, you starveling, you elfskin, you dried neat's tongue, you bull's pizzle, you stockfish! O, for breath to utter what is like thee! You tailor's-yard, you sheath, you bowcase, you vile standing tuck—

"A shot startled Burton and he almost lost his balance and toppled off the cliff. The bandit was even more startled. The bullet hit him in the throat.

Faris's brother, Hossein, stepped out, holding his second pistol on Burton, and his eyes glistening with venom. Burton couldn't suppress a chuckle; they were killing for the chance to kill him. But the moment of resignation passed quickly.

"'You've saved my life and I owe you a great debt,' he said.

"'What did you say to him?'

Burton knew Hossein had heard him, but also knew there was no reason for Hossein to understand that Burton had spoken English. Why would he know? No Englishmen came this way. And, no Americans, Reynolds.

"'I said that I forgave him.'

"'Hah!... hand me your pistol…'

"By the time they reached the canyon floor, the bandits had retreated in defeat. Pilgrims worked to move enough rocks to reunite the caravan and many poured across to congratulate Burton and thank the great Darwaysh for saving the Sharif. One of the Sharif's guard pushed forward to bestow on Burton the great honor of an invitation to join the Sharif at a meal. Burton told the messenger that Hossein had saved his life. But the messenger only repeated the invitation to Burton. Amidst the crowd of admiring faces, Burton only saw Hossein's skeptical and threatening gaze. If Hossein told what he'd heard on the mountain, Burton would be dead in seconds.

"Have you noticed, Reynolds, that when people meet a stranger they do the strangest thing? They ask questions. I wonder why? I suppose they like to hear stories. I prefer a different method. Any idea what that is?"

"You do the talking."

"Precisely!"

"And the lying."

"How well you learn, Reynolds. If there's going to be lying going on – and there will be – I prefer to control it. The Sharif and his five closest advisors, sage one and all though they were, sat with Burton and questioned the stranger that they might understand whom they were dealing with. Burton could feel their curiosity and decided he would be safer by volunteering his story rather than answering their questions which might catch him off guard. He knew if he failed, he was unlikely to live long enough to leave the tent.

"'Great Sharif, I am honored to be here in your presence and the presence of those you esteem and it would honor me further if I might be allowed to tell you how I became a wandering Darwaysh and found myself here today chasing bandits in the hills.'

"The Sharif nodded his assent. Burton had only the vaguest idea of what story he was going to tell, but he had promised to start, so start he did. And the worlds flowed."

"'I was a profligate and to feed my vices I lied and cheated and stole, and though I never murdered, murder was in my heart and I have no doubt but that I would arrive at that desolate destination someday. I could bend women and men to my will and knew a bit of medicine, enough to pass as a doctor if it would further my evil plots and connivances.'

"'To avoid authorities and the angry relatives of one of my victims, I traveled far beyond Islamabad to the mountains of Jammu amongst many Hindu and even Buddhists. It was there that I encountered a Darwaysh, and he was a man who had prospered as a doctor to the infidels and the holy and as a merchant dealing the many medicines he had discovered. This Darwaysh had a daughter, a beautiful woman and sweet in his eyes, but my eyes saw something else and she saw me with clarity, too. We recognized each other for what we were and our wickedness was clear as the mountain streams and just as delicious to us. She soon understood that I studied with the old Darwaysh only to further my plot to rob him.'

"'The Darwaysh was holy and good and I pretended I was the same and learned medicine from him and how to worship.

And I made love to the daughter, Fatima she was, in order to control her suspicions of me, but she was wily in her own right and seduced the plot from me and determined that I was taking the wrong tack and said that if I would split the booty with her she would guide me because she despised her father for his incessant goodness to others, even though he doted ever so affectionately on her. And if I didn't cooperate with her she would unmask me to her father. You know the honor among thieves is thin as the mountain air so I agreed to conspire with her.'

"'I continued my studies with this good man and saw him heal without discrimination, the good and the evil, the rich and the poor. Saw him pray with a pure sincerity that I had thought did not exist on this earth. I had always regarded illness as a weakness to be taken advantage of as does a tiger choose the weakest gazelle. And I learned that the need of the ill was great and the need of the lost souls was equally great.'

"'Perhaps Fatima knew I had a change of heart before even I was aware of it. Two days before we were to hatch the plot to kill and rob her father, I warned him of our intentions and of the malice in his daughter's heart. The Darwaysh wouldn't hear of any of it. He repeated his love for his daughter and assured me that all would work out for the best.'

"'While I was wondering how to thwart the attack at the appointed time the next evening, Fatima, along with another conspirator, a man, broke into the Darwaysh's bedroom and attacked him. Hearing the commotion, I rushed in and threw the attacker off the Darwaysh and in the fight that followed I killed the man.'

"'I could see in the Darwaysh's eyes that he did not want me to accuse his daughter to the authorities, so I refrained. He lay still for two days and then called Fatima and me before him.

He said he intended to divide his fortune between us. Fatima would have his money. He praised her for never having stolen a rupee despite knowing where his stash was hidden. Fatima ran away to gather the money and I was left alone with the Darwaysh.

"'"The Darwaysh said to me '*Good sees good and evil sees evil. And now you see both.*" He told me to take his Darwaysh cloak and his knowledge of prayer and the Koran and the medicine and set out to learn what I could of people both good and evil. And that is how I came to have the honor of your hospitality.'

"Burton and the Sharif exited the tent arm in arm and walked among the pilgrims together. Not so much as a murmur of dissent was heard. Burton's identity was certified and solidified and the only person mystified by it or doubtful was Burton, who had not the slightest idea where that story he told came from."

Delight rushed into Hodgson's eyes making him look like a mischievous bald imp – or the Djinn in the book. An old one, though. "His identity was secured. Secured! I could never have arranged it myself. Could Burton? He assumed he'd have to keep proving himself every day of the journey. As everyone did. Sometimes you just have to try, just keep trying and things go the right way. Or the wrong way. Keep it in mind, Reynolds."

23.

I read until midnight Burton's account of the approach to Mecca. The account of a battle with the Utaybah was there, but no mention of Burton's part in it or an interview with the Sharif. The pilgrims stopped to don the Ihram.

"Having pitched the tent and eaten and slept, we prepared to perform the ceremony of Al-Ihram (assuming the pilgrim-garb), as Al-Zaribah is the Mikat, or the appointed place. Between the noonday and the afternoon prayers a barber attended to shave our heads, cut our nails, and trim our mustachios. Then, having bathed and perfumed ourselves,- the latter is a questionable point, - we donned the attire, which is nothing but two new cotton cloths, each six feet long by three and a half broad, white, with narrow red stripes and fringes: in fact, the costume called Al-Eddeh, in the baths at Cairo. One of these sheets, technically termed the Rida, is thrown over the back, and, exposing the arm and shoulder, is knotted at the right side in the style Wishah. The Izar is wrapped round the loins from waist to knee, and, knotted or tucked in at the middle, supports itself. Our heads were bare, and nothing was allowed upon the instep. It is said that some clans of Arabs still preserve this religious but most uncomfortable costume; it is doubtless of ancient date, and to this day, in the regions lying west of the Red Sea, it continues to be the common dress of the people.

Having completed the rituals, they faced Mecca and prayed. They were exhausted and exhilarated, feeding on anticipation. They were solemn and they were giddy.

"The wife and daughters of a Turkish pilgrim of our party assumed the Ihram at the same time as ourselves. They appeared dressed in white garments; and they had exchanged the Lisam, that coquettish fold of muslin which veils without concealing the lower part of the face, for a hideous mask, made of split, dried, and plaited palm-leaves, with two bulls-eyes for light. I could not help laughing when these strange figures met my sight, and, to judge from the shaking of their shoulders, they were not less susceptible to the merriment which they had caused."

He finishes the chapter with a thorough description of the geographical formations in the area northwest of Mecca. Rocks. I skipped that part.

I fell asleep mulling over the differences in the two accounts. Hodgson's was the kind of candy that sticks. The kind that shapes dreams. It was in the middle of my dreamed grilling by the Sharif of Mecca that voices outside the tent woke me. I checked my watch immediately - 1:18. Only then did I realize the voices belonged to Hodgson and Ali. They were arguing.

Gently, quietly, I opened the doors to the balcony and stepped out, feeling as if I were breaking into someone else's room. It was dark as the sea; the hills made vague blots that might have been waves or clouds. A bit of light struggled from the room two balconies to the left of mine.

"After all, you are a thief, Ali."

"I was a thief."

"Stopping isn't the same as changing."

"And what are you?"

"I'm worse. Worse than any thief. We both know that. That's why it's so easy for me to ask you to do this."

"But I won't do it. Here, you take this."

"Don't be ridiculous." Hodgson sounded insulted.

"We'll see who's a thief. Good night."

The voices ceased. A door closed.

Hikers and bird watchers beat me downstairs in the early morning. They had finished their breakfasts and were packing lunches by the time I took a seat on the terrace with a view of the front door. I was a guard dog, ready to catch Hodgson in flight.

Ali came down carrying his valise. He gave no sign of seeing me, passing on to the desk to settle his bill. He directed the bellman to take his valise outside, then came onto the terrace and stood before me.

"I had hoped to see you down here, Mr. Reynolds. Making sure Mr. Hodgson doesn't escape again?"

"I think he'd try even if he didn't want to."

Ali winced at that and his mouth opened in surprise. He reformed his expression and said, "The problem is we never know what he wants until sometime later."

"I'm glad to hear I'm not alone in that. Won't you join me, Ali." I wanted to open the door to last night's argument but he declined the invitation.

"I thought you might want to share my carriage."

"Where are you going?"

"Mr. Burton's funeral takes place tomorrow morning. You'll have to leave today to make it."

"Is Hodgson..."

"He wouldn't be welcome. Well, you can always find a carriage driver in the afternoon. They want to return to Trieste for the night."

I sat there for two hours alternately reading Burton and deciphering the late night argument, making it fit with Ali's casual demeanor.

Burton and his companions entered Meccah at last and after some difficulty settled in at the boy Muhammed's mother's house. *"After the meal we procured cots from a neighbouring coffee-house, and we lay down, weary, and anxious to snatch an hour or two of repose. At dawn we were expected to perform our Tawaf al-Kudum, or Circumambulation of Arrival, at the Harim.*

"Scarcely had the first smile of morning beamed upon the rugged head of the eastern hill, Abu Kubays, when we arose, bathed, and proceeded in our pilgrim-garb to the Sanctuary. We entered by the Bab al-Ziyadah, or principal northern door, descended two long flights of steps, traversed the cloister, and stood in sight of the Bayt Allah.

"There at last it lay, the bourn of my long and weary Pilgrimage, realising the plans and hopes of many and many a year. The mirage medium of Fancy invested the huge catafalque and its gloomy pall with peculiar charms. There were no giant fragments of hoar antiquity as in Egypt, no remains of graceful and harmonious beauty as in Greece and Italy, no barbarous gorgeousness as in the buildings of India; yet the view was strange, unique and how few have looked upon the celebrated shrine! I may truly say that, of all the worshippers who clung weeping to the curtain, or who pressed their beating hearts to the stone, none felt for the moment a deeper emotion than did the Haji from the far-north. It was as if the poetical legends of the Arab spoke truth, and that the waving wings of angels, not the sweet breeze of morning, were agitating and swelling the black covering of the shrine. But, to confess humbling truth, theirs was the high feeling of religious enthusiasm, mine was the ecstasy of gratified pride."

What did Hodgson want stolen? Up to that point I had seen no way to explain Ali's cryptic remarks and warnings. A shared reverence for Burton united them, making any rift insignificant or too arcane to explore. But this argument demanded attention, and best of all, Hodgson hadn't gotten what he wanted. Reverence could divide, too.

"Few Moslems contemplate for the first time the Kaabah, without fear and awe: there is a popular jest against new comers, that they generally inquire the direction of prayer. This being the Kiblah, or fronting place, Moslems pray all around it; a circumstance which of course cannot take place in any spot of Al-Islam but the Harim. The boy Mohammed, therefore, left me for a few minutes to myself; but presently he warned me that it was time to begin. Advancing, we entered through the Bab Benu Shaybah, the Gate of the Sons of the Shaybah (old woman). There we raised our hands, repeated the Labbayk, the Takbir, and the Tahlil; after which we uttered certain supplications, and drew our hands down our faces. Then we proceeded to the Shafeis place of worship the open pavement between the Makam Ibrahim and the well Zemzem where we performed the usual two-bow prayer in honour of the Mosque. This was followed by a cup of holy water and a present to the Sakkas, or carriers, who for the consideration distributed, in my name, a large earthen vaseful to poor pilgrims."

When had Hodgson and Ali formed the bond between them? Ali was a boy during the pilgrimage. I assumed Hodgson had rarely seen Burton after the mission was completed, but perhaps I was wrong. Was Ali a go-between? Were there more adventures, more betrayals?

Burton didn't like the water of Zemzem. *"The produce of Zemzem is held in great esteem. It is used for drinking and religious ablution, but for no baser purposes; and the Meccans advise pilgrims always to break their fast with it. It is apt to cause diarrhoea and boils, and I never saw a stranger drink it without a wry face. Sale is decidedly correct in his assertion: the flavour is a salt-bitter, much resembling an infusion of a teaspoonful of Epsom salts in a large tumbler of tepid water. Moreover, it is exceedingly heavy to the digestion. For this reason Turks and other strangers prefer rain-water, collected in cisterns and sold for five farthings a gugglet. It was a favourite amusement with me to watch them whilst they drank the holy water, and to taunt their scant and irreverent potations."*

The pilgrims begin Tawaf – the circling of the Ka'aba seven times at different paces according to tradition. *"At the conclusion of the Tawaf it was deemed advisable to attempt to kiss the stone. For a time I stood looking in despair at the swarming crowd of Badawi and other pilgrims that besieged it. But the boy Mohammed was equal to the occasion. During our circuit he had displayed a fiery zeal against heresy and schism, by foully abusing every Persian in his path…;*

After vainly addressing the pilgrims, of whom nothing could be seen but a mosaic of occiputs and shoulder-blades, the boy Mohammed collected about half a dozen stalwart Meccans, with whose assistance, by sheer strength, we wedged our way into the thin and light-legged crowd. The Badawin turned round upon us like wild-cats, but they had no daggers. The season being autumn, they had not swelled themselves with milk for six months; and they had become such living mummies, that I could have managed single-handed half a dozen of them. After thus reaching the stone, despite popular indignation testified by impatient shouts, we monopolised the use of it for at least ten minutes. Whilst kissing it and rubbing hands and forehead upon it I narrowly observed it, and came away persuaded that it is an aerolite. It is curious that almost all travellers agree upon one point, namely, that the stone is volcanic."

Maybe I was too confident that Hodgson hadn't left, maybe he snuck past me or left in the night. Maybe Ali was a decoy. I slammed shut the book and rushed upstairs and knocked on the door two down from mine. No one answered. I tried the handle and the door opened.

24.

In the sitting room, a breakfast service lay uncovered, the omelet untouched. I moved forward, calling out to Hodgson and stopped at the bedroom door and pushed it open.

He was bent over a high backed chair, one hand resting on the arm for support. One pant leg was on and he seemed to be pausing in his struggle to engage the other one. His cheeks hung like thin florid slabs barely attached to the bone and his swollen lips seemed to have pooled the residue of blood before it flooded the floor. He reached again for his pants and missed. His head twisted and the bulging eyes, fighting gravity and the slippery liquid they lived in, swiveled my way for a moment. He wasn't old, he was age itself in all its grotesque cruelty. His free hand stabbed again and this time snagged the trousers and he inserted his leg. Neither of us spoke as he buttoned up and fixed his suspenders.

He smiled and his eyes narrowed to counter any pleasantness that might be taken from the smile.

For a moment the man I was six months ago appeared before me, a man who inquired about Hodgson's health expecting to get a straight answer.

"I thought you might have left, Reynolds. Snuck off without me."

He still held onto the chair and had not straightened up fully.

"Could I sneak away without hearing the rest of your story?"

"We'll find out."

He gestured toward the sitting room and waited for me to precede him. I walked fast so if he fell forward he wouldn't bump his head on my heels.

"We can order more food if you're hungry," he said.

I turned at that. He had straightened up, haughtiness acting as a hydraulic fluid to fill him out. But it couldn't hide the stiffness and discomfort. He lowered himself into a padded leather chair. I sat to his right on the couch.

"I saw Ali this morning. Before he left," I said.

He reached inside his coat pocket and extracted two folded sheets of paper. "These are for you, Reynolds. You've earned them. They'll help revive your career, I'm sure of it. Only think of me when you receive your promotion."

I knew better than to reach for them.

"This one contains three names. The top German spies in America. Two in New York and one in Washington, D.C. He works in the War Department. The second lists five Irishmen actively working with the Spanish government to undermine American influence in Cuba."

He set the papers on the table and I thanked him. "I heard you arguing with Ali last night."

His head turned sharply away from me and back, like a bird's. I had caught him off-guard.

"Did you?" Though the two words carried a tone that said, 'why should I care?'

"You asked him for something. He refused."

"I was thirsty for a gin. Ali knows it's bad for me. I'm fortunate to have such protective friends, don't you think?"

"You wanted him to steal gin?"

"Think of your homecoming, Reynolds. Those names will serve you well. I suggest you dole them out. Always overplay a good hand."

"Would you have given me these names if we didn't already have them? Maybe they'll help to keep me from Alaska, but that's all."

"What are you up to, Reynolds?"

"What do you want stolen?"

"I wasn't serious about overplaying your hand."

It was my turn to hand over a piece of paper. On it I'd written: *the number of Spanish battle ships, where they're deployed, the captains names and profiles, detailed plans of Spanish harbors, their vulnerabilities.*

Hodgson read it, folded it and put it on the table beside him. "I read Mahan. He's entirely correct. Naval power is the key to prosperity. It's like building a road across the globe and controlling that road. We could, could have, and I advocated it, charge everyone a toll just to set sail..."

"But how could you have read Commander Mahan? He was only published two months ago. I only know his work because he taught me at the War College. I've been with you..." I cut myself off because the answer was obvious: the British had stolen a draft of Mahan's work.

Hodgson carried on as if there had been no interruption. "The Americans want to supplant the British as master of the seas but first you have to defeat Spain. Defeat Spain in the Caribbean and then you become as powerful as we are there. Defeat Spain in the Pacific and you own an entire ocean." He stopped and sat back and regarded me with something that resembled affection. "I've been expecting this for a while, long enough to stop expecting it. This was your mission from the start."

"You taught me patience."

"Did I teach you greed? You ask a lot… And you don't know yet what I want."

"You sounded desperate last night," I said.

"Why me? Why was I given the honor of your presence?"

He knew the answer better than I did. Words were unnecessary. But silence is mightier than arrogance, condescension, disrespect; its cruelty is infinite. It's a room without walls where monstrous thoughts breed and attack and infect. Anything I said, no matter how barbed, would be a relief, something to refute, to enable the claim 'only this.' I was too weak for complete cruelty. Hodgson had earned the words.

"We saw the way you'd been treated. Shunted aside. Passed over. You know too much to be shunted aside."

"Too true. Too much, too well, too many. Too long, too."

"There should be more. You're still valuable," I said.

"Valuable? I was never valuable. Who is valuable? I'll tell you. I'll enumerate. Servants are valuable. That's why we keep them in their place. Can't do without them."

"And then, humored. The very act of accepting me as your student was the humiliation that we thought would make you turn."

It stung, but it was only a sting. His eyes left the room. What they saw I'll never know. When they returned, he said, "*There was a young man from the West, Garnering information was his quest, Into confidence he wormed, Until an old man squirmed, And for this he remained in Trieste.*" He shrugged dismissively. "At least it has a final line… All this, gathering all this information, would take time. Requests. Trade offs. Different departments."

"All the more reason why you're the man to handle this."

"You mean that no one will worry about giving information to an old man, shunted aside, passed over, humored?

"Yes."

"No. Your price is too high. I'll find another way to get what I want. I wonder if you will."

His hesitation was fine with me. The clock was moving in my direction. Hodgson surprised me then by talking about himself, his career. He'd been commissioned Lieutenant after Sandhurst – then called the Royal Military College. That was 1833. He was assigned to the Northern District of England under General Napier. Napier took to him and brought him along to India. Hodgson learned his craft during the war to conquer Sindh, the same war in which Burton proved so adept and valuable.

"But I tied my future to the wrong horse. War is a tiring business for old men. Napier left India in haste. I became a spy without a master, untethered. Good for my craft to be able to roam free, bad for promotions. I wasted time, Reynolds, don't waste time… I'm going to tell you something only Ali and I know of. There's a manuscript, the full story, everything that Burton did, everything he went through, the true story of him and Leda, of his Hajj, of his… of what happened afterward in Medinah, and after that."

"You think it's in the library at the villa?"

"I'm certain of it. I was searching for it when I collapsed. The widow would burn the entire place if I went back now, but… I've accumulated little, as you can tell, and I can hardly call many men friends. And no women. You've accurately measured the loyalty of the government to me after sixty years. The only thing on earth I truly desire – covet – is that manuscript." He looked away, ashamed of the rare moment of sincerity. Maybe it startled him.

"Why now? Why didn't you ask Ali to find it days ago?"

His face grew red and his lips pulled back on his teeth. "I'm feeling old, not feeble minded." He took a deep breath to compose himself, and winced. "Be good enough to wheel that food cart into the corridor, Reynolds. The smell reminds me of a particularly odiferous journey I took once on a fishing ship from Algeciras to Nice."

"No ice..."

"Whatever are you talking about? It was the crew."

I wheeled out the cart, returned, sat down across from him. I wished I had a cigar.

"You usually light a cigar around now."

"Would you like me to?"

"No need to be so angry, Reynolds. Never angry. You're only doing what you're meant to do. Don't be angry about that." He waited for me to protest but I just mimicked his smile. "Tomorrow is Burton's funeral. The villa will be empty. This is the chance. The festivities begin at 10:00 and will last, with all the huzzahs and flimflammery, over three hours. They've invited every windbag within three hundred miles."

Ali's vehement refusal made me hesitate, but that was all. He had lived the life and stolen, unlike me, much more than candy and kisses. I wanted the danger. "What would I be looking for? There must be a thousand volumes in the library."

"Closer to three thousand. The manuscript I'm looking for is hidden inside a plain and gray cover marked "A Study of Shakespeare" by A. Swinburne. It might not be in the library. Could be anywhere in the house. Get it for me, Reynolds. Find the manuscript and I'll give you all you ask for."

25.

The Hotel Antonia occupied a narrow three story gray stone building two streets above the harbor. I took a room under the name Marco Rinaldi and settled in with Burton as he completed his Hajj.

On the first night, the moon full, they returned to the Harim, more striking and glorious than in the daytime, and still crowded with pilgrims.

"What a scene of contrasts! Here stalked the Badawi woman, in her long black robe like a nuns serge, and poppy-coloured face-veil, pierced to show two fiercely flashing orbs. There an Indian woman, with her semi-Tartar features, nakedly hideous, and her thin legs, encased in wrinkled tights, hurried round the fane. Every now and then a corpse, borne upon its wooden shell, circuited the shrine by means of four bearers, whom other Moslems, as is the custom, occasionally relieved. A few fair-skinned Turks lounged about, looking cold and repulsive, as their wont is. In one place a fast Calcutta Khitmugar stood, with turband awry and arms akimbo, contemplating the view jauntily, as those gentlemen's gentlemen will do. In another, some poor wretch, with arms thrown on high, so that every part of his person might touch the Kaabah, was clinging to the curtain and sobbing as though his heart would break."

Burton could capture the places and the rituals without losing sight of the people. The people captivated me. He couldn't resist them and if he didn't like them at first – those hairy, gruff Turks turned out to be "*kindhearted and not unsociable men*" – he often found a way to get along, even if he had to be on guard while doing so.

On the second day they journeyed toward Mount Arafat. *"Most of the wealthier classes mounted asses. The scene was, as usual, one of strange contrasts: Badawin bestriding swift dromedaries; Turkish dignitaries on fine horses; the most picturesque beggars, and the most uninteresting Nizam. Not a little wrangling mingled with the loud bursts of Talbiyat. Dead animals dotted the ground, and carcasses had been cast into a dry tank, the Birkat al-Shami, which caused every Badawi to hold his nose. Here, on the right of the road, the poorer pilgrims, who could not find houses, had erected huts, and pitched their ragged tents."*

Burton figures 50,000 are gathered on the vast plain below the mountain (which is only a large hill), though the superstition is that the number can never be counted and if fewer than 600,000 souls attend, the angels arrive to make up the difference.

He camped there among the people selling food, the people begging for it, the thieves, the police and the soldiers to catch them and to steal from them, the women wailing, the men fighting, the women fighting, the drunks wandering lost, the men calling out the names of women – as a favor! – the grave diggers, the Egyptians drinking hemp and the singers in the tents. The splendor and the filth.

The cannons woke them in the morning and they climbed Arafat, prayed and returned to the tent. Here he sees the Sharif and his impressive entourage – not on the road as Hodgson describes – and soon after that the speech he has come to witness begins from a perch on the mountain but Burton is still near his tent, too far away to hear it well. The reason? A woman.

"But how came I to be at the tent?

"A short confession will explain. They will shrive me who believe in inspired Spenser's lines

'And every spirit, as it is more pure,
And hath in it the more of heavenly light,
So it the fairer body doth procure
To habit in.'

"The evil came of a fairer body. I had prepared en cachette a slip of paper, and had hid in my Ihram a pencil destined to put down the heads of this rarely heard discourse. But unhappily that red cashmere shawl was upon my shoulders. Close to us sat a party of fair Meccans, apparently belonging to the higher classes, and one of these I had already several times remarked. She was a tall girl, about eighteen years old, with regular features, a skin somewhat citrine-coloured, but soft and clear, symmetrical eyebrows, the most beautiful eyes, and a figure all grace. There was no head thrown back, no straightened neck, no flat shoulders, nor toes turned out, in fact, no elegant barbarisms: the shape was what the Arabs love, soft, bending, and relaxed, as a woman's figure ought to be. Unhappily she wore, instead of the usual veil, a Yashmak of transparent muslin, bound round the face; and the chaperone, mother, or duenna, by whose side she stood, was apparently a very unsuspicious or complaisant old person. Flirtilla fixed a glance of admiration upon my cashmere. I directed a reply with interest at her eyes. She then by the usual coquettish gesture, threw back an inch or two of head-veil, disclosing broad bands of jetty hair, crowning a lovely oval. My palpable admiration of the new charm was rewarded by a partial removal of the Yashmak, when a dimpled mouth and a rounded chin stood out from the envious muslin. Seeing that my companions were safely employed, I entered upon the dangerous ground of raising hand to forehead. She smiled almost imperceptibly, and turned away. The pilgrim was in ecstasy.

"The sermon was then half over. I was resolved to stay upon the plain and see what Flirtilla would do. Grace to the cashmere, we came to a good understanding. The next page will record my disappointment that evening the pilgrim resumed his soiled cotton cloth, and testily returned the red shawl to the boy Mohammed.

"The sermon always lasts till near sunset, or about three hours. At first it was spoken amid profound silence. Then loud, scattered Amins (Amens) and volleys of Labbayk exploded at uncertain intervals. At last the breeze brought to our ears a purgatorial chorus of cries, sobs, and shrieks. Even my party thought proper to be affected: old Ali rubbed his eyes, which in no case unconnected with dollars could by any amount of straining be made to shed even a crocodiles tear; and the boy Mohammed wisely hid his face in the skirt of his Rida.

Presently the people, exhausted by emotion, began to descend the hill in small parties; and those below struck their tents and commenced loading their camels, although at least an hours sermon remained. On this occasion, however, all hurry to be foremost, as the race from Arafat is enjoyed by none but the Badawin."

There is more – they travel to Mina for the throwing of the stones at the Devil. *"As the ceremony of Ramy, or Lapidation, must be performed on the first day by all pilgrims between sunrise and sunset, and as the fiend was malicious enough to appear in a rugged Pass, the crowd makes the place dangerous. On one side of the road, which is not forty feet broad, stood a row of shops belonging principally to barbers. On the other side is the rugged wall against which the pillar stands, with a chevaux de frise of Badawin and naked boys. The narrow space was crowded with pilgrims, all struggling like drowning men to approach as near as possible to the Devil; it would have been easy to run over the heads of the mass. Amongst them were horsemen with rearing chargers. Badawin on wild camels, and grandees on mules and asses, with outrunners, were breaking a way by assault and battery. I had read Ali Beys self-felicitations upon escaping this place with only two wounds in the left leg, and I had duly provided myself with a hidden dagger. The precaution was not useless. Scarcely had my donkey entered the crowd than he was overthrown by a dromedary, and I found myself under the stamping and roaring beasts stomach. Avoiding being trampled upon by a judicious use of the knife, I lost no time in escaping from a place so ignobly dangerous. Some Moslem travellers assert, in proof of the sanctity of the spot, that no Moslem is ever killed here: Meccans assured me that accidents are by no means rare."*

And then the triumphant moment of Burton's Hajj: he is lifted inside the Ka'aba and allowed to see the glories it holds. Not every Hajji receives such an honor and not every Hajji can afford the tip that is required, even for the men who lift him up and down. He is quizzed as to his origins and heritage and then conducted around the windowless building. It was close in there and he felt like a "trapped rat," but he managed to sketch out the floor plan without being detected.

I didn't want this to end – this man on this journey – and yet I wanted it to end here, on the Hajj. Wanted this to be the real story, all of it. This Burton, the man who could record all this with wit and genuine interest and sympathy, was the one I wanted to know. When faced with danger of being unmasked, he responds with his wits and bravery and charm. What if the manuscript I was going to search for showed him to be Hodgson-like: cynical, manipulating, and acerbic? The way I was becoming. Burton was wise without being cynical. He harbored few illusions about the individuals he encountered but even if he thought their goals or desires were misguided or useless or self-serving, he accepted the sincerity of their beliefs, even their compulsions. Detachment didn't cause him to drift into superiority. In posing as one of them, he treats himself as one of them. That's the trait that completes his disguise.

On a piece of plain stationary, I wrote: *Package secured. Advise when payment is ready.* I sealed it and addressed it to Hodgson at Opcina. Then I settled back and formed a compromise and wrapped it in a lie – I would find the manuscript but not read it – and fell asleep.

26.

Not a flagpole was bare and all flew at half mast.

At Café Szabo, the waiter, wearing a white apron and a mournful scowl, stopped by my table. "We are closing in fifteen minutes, Signore. For the funeral. Signore Burton's funeral."

The proprietor, who had given me the bread pudding to pass along to Burton, walked past in his black suit and narrowed his eyes like a villain in a melodrama. I thought he was going to demand his pastry back, or give me a bill for it, but he hurried on his way.

A moment later, Daisy Letchford and Frederica, the maid at Villa Gosleth, strutted past the café, toward the church. I joined them. Daisy's eyes coated me with disdain. But neither disdain nor the trappings of woe could injure her beauty, as she had done all she could to enhance it for this special occasion.

"There is no seat for you in the church."

I tried to look disappointed and remain credible. "Are you sure?"

"I made the arrangements."

"Well, I must pay my respects as best I can."

We heard the procession before we spotted it. A military band pounded a beat and hit many of the notes to Handel's Death March in the correct order and it was with appropriate dread that I moved closer to it. We turned into the plaza and saw the military officers and the governor who were lucky to be marching behind the band. Those three American sailors leaned against a wall, openly ogling the women as they passed. Traffic was thick enough that they would have a tough time reaching me. Still, I kept an eye out for them. A tense group of orphans preceded the band toward the church and bore the full brunt of its talent. Already parked in front of the church were the mountains of wreaths and flowers and, closer, the coffin, covered with the Union Jack.

The crowd behind us pushed forward. Daisy and Frederica struggled toward the lane guarded by infantrymen which would allow them entry to the church. I cleared a path for them and before departing asked that they give Mrs. Burton my sympathy. Daisy did not reply.

Despite struggling against the tide of mourners it took only ten minutes to make it to Villa Gosleth. Ali's key, provided by Hodgson, let me in. Now that the corpse was gone, the plasters, the electric generator – even the cat was absent – the place felt more tomb-like than ever. Even the air was dead.

Light from the garden spread across much of the library floor. Letters and cards of condolence filled a basket beside the desk and a large pile of outgoing mail was stacked high on top. Hodgson had said 'plain and gray' cover. Several hundred volumes fell into that category, very few had titles on the spine. The library was organized two ways: by subject – books set in Africa, Arabia, books on religion and so on – and by authors name. There were four Swinburne volumes, two in plain and gray covers. Neither had the manuscript I was looking for. The poetry section held two more Swinburne volumes. Neither held what I wanted, though the poems were beginning to capture me and I resolved to read them someday.

An hour and ten minutes passed. I went upstairs to Burton's rooms, the hidden cavities of the tomb where treasure, surely, was stored. The shades were drawn. I lit a lamp. The desk was tidy: on the left side lay a thick stack of writing paper, an inkwell sat on the right, a thick gray blotter separated them, upper right a basket held six sheets filled with elaborate descriptions of the history of the people of Trieste. It was all neat. Too neat.

There were six drawers. Two on the bottom right were filled with drawings – desert scenes, jungle scenes, camels, donkeys, leopards, and people of all kinds. A gray folder contained drawings of rock formations and I was about to put it away when a page slipped out – a drawing of a woman. The folder was filled with women dressed and undressed, Arabian and Indian and African and European. The other drawers contained letters and writing in languages I could not identify and drafts of prose and drafts of poems. It was too easy to be distracted by it all.

The bookshelves held about three hundred books. No Swinburne. I went into the bedroom. Burton might have been reading "*Incidents of Travel in Central America, Chiapas and Yucatán*" by John Lloyd Stevens, or it might have been placed beside his bed by Mrs. Burton.

Three small bookshelves held books in numerous languages. None bore Swinburne's name.

Two hours.

I moved to his dressing room which faced the street. It was still quiet outside.

But I was no closer to finding the manuscript and decided there was no reason to stick to Swinburne. After all, the instruction had come from Hodgson.

Burton left his work out on his desk and in unlocked drawers which meant he trusted his wife not to go through it, or didn't mind. She hadn't interfered in his new translation of

"*The Scented Garden,*" which she now intended to destroy. So, in life, the safest place to keep the manuscript would be on or in the desk. Did Burton know he couldn't trust her in death? Did he care? We all leave unprepared.

I revisited the desk drawers, the ones filled with papers in other languages, with other writing systems and pulled out everything. I recognized Arabic but there were other writing systems, too. A quarter way down the second stack I found a typed manuscript in English. I quickly leafed back to the first page and began to read.

"This is the true story of how I fell in love in Persia, how my love was murdered by those she trusted most, how the vile forces of the crown exploited my grief and sent me on a mission to al-Hijaz to steal a stolen woman, and how I bounced from hell to heaven and back."

I couldn't release the page. With my other hand, I leafed through to the end of the last page in English not worrying whether it was all part of the same manuscript. I set it all aside and returned the rest to the drawer. From the street a man called out "Annamaria, hurry up. Enough chatter." Annamaria told him to worry about his own tongue. I peeked out the window. People were filtering back from the funeral.

I didn't see an envelope in Burton's rooms and didn't waste time hunting around but returned to the library, found one and stuffed the manuscript inside. I slid it inside my coat and passed through the rotunda to the door.

The street was crowded and worse... Mrs. Burton's large black carriage turned the corner. Now the villa was my tomb. I rushed back into the library and addressed the envelope to Marco Rinaldi at Hotel Antonia and slipped it into the pile of outgoing mail. Then I took down a volume of *Arabian Nights* and sat near the garden doors.

27.

"I couldn't get inside the church but I wanted to pay my respects nevertheless."

Daisy said, "I locked that door!"

Mrs. Burton said, "What were you looking for in the library?"

"I was reading this…" I waved the book toward them.

"I'm certain I locked that door." This time Daisy almost growled.

Ali stood silently beside Mrs. Burton.

Mrs. Burton said, "Perhaps Mr. Reynolds searched for another copy of *Scented Garden*. He wouldn't be the only one." She looked directly at Daisy. "Is that why you're here, Mr. Reynolds?"

Daisy burst. "You don't think that I… ? That I could conspire with him!"

Mrs. Burton looked to Ali. "I think the first step, Mr. Reynolds, would be for you to open your coat, so we can be sure," he said.

"You can search me if it will satisfy you."

"Open your coat, please," Ali said.

I took off my coat and showed both sides of it before putting it on the back of a chair. I held up my arms and moved forward. "This is exciting, isn't it? I haven't been searched since

I stole a peach from the grocer in Hartford. But I handed that off right away. Unfortunately, my accomplice ate the peach. What do you think I've stolen? Ali, what do you think I'm looking for?"

Ali and Hodgson never intended me to find the manuscript. They only wanted me to be caught looking. Then Ali, pretending I searched for *The Scented Garden* and failed to find it, could offer his help to the frustrated widow and use the unlimited access to the library to search for the manuscript about the Hajj. Their plot infuriated me. Foiling them delighted me.

Mrs. Burton said, "There's no need for Mr. Reynolds to be searched. I'm not hiding the fact that I intend to destroy Mr. Burton's work on the new edition of *The Scented Garden*. My husband would approve. He appeared to me, Mr. Reynolds. Not once, not twice, but three times. And each time he told me to destroy the manuscript. I am bound to do so."

My head was pounding with one question: why didn't he tell you where he hid it? But I detached my tongue from my wit and tried to think about what an excellent job Burton had done of keeping the manuscript from her.

"Allo, allo?"

We all turned to the door where the postman was using all his strength to keep his overstuffed bag from dragging along the marble floor. He abandoned it next to the desk and gestured to Daisy: you unload it. Then he waved toward the door and a boy struggled in carrying an even heavier bag. The postman bowed and delivered a stream of even heavier condolences, reminiscences, encomiums, salutations, from himself, his wife, his entire family and everyone on his postal route.

Mrs. Burton welcomed the balm. She shifted her eyes from the postman to his copious delivery. The measurement seemed to satisfy her. When the man was done speaking he did some bowing and was almost out the door without performing his most important task – the outgoing mail.

The pile on the desk was off limits to me. I reached into my coat pocket for the note addressed to Hodgson.

"Excuse me, before you go. Could you take this for me, please?"

The postman smacked his forehead with his palm a few times and took my card and ordered the boy to pick up the pile on the desk.

When they left, I said, "May I make a suggestion? Perhaps Ali could help you search for the manuscripts. Surely, he can be trusted and he knows Mr. Burton's work intimately. If the drafts were disguised amongst other papers, or even just misplaced, he'd be the best person to find them."

Ali's eyes shot flashes at me. I didn't duck. He understood now that I had puzzled out the scheme to make me a stalking horse. I hoped Mrs. Burton gave him access and made him examine every line of every document in the house.

I smiled to confirm to him that I had found the prize despite his and Hodgson's lies.

28.

It started this way:

There are many gods. There is one god. There is no god. Gods are merciful. Gods are cruel. Gods are indifferent. Their indifference is merciful. Their indifference is cruel. Their indifference is absolute.

This is the true account of a spy mission I undertook at the behest of Major William Hodgson. Of how my pain was exploited, and how my ambition controlled me and how I was betrayed by Hodgson and ultimately by fate. There can be no instruction taken from this account except to marvel at the indifference of the universe to the passions of mankind.

It was all here, and with chapter headings:

In which I am struck by lightning, live for the first time, love is betrayed and I am plunged into hell.

In which the Devil visits my Limbo in Herat, a proposition to release me.

I am recognized. A new servant joins me. I fall in and out with thieves.

A new friend and his guardian Saad.

A nighttime encounter with death and a mysterious hint at my future. Unbearable anguish or unending delight..

Being watched and watching.

A change of plans.

I raced through it, past Faris and Barzouki and the brothers, past the Sharif and the fight with the Utaybah, and shuffled ahead to Mecca where Hodgson had left off. I pulled down the shades and lit the lamps in my tiny, fetid room – and lit candles to deal with that problem – and ordered up a pasta and a bottle of wine from the restaurant next door. And I began to read.

CHAPTER TWELVE: In which I enter a closed shop and find what I'm looking for and what I hoped not to find.

Once, in Bombay, Mr. Collins, an Episcopalian minister told me, "If you pretend to have faith, you will have faith." We heard laughing round the corner and a voice said "Oooh, what passes for wisdom these days." We investigated. There sat a skinny young man, a Hindu monk of the Kalamukha, and the minister scolded him with all the disdain he could muster – in other words, a flooding river of disdain for Hindus, Buddhists, Muslims and even Catholics. The monk looked at me and said, "You don't seem to be as angry as your friend. Would you act angry, please?"

Without preface, I started in, "How dare you defy this man of learning and degrade centuries of wisdom handed down in families, in churches, and… pubs…. You, a peasant, a beggar, no wonder you wander from corner to corner…." Sillier and sillier it got, no matter how hard I tried to insult the man, no matter how I made the veins in my neck distend.

He ignored Mr. Collins and smiled at me. "Eventually you might fool yourself into believing you are angry enough to fool others, but the day will come when you admit the truth – that your anger is baseless, a pose, and then you'll only feel shame at the time wasted avoiding the truth. Think of someone pretending to be sad. He just appears foolish. Think of someone pretending to be happy. He just accentuates his sadness. So someone pretending to have faith just increases his emptiness."

Collins cursed the monk out again.

"Which often results in misdirected anger," the monk said.

Now, as we flowed down from Arafat to Mina, my pious disguise had solidified into a cast and only I knew how flimsy it felt from the inside. The brothers flanked me, as always, and even if my cast cracked, I was the safest person there. They were my bodyguard, unpaid yet vigilant, waiting for some mysterious signal to turn on me.

We threw our stones at the devil and then a voice boomed and there was no shelter from it. "I am Sa'ad the Demon and I can throw harder and sharper than any man. Who dare come forward and contest with me?"

Duck, you poor Hajjis, cover your heads!

Instead, they swarmed, drawn to the confidence and the challenge, as I would have been not long ago. I didn't see Barzouki and didn't go searching. Had it only been little more than a week? It felt like months, and my instinct was to extend the separation for now. This was reveille. I'd be awake and ready the next time.

Propelled by their exhilaration and exhaustion, the Hajjis created their own irresistible current back from Mina, hearts and purses empty, and I slid along with them. I had eaten with them, cured them, listened to their prayers. I had lied with every breath and many loved me. What did I feel? They were grand and meek, consumed by doubt, overwhelmed by their certainty, belligerent, gentle, kind and cruel. They hated and loved their enemies, hated and loved in the same breath, both with such sincerity that any man or woman could only return the same with equal fervor.

But I was an imitation, a replica, a counterfeit walking among them feigning all honesty and even dishonesty. I couldn't give the Hajji experience any meaning beyond experience itself. It was geography, procedure, ritual, friendships, enemies, personalities, affectations, fears, but no feeling. No feeling. I couldn't dress it all in inspiration or insight. I couldn't erect a façade to protect it, because that edifice would crumble long before I reached home. And then I'd be doubly stripped: of faith and of my identity, the identity that protected me from much more than just the zealots.

Yet, I was lucky. My disguise would stay in place, while the veneer of the Hajjis wouldn't last any longer than the visions and revelations they claimed visited them, the bubbling embellishments included. Did the shepherd who claimed to own the flock dread the dissolving of his disguise as he neared his home? The clerk who pretended to own the business? The glazier who paraded as a man of property? How many decided not to go home at all, as I told myself I would have, enjoying their transformation, believing others believed it, and believing that when they stopped moving they could sell strangers on their self promotion? Most would crumble and return home to collapse with relief into their former status.

There wouldn't be any relief for me, only dread of being stripped of my robes to become again the Lieutenant Burton who was drowning in the desert in Herat. The dread clung like a hair shirt. Relaxation was an enemy. Comfort as a Darwaysh would allow bad habits to seep in, and some of them might be British habits I'm hardly aware of.

It was the secrets that kept me going. The secret that I was an imposter, the secret of my mission, the secret of how little I cared that I was both a fraud and a spy, how little I cared for religion and my lack of it, of how little I cared for my mission as a spy. The secret that I cared only for the next danger: The next secret that might be the final secret, despite it's unimportance to me.

On my first day in Meccah I made an excuse to stroll over the At Taysir district, west of the Ka'aba, to the print shop where Hodgson had directed me to pick up my invitation to Prince Rashid's festival. Strung along Al Safah street and down an alley, a long line of customers waited impatiently for their turn to have one of the three scribes write letters back home about how well they endured the journey, the friends and important contacts they'd made, their thrill at first seeing Mecca, the glory of the Ka'aba and the many times their relatives names were mentioned in prayers. There were too many for me to make my approach, and I didn't want the invitation at that point anyway. Now, after my own private tour inside the Ka'aba I made an excuse to get away from Boy Muhammad and his mother's guests and returned to the store.

The street was empty. The alley was empty. The store was closed. It was as if the district had lived its season and would wait a year to bloom again. Shadows covered most of the street and, though the air was still, each window shielded movement and every other curtain fluttered. The feeling that eyes were upon me – I'd had it since arriving in Alexandria and had seldom been wrong – almost convinced me to pass by, but bold is better so I knocked on the door, making as big a racket as I could.

The door cracked open wide enough to reveal a nose and one eye. I was reluctant to give him too much information but when I mentioned Prince Rashid the door swung wider. The printer was young and tall – I'd expected someone older – and he hardly reacted when I introduced myself. And then, after tea, and the obligatory recounting of my Hajj, I extracted my passport and held it out to him. He held it long enough to read it all three times. We were only inches from each other in the cramped room and the air felt heavy, immovable. Beyond the curtain I could see his cot and the stacked writing tables that he set outside in the stall for his scribes to work at and the rolls of paper neatly piled on shelves.

He handed the passport back to me. He smiled and stood. I didn't like his smile, though, and behind his rote politeness lay a knowing snideness. He took a key from a box on a shelf and crossed to a desk and used the key to open the middle drawer. He withdrew another key and opened a bottom drawer. From it he extracted two folded sheets of parchment. He laid them before me. Each bore a seal at the top and in large letters the name 'His Royal Highness Shaykh Rashid al Thani', beneath it was a description of the event, the location in Medinah – his palace – and the name of the invitee. One invitation was for Shaykh Abdullah, the Pathan. The other was for Mirza Abdullah, the Persian – my original identity, the one I had abandoned in Alexandria.

"I have two invitations," he said, and again his insinuating tone nicked me.

I had left a letter about my name change with my host in Alexandria, addressed to a cover name – Hosni Boutros – at a hotel in Greece. That was the method Hodgson had arranged for communication. I hadn't worried about the inefficiency of the method at the time.

The printer waited. Somehow he was connected with Hodgson's network of spies but that did not mean he was trustworthy. To know I changed my identity was to know I was an imposter. I picked up the invitation for Shaykh Abdullah and said, "I don't know this other man." I folded the invitation and tucked it inside my belt.

The printer smiled again, knowingly, and reached for the other invitation. I grabbed his wrist with my right hand and his robe with my left and pulled him across the desk toward me. "Who told you my name? Who?"

"Please, please… I don't know."

I jammed my grip up to his throat and squeezed. Rough sounds rumbled up as he tried to breathe. "Who? How was it given?"

He couldn't speak but I held on anyway to convince him I was serious. His hand reached back on the desk toward a thick paperweight. I let go and grabbed his arm and twisted. I asked again.

"Please. A boy came, a servant, I thought, maybe twelve years old, he came and asked for a letter to be written. As I worked he passed along a scrap of paper that told me to make an invitation for Shaykh Abdullah. I swear. I've never seen him again."

"Did the note say anything about Mirza Abdullah?"

He didn't answer and I pulled his arm back tighter and pushed my forearm against his throat, though I knew the answer. At last he gasped, "No," and I released him and threw him into a chair. I tore up the second invitation and kept the pieces.

"Did you know the boy? Seen him before?"

"No, never. And not since."

"Why did you believe him?" I spoke softly, as if we were conspirators, so that the answer would come back softly.

"He gave the code." It was a whisper. I waited. "Please. I'm not allowed. It is not allowed."

I pitied him. Without his scheming manner he was like a skinny dog shorn. I stepped closer and looked down on him. He pleaded, but it was only meant to delay the inevitable surrender. At last he spoke: "The boy said, 'I'm told there will be clouds tomorrow', and I answered, I'm certain you're right."

I stifled a laugh: so much to be hidden beneath such a thin shroud. "You would do well to keep your thoughts to yourself and only carry out the job you are ordered to do. If any word of this spreads I will know where it came from. Goodbye."

But I turned back before closing the door. "Tell me, did you sense the boy's master was nearby?"

"I didn't see anyone," he said.

"But did you sense it?"

He thought for a long time, long enough for me to believe the answer. "I did."

CHAPTER THIRTEEN: In which we depart for Medinah, attempt to solve a mystery, and arrive at the festival.

One was the same as a thousand to me. Ten thousand. Someone knew for certain that I was an imposter and that I was attending the Prince's festival. It would be easier for me to pick the agent out of a crowd than try to think of a man who could resist the temptation to use that power over me. Or surprise me with it. Or sell the information. I assumed the contagion had spread, that the infected might not yet be aware of their exposure but were spreading the knowledge nevertheless. But, an unexpected feeling took hold of me; I was delighted. Whatever gloom leaked through these cracks in my future was washed out by the danger boosting me. And the surge drowned the fatigue and the natural vacuum that hit everyone after this ecstatic journey. Now every face had meaning, and every comment held several meanings. I was alive.

Ali listened to my predictions about 'clouds tomorrow' as if they were cryptic wisdom, at first, but soon he just shrugged and went about his tasks packing the camels. He had latched onto me as soon as we met, outside Suez. Could I have been his assignment and my vanity prevented me from seeing it? Gamil had owned him but that wouldn't preclude Hodgson, or one of his agents, from recruiting Ali. The promise of freedom would be incentive enough for Ali to accept the mission.

The Boy Muhammed had attached himself to me and made a suspiciously gracious host and guide in Mecca, but he showed no awareness of Faris's death. Old Shaykh Abdullah, Shaykh Hamid, there were a few others whose behavior was worth reviewing and discarding. I came to the conclusion that any conclusion that didn't sound like Barzouki was a mistake.

Barzouki was neither friend nor ally nor enemy. He wasn't good or evil. He was just an ambiguous piece of a puzzle I was certain I would solve. Designating Barzouki a spy of some sort – allegiance unknown – explained that he had killed Faris but not why he killed Faris. I didn't presume it was done for my benefit.

No sooner had I admitted this than our desultory group was roused by a familiar booming voice; Sa'ad ordered weary post-pilgrims out of his way – Barzouki's way – and all in an effort to reach me. We embraced as old friends and Sa'ad lifted Ali over a nahked camel to give him a kiss. The others drifted away, shaking their heads, in no mood for any pleasantries that might delay our departure.

"I thought I would never see you again, Darwaysh," Barzouki said. "I was so sad throughout the Hajj. So sad. I learned so much and no one to tell it to. No one who would understand me the way you do. No one who could teach me as you could."

"But that woman could," Sa'ad said. "My little Omar is a man now!"

There were prostitutes in Mecca, particularly active after the return from Arafat and Mina when men could begin de-purifying themselves.

After the ritual recounting of our inspiring experiences, I asked Omar if he was returning to Medinah to begin the apprenticeship his family had arranged for him.

"Even better, Darwaysh. I've been invited to the fete at Prince Rashid's palace. I'm going to meet influential people from all over. My fortune is assured."

His ebullience attracted the eyes of the others and made them shake their heads, but I wasn't going to lecture Omar about being presumptuous. His invitation made me feel my own destiny closing upon me, murkier than ever, too murky to presume anything other than dread, which I cloaked in humility. Maybe some would try to believe there was a silent hand beyond this supposed coincidence but I saw Barzouki; his ingenuous prattle only focused my wariness. Why chase phantoms? Why believe in anything else?

"Perhaps Faris's brothers are invited as well," I said, but Omar ignored that.

My unsubtle queries were turned into a mockery by Sa'ad, of course. "It's poetry, Darwaysh. I shall quote you around the known world. There will be clouds tomorrow!" He made the phrase a popular topic among the caravan. It could never be used again as a secret signal. Perhaps that was his purpose – to put it to rest because he was the secret agent. No one would suspect him. I had great difficulty with the thought. How could Sa'ad be trusted by the likes of Hodgson?

Omar boasted the entire trip, stepping on Sa'ad's toes as he did so and leaving the loquacious giant to telling stories of his own past adventures. Everyone preferred those. They might not have come any closer to the truth than Barzouki's pretension but the delivery was joyous.

"They say Prince Rashid keeps a harem. I have visited a harem once in Izmir at the grand palace of the beneficent Selim, grand nephew of the Mahmoud. Women of all sizes and types frolicking in the baths and only one man to service their needs. A great waste. A great waste."

I asked what brought him to the harem.

"Selim wanted to know if he could trust me. It was a test. I tell you Darwaysh there are days I wonder if I made the right decision."

Day broke just as we finished our ascent of the famed and treacherous basalt steps leading up to the plain on which Medinah rests. We dismounted in awe at the sight – pink and purple in the mist and dew – even those who were coming home and those who had visited previously stood reverently. Barzouki and I, along with Sa'ad and Ali, parted from the travelers and set sight on the four towers surrounding the shimmering green dome of the mosque where the Prophet's remains are buried. Past there, through a palm grove, cool and moist, we found a white washed wall, ten feet high, which curled above a wadi and we followed it. At times, just the other side we caught glimpses of other walls of varying heights belonging to the many buildings comprising the palace.

Soon we didn't need the wall to guide us; the grunting of the camels led us to the staging area outside the front gate. And chaos. A few dozens guests, and several more dozen servants, milled among the nahked camels while waiting for the palace servants to examine their invitations before allowing them through the black wrought iron gate. There was a competitiveness to it all, some gushing at the servants like tradesmen, others standing haughtily as if they could fool the servants into believing their inflated importance. Everyone was dressed in fine clothing, clean and smooth. My Darwaysh robe stood out and I thought about how to shed it before sneaking into the harem – if that was what I'd have to do.

Sa'ad cleared a path and Barzouki rushed through it with his invitation. A servant took it. Ali waited for a chance to present mine. My attention turned to a contingent of Russians.

Two wore woolen suits and one wore a heavily beribboned military uniform, grey it was, trimmed in red. They all seemed to have rudimentary Arabic which they spoke with comical confidence. A servant flattered them for a moment and explained that because they were such esteemed guests they had been awarded much coveted rooms inside the palace and would they please follow him. The military man stopped his compatriots; he thought they should stay in a tent, one tent, together. They gathered and conferred in Russian but I wasn't close enough to pick out what they were saying. The military man won the argument and the servants, though surprised, indicated that the Russians could have whatever accommodation they desired.

The big gate swung open and they were ushered through just as a cry went up from the courtyard and shouts followed. Two armed guards grabbed a young man in a fancy, embroidered jubbah. He started by demanding to be released and to see the Prince himself and claiming it was all a mistake, but he quickly advanced to cursing them and threatening an eternity of pain. He quieted down when a thin, sharp faced man in Turkish pants and a short, dark red coat approached. His mouth was held tight in a grimace of permanent disdain. He wore a shiny *kilij* – a scimitar – that clanked against his leg as he walked. He didn't seem to mind. The man had no hair on his face, not even eyebrows. He was a eunuch. The first I ever saw.

The young man tried arguing more but fear made his voice falter. His demands faded to meek requests. The eunuch held out the young man's invitation and ripped it in two. I couldn't hear what he said, but, like a wave, word – actually one important word – rolled along from mouth to ear: Persian.

Two more servants appeared and each grabbed one of the man's legs. His back was lowered to the ground and his legs held in the air. A servant rushed forward with a bullwhip but the eunuch shook his head. Another servant approached and handed the eunuch a rod made of sliced palm, sharpened at the edges and with a leather cord wrapped at one end to make a handle. The servants made their moves smoothly and without orders, as if it was a routine, like putting up a tent. The little eunuch proceeded to whip the soles of the Persian's feet. By the eighth stroke, the blood pored out as if a canteen had been tipped over. It was a large canteen, though, and never stopped, even after the twentieth and final stroke. The man was dragged through the gate, past us, and dumped into the wadi where he lay untended and moaning.

While he wiped blood from his hands, the eunuch stared at the faces of the guests who dared witness the spectacle, as if he could identify the next imposter. A voice spoke in front of me, the servant who had taken my invitation. "Please, Darwaysh, can you confirm how you came by this invitation?"

"The Prince's son, Majid, invited me. I'm a doctor. I treated him in Alexandria, though I don't think he'll be here this week." Indeed, I had arranged an introduction in the least suspicious way – I treated the boy's hangover. The boy had nothing to do with the invitation but he would not remember that.

The servant turned to another servant who held a list and nodded his assent. The first servant said, "Come this way, please. You may choose any tent. Any tent that is unoccupied."

He gestured for me to follow him through the big gate. The eunuch had settled his attention on me and I returned it. To the servant I said, "Thank you. My servant can choose for me. First, I must help…" And I gestured toward the Persian moaning in the wadi.

I turned my back on the eunuch, fetched my medicine box from our pack animal and attended the poor man. No one would help me carry him to the shade of the wall so I picked him up myself and as I toted him I saw the eunuch summon the servant and speak to him. While I was bandaging the Persian's feet, the servant came to me and told me there was a change in plans, I would have a room in the palace.

And so I got what I wanted.

CHAPTER FOURTEEN: In which I explore the palace, am guided to the harem and introduced to two beasts.

Barzouki and others were in the baths by the time I got there. He introduced me – with lavish compliments – to a few of the guests but my mind was elsewhere. A fine silk robe was provided while my Darwaysh robe was taken for cleaning. Bassam, a servant just about Ali's age, escorted me back to my room through the maze of corridors of buildings jury-rigged together, up and down stairs, across courtyards. He informed that I'd be fetched for the opening reception in a few hours and there I would meet Prince Rashid.

Nothing in our traverse looked like it could be the harem. I waited five minutes then set out to explore on my own. The walls of the corridors were beautifully decorated mosaics, but all design and no depiction; I couldn't hold on to any of it. It would be easier to find my way in a dark forest. I might have gone down the same route three times. No one passed me. No sounds came from behind the countless closed doors. My own room was lost to me.

I turned down a corridor of yellow and purple tiles, no windows. At the end a guard was seated in front of the only door in the long hallway. When I came close to him he jumped up and put a hand in warning. I kept coming and said, "My room is that way. I must get back there."

He ordered me to stop. I repeated my lie a few different ways. His hand moved to his *kirjil*, but his eyes rose past me and filled so quickly with fear they seemed to change color.

I turned.

Bashir, the eunuch, stood just a few feet behind me. He held the bullwhip in his left hand. "Let him pass," he said.

That order seemed to terrify the guard, but he was more terrified of disobeying. He opened the door and made an effort not to look outside.

"Your room is not out that way. But you may pass into the courtyard if you wish," Bashir said. His voice was thin and raspy making the polite words sound like a challenge.

He followed me out. Three small palms grew in the center of the courtyard. Flowers, red acacia and blood lilies, lined a path across the across the rectangle, but the flowers had been torn up in spots and no one had bothered to clean up yet. A large stone building towered about thirty feet opposite us. It was about that wide, as well. A heavy wooden door added to the fortress like appearance. Above the door a wooden awning jutted forward providing shade for the guard and the two large wooden cages on either side.

This guard also leapt up when he saw me and also melted a bit when he saw Bashir behind me.

"Is this what you were looking for?" Bashir said. The words squeezed from his throat.

"It doesn't look like my room."

He walked past me toward the guard, confusing him with the swiftness of his approach. The guard flinched back against the wall. Once Bashir reached the shade he spun to face me. His lips stretched becoming think razors. His hand opened slightly and the whip unfurled, slapping the dust.

"You were searching for the harem. This is it. And this is all you'll ever know of it. You might think you can overpower just one guard, but there is more..."

Bullwhip in front of me, I did not know what threat lurked behind and the urge to find out burned more the more I fought it. Bashir reached out with his free hand, his right, and gripped the handle on top of the cage. He lifted the door. Nothing happened. The cage was dark. Then a low gurgling growl bounced from inside. A head poked forward. A leopard's head.

He only had eyes for me.

Staying low, head between his haunches he stepped out of the cage, stopping to bare his teeth before reaching the sun.

The guard had sidestepped behind the other cage.

Bashir tightened his grip on the bullwhip. "If anyone other than me or Prince Rashid, or the guard on duty steps into this courtyard both cages are opened. Now I only let one leopard out because you are a guest of the Prince and I find it easier to control one cat at a time." He paused, transferred the whip to his other hand and grabbed the handle on top of the second cage. Again, his thin, bloodless lips sharpened themselves. "I think you'll find the way to your room more easily now... if you dare to turn your back."

"It looks to me that you've put yourself in a bad position," I said. "How are you going to explain to Prince Rashid why you killed one of his guests? Maybe you'll try to blame it on the poor guard, but no one will believe that. I'm sure word has already spread that you invited me out here."

He stood in the shade and I stood in the sun. If he would wait, so would I. Perhaps we were waiting for the same thing – his obedience to the Prince to overwhelm his hatred for me. I didn't want to turn my back to either beast. The cat might not have been thinking about the consequences of acting. We waited. The cat crept forward. We waited. The cat lowered its body, as if ready to pounce.

Bashir cracked the whip. He shouted, "*Iirjae*! *Iirjae*!"

The cat was startled but seemed to understand the command to return. The whip cracked again. The cat slunk meekly back into the cage.

Bashir, eyes on me, gathered in his whip.

CHAPTER FIFTEEN: In which I meet Prince Rashid and he meets me and I am betrayed.

An hour later, Bassam knocked on my door and delivered me – after the requisite mystifying twists and turns – to an enormous central atrium. The walls were tiled in yellow, green, blue, red, purple and the pillars were painted in a softly curving and suggestive style. Risqué for Arabia. The cushions matched the colors on the walls. Many of the guests had already arrived. The Russians huddled together, apart from the rest.

I avoided Barzouki and mingled with the guests – a professor of philosophy from Beirut with bad teeth, and horrible, cloying sincerity, a lawyer from Istanbul, a trader of lumber who talked of the forests he coveted in Greece, a chef from Jiddah, a dealer in arms who wouldn't admit to his trade, though he revealed it by boasting of his profits and important customers.

A smooth man in his thirties, I judged – though already losing his hair – entered the room and asked for our attention. "Welcome to all of our guests. I am Zafar bin Salman, factotum to your host. Prince Rashid will arrive presently and prefers to greet each of you individually. Please carry on, enjoy the evening, and if you need anything please allow me to help you."

With that he turned to the arcade on the left just as Prince Rashid entered the atrium. The Prince was taller than most, tall as me. Mid forties, I guessed. His hair was thick and combed back and his beard was trimmed so that it ran along his jaw to his chin, revealing his clean cheeks. His face was unlined, untouched, it seemed, by worry or sorrow and the smile in his large eyes confirmed that. Zafar took him first to greet the Russians.

Conversations quickly became distracted as most eyes followed the Prince, each guest hoping to be the next to be honored with his greeting. The Prince moved deliberately, giving each party its due. Barzouki sidled up to me and said, "I think you and the Prince will be great friends, Darwaysh. You are both men of the world." And he slid away before I could answer and I did not come close to him again before I was tapped on the shoulder by Zafar. I turned to face the Prince.

"Darwaysh, I understand that you cured my son in Alexandria. I must thank you."

"It was my honor and you have repaid me many times over by allowing me into your house."

"Unfortunately, he could not honor us as well. Might I inquire, what disease he suffered from?"

"I'll tell you the symptoms. I'm sure you can diagnose it as easily as I did. He was lethargic, wanted to stay in bed, refused all nourishment, spoke often of suicide, wished the world itself would end, drank immoderately, babbled his pain to strangers, walked back and forth on a certain street…"

"He was broken hearted?" The Prince laughed. "What a relief. But how did you cure him?"

"I have pills which I make out of sugar."

"That worked?"

"They work when they're administered by the right nurse. The cure took hold very quickly. I'm afraid she is the reason he isn't here now. He's followed her to Italy. I expect a relapse."

The Prince laughed again and clapped me on the shoulder. But his smile faded quickly. "Nevertheless, he must decide who he is. Much awaits him here. And plenty of women, too. He could be a man of responsibility, a man of influence, a man of great wealth, instead of a man changing himself day to day, drifting in and out, chasing beauty..."

"You sound envious."

His expression hardened and the smile evaporated from his eyes so quickly they seemed to sizzle. But the lightness re-formed and he clapped me on the shoulder again. "You know me, Darwaysh. I like that. I like that."

"All year round the lover is mad, unkempt, lovesick and in disgrace. Without love there is nothing but grief..."

He finished the line for me. "In love... what else matters? You quote Rumi! How delightful. I have an original manuscript here in the library. Come, I must show you."

"The Masnavi? All volumes?"

"Yes! You must see it. Come."

"What a great treasure!"

He took my arm and walked me toward the rooms on the right side of the atrium, opposite the side from which he had entered.

"Wait, my Prince! Don't go! For your own safety."

We turned. Barzouki rushed toward us. The guests all stared. Two guards rushed to grab Barzouki before he could reach the Prince. Barzouki didn't struggle and he didn't look at me.

"That man is not a Darwaysh, not a doctor. He's not even a Muslim. He's an Englishman and he's here to kill you."

Prince Rashid still held my arm. "Do you know this man?"

I pulled loose. Something crushed my head. I thought I saw the eunuch as I fell.

CHAPTER SIXTEEN: In which Enlightenment clears my head and a bargain is made.

The only sound was a clock ticking. I turned to locate it. I saw Bashir. He nodded to a big guard who put a hand on top of my head and turned it back toward the Prince. To resist would have meant a broken neck.

I didn't speak. Didn't want to speak. Wanted to wait for the picture to form. Hodgson constructing the nimble plot, recruiting Barzouki, confident this climactic moment would come. I was a broken-hearted lover hiding out in Herat living only for his ambition and Hodgson knew what to do with a man in that state. The truth slammed me all at once and then unfolded itself slowly, a mosaic as intricate and horribly beautiful as any in the palace.

The Prince said, again, "I will listen carefully as these might be your last words."

The library was windowless, still and quiet as a library should be. No one looked at the books but me. The pieces clicked into place one at a time. Everything fit. My mind ran along two parallel planes. On one I reconstructed the trap I'd dived into and looked for cracks through which I could escape. On the other plane loomed my fear and, more surprising, my relief alongside it. They blended to form a cocktail that coursed through my veins and lifted me. I'd been longing for this moment since Leda had been murdered without knowing what I longed for. Not for any silliness about meeting her again in a better place, but to sear me, to peel off the skin I'd donned after her death and allow me to feel again.

The Prince put his palms up. "Nothing to say? At least plead for mercy. I won't grant it, but you'll die knowing you tried."

"He's here to kill you," I said. "Barzouki. He's here to kill you." The truth of it sent a surge of energy through me and I began to rise. A quick end was put to that. The Prince signaled the guards to back off. "That's the only way. I'm just a stalking horse. That's the only way he could know who I am. Richard Francis Burton, by the way. It's brilliant. This whole venture, my whole trip, is just a side show. I shouldn't have thought them capable of anything so brilliant. Who wants you dead?"

"Slow down Richard Francis Burton. You're saying..."

"I'm saying that someone in the British Army wants you dead so they have arranged to send me on a geographical mission posing as a Muslim and then, when I arrive here, they unmask me and so gain your trust. It's the only way. My identity was perfect. Only the people who sent me knew it.... Do you know a man named Hodgson?"

The Prince did not answer. He did know Hodgson. "He wants to kill you," I said.

"And why would he want that?"

It was my turn for silence. I was baffled but I was certain I was right. At last I said, "What are those Russians doing here? Do you have some kind of business with them?"

"I've been selling gypsum to Russians for years. My father sold them gypsum. The English never cared before." He wore the willful naïveté of the rich and powerful, the ones who want to avoid the responsibilities of their power and to pretend a simple honesty and forthrightness. Naïveté as an indulgence. Who amongst his followers would ever refute that pose?

"But the Russians don't come here too often…" He didn't answer. "What else are you selling them? What have they come for?" He didn't speak but it was easy to see the answer dawning on him. "Copper?"

He nodded. "Copper."

"Copper makes bronze and bronze makes cannons. There's a war coming. England and France against Russia."

Prince Rashid paced around to do his thinking. Bashir stared at me, probably measuring how long it would take for all my blood to drain, knowing, as he did, from experience.

"Well, perhaps your Darwaysh identity was perfect and perhaps it wasn't. Perhaps you are a stalking horse. What we know for certain is that you are English and you have been lying. The rest… is a story."

"You're right. Absolutely right. You must trust your senses and not my ramblings. And if you do you'll be dead within days."

Bashir took that as a threat and knocked me out of the chair. Prince Rashid gestured him to relent. "You may rise," he said.

I rose.

"You tell a complicated story but there is a simple way to find the truth. If you are saving my life then you'll be well rewarded despite your... disguise. In the meantime, you'll be cast into the pit. How long do you surmise it will take…

"Omar Barzouki."

"Omar Barzouki to make the attempt on my life?"

"Three days." Maybe the wait had been too long and that accounted for my exuberance. I had no reason to believe my clock accurate except that I wanted it to be.

"Well, then, if, within three days, Barzouki attempts to kill me, you will be released and rewarded beyond your imagination. Anything I possess will be yours."

"What? For instance..."

Bashir raised his whip but the Prince said "No!" and Bashir froze his arm in motion. Bashir was well trained.

"Are you negotiating with me? I do like you Richard Francis Burton. Tell me what you would like... should you survive."

"I'm told you keep a harem..." I smiled at Bashir to taunt him.

"Is that all? A woman in exchange for saving my life? I'll give you that and more. On the other hand, if Barzouki proves true, you will never leave the pit and your death will be agonizing, also beyond imagination."

"That's fair. It's the best way. You're a wise man."

"Wouldn't it be a shame if you died in the pit and still turned out to be right? No one has ever lasted two days."

"Then I shall be the first. I hope you survive me being right."

Prince Rashid laughed and clapped me on the shoulder. "Take him," he said, and turned his back.

CHAPTER SEVENTEEN: In which my new accommodation is explored. Visitors arrive. And I confront a new lodger who saves me.

On the backside of the palace grounds we followed our shadows courtesy of a sharp half moon across a barren yard bordered on three sides by a stone wall which curved in a wide arc from the edges of the palace kitchen. The wall was about eight feet high, but it wasn't going to spread its shade enough to help me.

Though I had no dreams to condemn me, my colored robe had been stripped away and I was to be cast into the pit. A guard, one of four, gestured for me to sit. I could not see the bottom and so imagined it had none. Has anyone been rejected at the river Styx? Certainly not on the basis of merit. If you were sent back, would life, no matter how miserable, seem like heaven? Survival, I knew, was not a matter of motivation or determination, and no, it wasn't destiny, either. I would struggle against death as long as I could, as all men would. Each to his own limit. Survival balanced on the thin edge of chance.

A guard took my right arm, another my left and they meant to lower me inside. I thought that was a gentle approach for a nasty punishment. So did Bashir.

In his hissing, thin and always surprising voice, he said, "Drop him." The guards didn't hesitate.

When I recovered and looked up his face filled the space blocking the light of the moon, and though I couldn't make out his features, I could feel his nasty slit eyes and sneering lips radiating a midday hatred. He said, "We roast English pigs and let the vultures eat them."

His face was removed and a metal grate was slid in place.

There was no time to dote on Bashir's animus. I felt around for a sharp rock and began digging a hole about a foot in diameter and just a few inches deep in the middle of the floor. I stripped off my robe, and then my shirt, which was made from cotton, and re-donned the robe. Using four stones, I stretched the shirt across the hole. I called out as humbly and kindly as a I could. "Hello? If it may be permitted, please may I be allowed to have a cup?"

A voice replied: "Each day you will receive one cup of water."

"But I would like to have the cup, just the cup, now, please."

Perhaps I heard mumbling, perhaps it was just the sound of the wind sneaking onto the palace grounds; there was no wind down there. Legs spread so not to disturb my shirt, I sat against the wall. Eventually, a clattering sounded above, and the cup, dangling from a rope, descended. I whispered a thank you, and placed the cup in the hole underneath my shirt. It was chilly down there which only made me think about change and making things last and how people fear one and disdain the other.

I fell asleep.

The sun, dripping silently down the wall of the pit, woke me. The shirt was damp with dew and the cup beneath it held a few drops. I wrung out the shirt into the cup, drank what little there was and put the damp shirt over my head. I tied the cup to the rope and rattled it, hoping they would fill it right away. They didn't.

The sun found me so I hid under my shirt. Eyes closed, visions of the past, no dreams, the air heavy, the air still, the air heavier, the air pressed by the sun, compacted, the air heaviest, breath won't come in, won't flow out.

Eyes closed. Open. The sun seeped like sludge across the floor. Eyes closed. Eyes open. Eyes closed. Where were the skulls, the fingers and toes? I took this to mean they used the pit often and so kept it tidy. I had prayed all across the desert and into Meccah and never meant a word. Never believed. I couldn't. You can pray for the sun to rise and set. For the moon to wax and wane. Even the capricious wind. You can pray for life, it's been granted. Health is a shadow and for love pray to yourself. The best prayer, the only prayer certain to be answered – and the answer is certain – by each and every god is the prayer for death. For Barzouki's, for mine. There was no reason, no possible tale I could tell wherein I wanted the Prince's death; his death was a trigger for my own. And I knew, I know, that every prayer is only a prayer to time; a prayer for a death now, any death, is just a prayer for an alteration in time, very often, a just adjustment to time.

Eyes open. The sun dripped upward, just as slowly, slower, drip, drip, drip, eyes closed, eyes opened, drip, closed, open, drip. Closed, open, drip – up, it climbed the wall, and out the way it came in, right through that metal grate. Close, open, drip. Close, open.

The cup rattled down. I drained it, fearful of spilling any if I hoarded, and detached it for the next morning's dew.

The visitation of the voices waited until the second night. Many voices. Never Leda. Never Hodgson. My father speaking his disgust, his anger, Isabel filled with hope, this officer and that, fellows and superiors, many women, no friends, poets in English, Farsi, Arabic, Pashto, French, Italian, a jumble of sense battling nonsense.

Barzouki's voice came. "Darwaysh... Richard Francis Burton... Lieutenant Burton. It's me. Your friend. You fooled the Sharif of Meccah. Foolish you. That was dangerous, but I knew. It was I who tricked you. Many times. Many times. Poor, inept Omar Barzouki robbed by thieves in Suez. I waited, came out of a shop, opened my purse in front of them and counted the coins. I walked between buildings, luring them, just as I lured you."

"Why did you kill Faris?"

"But Suez was not the first time we met."

"Faris..."

"Think Lieutenant Burton. Who helped you? Who pushed you along your journey? Think, Darwaysh. Think of Cairo. The wakaleh. A drunken Darwaysh and a drunken Turk..."

I looked up and a face appeared. One hand covered the left eye and the hair was wild, falling over the face, obscuring the other eye.

"I spirited you to the Greek quarter and fetched your belongings. Just an eyepatch and a haircut. You're not the one who is a master of disguise. It's me. It's me."

"Faris. Why did you kill Faris?"

"To protect you. To make sure you reached this moment."

"Faris was not a threat."

"I must go now, Lieutenant Burton. We won't meet again."

Again, the sun melted across one wall. I drank my dew and covered my head. Ali's voice drifted down. I did not believe it and did not trust it and did not look up.

"Darwaysh, Darwaysh, oh Darwaysh please show a sign that you're still alive."

I would not be tricked.

"Oh Darwaysh. I don't care what they say about you. I am still your servant. Barzouki and the Prince are like brothers reunited now, spending every minute together. The Prince is enthralled they say. How can I tell him? Darwaysh, please."

I removed the shirt and the long candle of light embedded in the wall made me squint as I looked up. Ali was there. Or, rather, I saw Ali there.

"Run, Ali. They'll kill you after they kill me. Run now."

"I want to help you."

"Maybe there will be clouds tomorrow." I tried to chuckle but the noise I emitted sounded more like my death rattle than a chuckle. "Run, Ali. I release you."

"I will leave with you when you are released."

"What day is it?"

"This is your third morning in the pit. Are you going to die, Darwaysh?"

"Run, Ali. I'll find you."

The sun oozed across the floor. I dozed. I woke. I dozed. I woke. Eyes open. Eyes closed. Eyes open. The sun met the opposite wall and dripped upward. Beneath the thin, clean sun painted line, a rock I hadn't noticed before appeared. Red, reddish, flat on top. Shaped like an arrowhead. Two black dots on the side facing me. The color of the cliffs between al Hamra and Mecca. I could not close my eyes. The black dots blinked. I wanted to blink. My eyes would not close.

How did it get into this pit? What previous tenant brought this black dotted red rock? Facing me. Out of place.

The sun teased the wall, each drip revealing more of the red intruder, coiled in layers in a nook, and sketched along its back white rectangles lined in black.

My legs straddled the hole in the middle of the floor, my water hole. My foot was only a foot away from the arrowhead.

The black spots blinked.

Eat or be eaten. Whether 'tis nobler in the mind to suffer the fangs and venom of outrageous fortune or to take arms... what arms? The black spots were not seductive but they were temptation itself. Temptation to return the shirt to my head and wait... to lose the name of action.

The sharp edged rock I'd used to dig the hole lay near my right hand, which felt stiff and clumsy and slow. But I slid my hand – it oozed, too – onto the rock and let my fingers search for the sharpest edge. None felt sharp enough.

His head was already in the shade. What would he do when the light evaporated? I wasn't certain I'd be able to see him at all in a few minutes. Would time stop if I prayed for it? Slowly, I bent my knee, drawing my foot away from the arrowhead. The sun reacted and withdrew further. My other foot inched back.

Was he as hungry as I was?

The arrowhead moved. Slowly. And an unending cord of white rectangles lined in black slid toward me. I could not move without commotion and thought I would lose my balance if I tried to jump aside. The arrowhead entered the shallow pit I'd dug. It turned to my right. The body coiled in the pit, the white spots circling on each other. The eyes no longer faced me.

The sun backed up the wall like a coward. The snake settled in the pit, comfortable between my frozen legs and I tried not to shiver with each deafening clang of time.

Shirt in my left hand and rock in my right, I pounced. Slammed the sharp edge of the rock at the base of the arrowhead and put all my weight on it, rocking from side to side and hoping it was cutting through. The mouth opened with a strange yearning. It closed and opened. I pressed down, digging deeper. The body whipped around at my arms. I kept my weight pressing down until I could feel the grit of the floor and in one motion I swept the head against the wall. The mouth still opened and closed. It was dangerous still. I threw my shirt over it.

The body still twitched, too. The dead snake had more energy than I did and I thought if I waited for it to stop I might fall asleep and never wake. Using the sharp rock I tore two creases in the skin at the neck and peeled the skin back. Just far enough for me to dig my teeth in.

CHAPTER EIGHTEEN: In which I wake in Paradise. My host proves true and I lie to him and we solidify our friendship.

A small dark man sitting in the corner to my left moved a fan up and back and I breathed in jealously, hoarding the breeze. The room was vast. Light billowed through the row of small windows on my right. The silk of the velvet cushions on which I rested felt cool.

The door opened. Two women, eyes only beneath their niqab, stepped inside. A young girl followed shyly. I said hello. They scurried away.

I struggled to sit up. I poured water from the jug next to the bed and drank and felt how parched my lips were.

The exertion put me back to sleep.

I woke to find a soft finger dabbing salve on my lips and gentle, dark eyes close to mine. Behind her stood an old man with wild gray hair. "Ho, ho, he wakes. My medicine works. Someone fetch Prince Rashid," he said.

The exertion put me back to sleep again.

The nurse was still by my side when I woke. The Prince was summoned again and this time I managed to keep my eyes open.

Movement meant pain, even drawing a breath, but every sensation was delicious because the moments in between were lovely and unreal - just lying on soft cushions under a cool fan.

So I did not ask any questions that might have collapsed the spell. The Prince talked and I listened.

"You are healing well at last, Richard Francis Burton. Our doctor was not hopeful. Perhaps if you could have treated yourself, I'd have been able to talk with you sooner. Are you comfortable? These were my father's quarters. No one else has ever stayed here. It's quiet in this part of the palace. Although I understand that my sister and her daughters disturbed you today. They had never heard of England or Englishmen, but once they did they had to see one. My niece reports you did not disappoint them."

He paused while tea was brought in and insisted on pouring a cup for me. The servant's eyes popped out at that sight.

As he went on, I got the sense he was drawing out the story to tease me. "My guests were curious, too, but they were kept from the pit. I thought having strangers watch your travail would be barbaric. The festival was a success nevertheless. You provided added excitement. Don't know if this will please you, but your legend is going to spread across Arabia, though the story might undergo some changes. Knowing some of my guests, they've already concocted versions in which they unmasked you themselves and wrestled you into the pit. No one knows what really happened. I wonder if you do."

"I'm not even sure I'm alive."

Prince Rashid signaled and a servant came forward with a tray. On it lay a small purse of reddish snakeskin with white rectangles outlined in black.

"It was the snake that saved you. You took quite a chance, though. If you'd had cuts in your mouth the venom would have entered your blood and killed you within an hour. I'm thankful I didn't allow Bashir to beat you before you were sent down there. You managed to gnaw almost half the snake. We found you with it clenched in your fist and the head smashed under a rock. You were down there well into a fourth day. I had ordered your release but my servants moved slowly, thinking you were already dead.

"Barzouki told me quite a bit about you. It is my hope that when you recover your strength you will enlighten me as to how much was true. We spent our time together, Barzouki and I. Keep your enemies close, yes. We visited the Prophet's tomb and the Baq'I Cemetery. He was given many opportunities to kill me but he showed no signs of ill intent. He was quite solicitous, and boring, but hardly seemed dangerous.

"Barzouki said you met in Suez and he was suspicious of you immediately. He saw you speaking angrily with another man and threatening him. Barzouki interviewed that man who revealed your true identity and your mission to kill me. Soon after, the man was killed on the ship to Yenbo. Barzouki didn't witness the murder but he saw you two alone on the ship before the other man disappeared, presumably into the sea. Soon after landing at Yenbo, you left the caravan and traveled directly to Meccah – this before Barzouki could decide how to proceed. He feared you, he said, and when you joined the caravan to come here to Medinah, he resolved to wait until he was in the presence of my guards to accuse you."

I jerked forward abruptly and fell back at the effort. I'd assumed Barzouki would lie but the smoothness of his transformation of the truth alarmed me. The Prince chuckled. "There's more to the story," he said. "But you need your rest."

Before he left I inquired about Ali. The Prince said he would send him along.

A servant brought dinner and I managed to move myself unaided to the diwan. Another servant lit candles and a third still swung the fan in the corner. Ali came in. He fell to his knees beside me and took my hand and prayed and cried. "I didn't know, Darwaysh. No one told me anything. I didn't know until just hours ago." He hung his head. "I thought you were dead."

"Taste the lamb, Ali. Lamb mandi, as good as I've ever tasted."

He resisted at first, pretending not to be hungry but when he saw that I could not eat more, he acceded.

"I told you to run, Ali."

"Darwaysh…?"

"I told you to run and that I'd find you if I lived." He stuffed a piece of lamb in his mouth and squinted at me, puzzled. I quoted him: "I don't care what they say about you. I am still your servant. Barzouki and the Prince are like brothers reunited now, spending every minute together. The Prince is enthralled they say. How can I tell him?"

"But how do you know this, Darwaysh?"

"You told me. At the pit."

Ali shivered. He sank into himself as if he'd just heard that he would be returned to Gamil and the thieves. "But I was locked up in a room with Sa'ad."

"Did I visit you in that room?"

Ali kept his eyes on the floor and nodded his head. When he looked up, he said, "I'm sorry I doubted you, Darwaysh. Never again."

In the morning I grew restless and paced the room wondering how to proceed if the Prince reneged on his promise of a woman from the harem. Stealing a woman would be far more difficult than surviving the pit. Every attempt I concocted ended badly for me. My talent was for disguise: a eunuch? I could shave and dress the part but confronted with the wonders of a harem for the first time I might give myself away – and lend a tempting, and tender, target for the guards. Suddenly, the vast room felt like a tiny cell but when I opened the door, a guard blocked my way and shut me inside.

Wondering if I was a prisoner, I paced and my curiosity forced me to test the door again. This time the Prince was just arriving. He took my arm and guided me to his gardens.

We passed through the large atrium and along the arcade to the west end of the grounds. We stepped outside into another world. Acacia trees lined the walkway and patches of blood lilies, purple on the inside, dotted the way along with other flowers I had never seen. I wanted to know more about Barzouki but didn't want to ask. Prince Rashid wanted to know about relations between European countries and Russia. He was searching for angles to play them one against the other.

"They fear Russia because it's big and wants to grow, and the weakest spot is on the Black Sea, so the English and French will ally with the Ottomans as if adding paint to rotting timbers will help the house stand."

"But don't the Europeans fear and hate each other?

"They do. And after they block Russia they'll turn on each other again. The entrenched against the upstart. Or the other way around."

We sat in the shade of two acacias near a round cluster of white flowers whose scent reminded me faintly of jasmine. I was tempted to catalogue the entire garden but that part of my journey was over. A servant appeared. The Prince looked at me. I nodded. The Prince nodded. A moment later tea appeared along with dates.

"I understand Barzouki's mission then," the Prince said. "But what of yours?"

I had decided, in my most over-confident moments in the pit, that a lie was the safest answer to this question. The truth risked Prince Rashid's anger. He might alter his bargain and offer any woman other than the one I was assigned: the English had just attempted his assassination – why help them?

"I assume you've found my notes and read them."

He laughed. "The notes are fascinating. You don't seem to regard us as barbarians the way most Europeans do."

"You didn't read carefully enough."

He jumped up and his eyes shifted so completely they could have been a new set. "It's not too late to return you to the pit, Richard Francis Burton."

"Of course, you're barbarians. As am I. As are all peoples. Admit it, you find Europeans to be barbarians. They worship the wrong god. They dress in the most bizarre fashion. Eat food that would make you sick to even think of partaking. Your Sharif uses green umbrellas and wears elaborate robes and my queen wears hoops under her skirts and uses black umbrellas and each regards the other as a barbarian and each is correct. In China they eat dogs. Indians worship cows. Africans decorate their faces the way you decorate your walls. Barbarians. If you spent a week in a typical English village you'd jump into the sea and swim back to Arabia. Everyone has different gods and obeys his superficial customs and ignores his commands not to kill. Barbarians. In Kashmir, before a couple is married, the relatives come to the house the couple will occupy and spread a special mud on the floors to beautify them. You keep a harem. A Frenchman keeps a mistress. An Englishman sits in the sun on purpose. Barbarians."

"So if everyone is barbaric then no one is. Is that how you escape the insult? What do I care what you call the others?"

"That is how I show my respect."

"I owe you Richard Francis Burton and I will pay my debt, but don't push too far." He started away, but turned back to make sure I understood his pride. "How lonely your wisdom must make you. It is my anger, jealousy, and greed that make my people love me. They can recognize me through my flaws. But who can feel brotherhood with the wise man?"

"Maybe you'd like to duel me to settle the insult?"

"So you can confirm my barbarity?"

"Yes."

"Ha! And yours!"

"Exactly!"

He came close to me. I wasn't sure if he was going to stab me or hit me, or whether I should respond in kind. But he clapped me on the shoulder and laughed. "Well, at least your wisdom is tempered with recklessness. That I can recognize."

I wanted to tell him the truth and I hated the Englishman in me that lied so smoothly for a cause.

He sat down again and it was as if I had never insulted him and he had never been angry. "So then, it's a geographical mission? No spying?"

"Some think they're the same."

"But no killing?"

"No killing. Not you. Not the man on the ship. Faris was his name."

"Is any of Barzouki's story true?"

"The man did recognize me, but he didn't want to expose me. He recited a riddle: 'I have information which could bring you unbearable anguish, or unending delight.' But he never got the chance. He repeated the words when I found him, stabbed, onboard ship. He meant me no harm and I did not hurt him."

"So you have a mystery that lingers. And so do I."

"What is yours?"

"Whatever it is that you're holding back from me. And why."

I met his eyes. What reason did I have not to reveal my purpose? Loyalty to the crown? Loyalty to Hodgson? The image of Hodgson as my mahout bubbled up and I almost chuckled. Some men are like elephants and will obey no matter the treatment they receive. They need that constancy. But not me. And spies are trained in betrayal – or chosen because of a natural talent for it. And they develop a taste for it. Nevertheless, I hesitated. To betray my mission I would need to trust the Prince and I didn't know him well enough.

"Well… perhaps in time," he said. He rose and I did, too. "Can you ride tomorrow? I'll resolve another mystery for you. We leave early."

CHAPTER NINETEEN: In which Barzouki unmasks himself and, failing at a bargain, rides off to meet his destiny which arrives from the sky.

We left before dawn, riding into the rising sun and up a steep incline to a ridge and across it. In the valley below stood two small stone huts flanking a well. Three tents stood just behind the huts. One proud hawk rode on Prince Rashid's wrist and two more were carried in their cages by his servants. We talked of the beauty of the desert and its lovely smell and the exquisite freedom the Bedawin must feel. The Prince insisted we stop for my sake. I pretended not to need the rest, but I was grateful. The Prince and Zafar, his factotum, joined me under the shade of a half tent, while a servant prepared tea.

The Prince stroked the chest of the bird that perched on his wrist. "She's a falcon. Very fast. My favorite. She was less than a year old when I captured her. Best I've ever had. Have you hunted with falcons, Richard Francis Burton?"

"I haven't."

He handed that bird to a servant and removed another bird from its cage. This one was bigger than the last. "This one is a hawk. Bigger, stronger. The falcon kills with her beak. This one kills with her talons. Watch..."

He unhooded the hawk and removed the jesses and whispered to it before lifting his wrist to signal the bird to launch.

A servant handed me a telescope and I followed the flight. The hawk soared and circled, rarely flapping her wings. The circles became a spiral, moving lower and lower, as if she were along a road only she could see or feel, and her dive seemed inevitable as the wind. I never saw the hare until it was struggling in her talons.

While the bird enjoyed her prey, the Prince raved about the glory of the spectacle. Then he said, "Zafar and I discussed ways Barzouki might try to kill me. I thought he would use the guests as cover, use the crowd. Zafar guessed that he would be patient and wait until there were few others around."

"I wish you'd been right."

"He had his chances, even on the hunt, but he made no moves against me. So we arranged for one of my birds not to return. I decided to ride out with Zafar and just one guard and asked Barzouki to join us. It was an honor he could hardly refuse, though I warned him it would be grueling at midday. We located the falcon and decided to rest until the sun lowered. But after we put up our tents, we spotted bandits on the ridge. Zafar and the guard gave chase, leaving me and Barzouki alone. We ate and I said I was tired and retreated to my tent. Soon after, Barzouki slipped out of his tent and into mine. He was excellent at sneaking around but not so good at knowing he was being followed by four other of my guards. He stabbed me as I slept, numerous times. Except he was stabbing cushions. There…"

The bird was finishing his meal. A servant went to her and gently slipped the hood back on, and then attached the jesses to each leg.

"Would you like to speak with Barzouki before he dies?"

The steep, rocky slope down toward the well made slow going but I didn't mind; it gave me time to prepare for the fire that would flare when I saw Barzouki and maybe control the flame. A guard opened the door to one of the huts and a horrible stench spewed out of the darkness. The light hit two legs from the knees down perpendicular to the door. The guard might have been hoping I'd go inside but I didn't move so he had to pull Barzouki out.

He was missing teeth and blood had dried across his robe. He held his cup out with the plain simplicity that he always affected: an eager innocent in need of help. The guard filled it with water without hesitation. They'd been keeping Barzouki alive for this moment. After he drank he said, "Well, Burton, the Prince has made a mistake at last. We can finish him off together. I've been thinking about this. First, you have to convince him to let me live. Explain it to him, he's just a desert rat in silkier robes. Just explain it. Tell him I was only following orders and it's over. If you don't hold a grudge why should he?"

"Who else knew. About me?"

"Tell him we'll work for him against the English. Be his spies. He'll believe that. Tell him we'll feed him information about the English, their intentions. Tell him it will help him raise his prices."

"Who else knew?"

"That's not what you want to know."

"When were you told?"

"Who cares?"

"I do!" My voice rose and Zafar started forward from the well but Prince Rashid stopped him.

"You need me, Darwaysh…" For that he used his obsequious persona, but his contempt pushed to the fore. "You think Prince Rashid is going to let live an infidel who defiled the holy city? And if he does keep his end of the bargain how far will you get now that others know? You have no choice but to team up with me."

"Who told you? It wasn't Hodgson."

"Ask the question you want to. Hodgson didn't think you had the nerve to kill. You needed me. You still do. Go ahead. We both know what it is."

"Who told you?"

"That's not it. Ask the question you want to, Burton. Go ahead."

I turned to look at Prince Rashid standing with Zafar near the well. The falcon was back on the Prince's wrist. The Prince gave me the slightest nod and I understood its meaning.

A rigid, angry smile had formed Barzouki's cracked and peeling lips into a mocking mask, filthy and grotesque as an unearthed relic.

"Go ahead ask. We both know." Barzouki said. "You want to know why I killed Faris. Arrange it for me with Prince Rashid and I'll give you what you want. Speak with Prince Rashid. Arrange it for me and I'll tell you why I did it. 'Unending delight or unbearable anguish' that's what Faris said, or was it the other way around. What's the solution, Burton? When I die, so does the answer."

I wanted the answer, but it was the temptation of the damned. He would never deliver the truth – if he knew it at all. And regret would rot me. "One more thing, would Sa'ad be joining us?"

Barzouki's eyes grew wide with mocking wonder. "Sa'ad? Is he still alive? You can have him. I'm certainly done with him. But don't count on him keeping a secret. Bring the Prince over and tell him. Make the deal and then you'll know. I promise. Just call him over here."

I signaled the Prince. He and Zafar came forward. "I'm done with him," I said.

I walked away, past the well, past the guards and past the camels, kept walking, forcing myself to be too far to give in. When you refuse the devil, you always think you'll get another chance, another offer. A final refusal feels like a penalty of a different kind. When I turned back, Barzouki was mounting a camel. No one was raising a rifle or trying to stop him. Without delay he rode away, east, toward the mountains. Prince Rashid said something to a servant who immediately ran over to hand me a telescope.

The falcon took off. She was sleeker than the hawk and rose faster. I had to adjust to the speed to keep her in sight. She made a wide arc far ahead of Barzouki and when she circled behind me I shifted my gaze to Barzouki. He wrenched himself in the saddle to try to locate her. For the first time I saw him without one of his masks. Fear fought with hope. He wasn't the innocent would be philosopher or the cynical killer trying to connive his way back to life, he was just a terrified animal scurrying for safety, a rodent reacting to the threat, fleeing the falling shadow.

I didn't see the bird again until her beak plucked his left eye from his head. He fell. She rose and circled and dove again.

CHAPTER TWENTY: In which I say goodbye to a wise friend. A visit to the harem. And the laws of nature are suspended. The prophecy is revealed – Unbearable anguish or unending delight.

Feeling stronger, I wandered restlessly around the palace and grounds. Servants appeared at every turn and I purposely retraced my steps to baffle them and give them something to report. My physical pains abated but I ached to acquire the concubine and leave. Pushing the Prince would be as productive as waking a bear. I told myself I was reconnoitering but any kind of raid on the harem seemed suicidal. Much of my time was spent in the library. I kneeled beside the pit and looked down to see what my visitors – if they had, indeed, ever visited – saw. A commotion near the front gate attracted my attention while I was on my way to the garden.

It was Sa'ad. Three burly guards stood around him as the chains were removed from Sa'ad's legs. The guards were cautious. A camel was nahked next to him, and it looked like everyone was wondering how they were going to get Sa'ad onto the camel and out the gate.

His monologue of threats and boasts changed when he saw me. "Darwaysh, Darwaysh! I would not have left without seeing you. That's what I told these beasts."

Sa'ad kicked off the unlocked shackles. I took his arm and walked him away from the guards.

"You saved me, Darwaysh, so I'm told. Darwaysh, I will call you that because a man is judged by his actions, not his birth, otherwise Sa'ad would be judged a dung beetle rather than a great demon. I must wander now and try to understand what befell my beloved Omar."

"He misused you, Sa'ad. Perhaps more than he did me."

"He was a great man. He taught me to read. Well, he tried. He thought, I, Sa'ad the Demon, could learn to read. He was a philosopher, so maybe this world meant too little to him. Why do you look at me so, Darwaysh? Does love end with death? I think you know better."

"You're right, again, Sa'ad." I tried to smile but his question echoed like a curse.

"Death is not the enemy, and not a thief. If it were, life would be unbearable."

"Sa'ad, I'll be leaving soon. Why not ride with me to Jiddah? I would be honored."

"Sa'ad the Demon must ride alone for now. To redeem myself. To search the earth for truth. To discover love. But we will meet again. I know this, Darwaysh. This I know."

Bassam, the boy servant, fetched me at dusk, and led me through the maze of corridors to the courtyard fronting the harem. The rumbling cats stirred indifferently in their cages. Bassam backed off at the sound. The harem door opened revealing a more formidable obstruction: Bashir. I walked forward to face my fate, just hoping that Bashir wasn't planning to trim me in his image.

The heavy brown curtain at the end of the short corridor parted as Bashir approached and two eunuchs held it wide for Bashir to slip through untouched. I followed into a large, square lounge, with a ceiling at least thirty feet high. Diwans covered with silk cushions were clustered in two groups with small tables of carved mahogany. Tall candles burned in stands in the corners of the room. The eunuchs stood their ground at the curtain. No one else was around and the room looked as if no one had been around for a while. Bashir moved to the other end of the room and waited for me. When he turned, the curtains were parted again by two more eunuchs. We entered an atrium.

The walls went up thirty feet in here, too, and stairs led to a gallery that encircled the room. Large, lush tapestries hung from just below the gallery. Two were clearly French, depicting women – nymphs – being surprised in their nakedness around a watering hole. A few were Roman scenes: also, women barely clad in nature. On one side hung three long tapestries of Arabian scenes: a woman at the well eyeing a rider just arrived; two women holding hands and walking through a garden; two riders haggling over a woman who stood between them.

It was all the more delicious knowing that art such as this was forbidden; a collection kept private not out of greed or the threat of theft, but for the danger it posed to the Prince's life. I understood him better then. Enormous candles stood at the corners of the three slim pools and the water sparkled with silent explosions of light.

Bashir and I were alone in the room. He stopped before the curtains at the far end, but they did not part this time. He faced me, arms crossed, the flickering candlelight breaking his face into grotesque and threatening shards crashing against each other. Wonder overwhelmed any concern I had about Bashir. Maybe the candlelight made me look fearsome, too. Instead, I concentrated on what the room would look like with harem women bathing as Prince Rashid chose which chair to lounge in while he made his selection for that night.

I didn't see the Prince enter.

"I love the harem now, at this time, just as the light is fading, and the candles make soft shadows. Stimulating, isn't it?" He had entered through the back curtain and now moved past Bashir and toward the baths.

"I've been alone in here with Bashir."

Prince Rashid said, "That will soon be erased from your memory. Please sit."

I chose one of the chairs with my back to Bashir. Prince Rashid sat beside me.

"I allowed two of my brothers in here a few years ago. No man other than me has been here since. The women might be shy. Some – I can think of a few – might be quite eager to see a strange man. I won't say more in that regard. You should follow your own desires in making your choice. Only one, mind you."

"Unless I save your life again."

"I think I'll find gold easier to part with."

He lifted his hand and signaled without turning around. We didn't speak. A breeze touched our backs and the candles shivered.

A shadow passed on my left and a woman came around and walked beside the pool to the far side. She wore a standard black abaya. No head covering. Her hair was mostly gray. She was medium height and heavy.

Prince Rashid was watching for my reaction. "Yasmin served my uncle. She has been here since I was a boy. When I first saw her I thought I'd been struck by lightning and transported to heaven. Now she is mistress of the harem."

Yasmin stopped opposite us and called out, "*Abda*." Begin. I glanced again at Prince Rashid. He stared straight ahead, so I did the same.

They came from behind us, singly, spaced by a few seconds, moving slowly as in a procession, and Yasmin guided them into a line facing us from across the bathing pools. They wore abayas of white silk, thin, but not sheer, belted they were or tied at the waist to accentuate the women's shapes. Each wore a black niqab. They were barefoot.

"I have made rules, Richard Francis Burton. Each will remove her niqab, one by one. Then, if you can not decide, you may choose three who will reveal more. Are you agreeable? Am I being fair to you?"

"Most fair."

They began coming forward in twos, parting the gray dusk between the pools, the yellow candlelight tickling their white robes, and promising the truth as they advanced: all that is hidden is also revealed. The concubines stopped before us and removed the niqab. Some proud, some shy, some seductive, some fearful. Black and white, short and tall, plump and thin. Some lingered just a flicker longer before us, seeking to please the Prince, or seeking his approval – I was merely a curiosity. Were those his favorites? I bathed in the moment. What did it mean to be the Prince? To have pleasure at your command. Different pleasure with each concubine, if only slightly. Each with her surprises, the timid becoming brazen, the daring being meek. Who was playful, who was hungry, who was interesting? Did the Prince find pleasure in giving it? And, did he delight in the variety of ways pleasure was enjoyed?

In the second set, a blonde revealed herself. My Moldavian, I assumed. She had eager blue eyes and only for Prince Rashid. I looked at him as he smiled back at her.

"I see now why you're so grateful to be alive," I said.

He sighed. The procession continued. The fourth pair halted before us and removed their niqabs. Blondes! Both of them. Both with dark eyes. My spell was broken. My Romanian was limited. I said, "Esti superba." But they were being led away and I got no reaction other than an odd look from the Prince.

The fifth pair came – no blondes – and I felt nothing other than relief. They floated back to the line. Yasmin tapped the last pair. One started forward, but the other did not move. Yasmin barked. The first woman rushed forward obediently at the command and stood in front of Prince Rashid. The second woman still remained locked in place. Prince Rashid stayed calm, as if he expected this. Yasmin gestured angrily and two eunuchs appeared. They grabbed the recalcitrant woman by each arm. Yasmin gave the order to march her forward. She did not resist. If she had, someone would have ended up in the bath. When she was standing in front of me, Yasmin ordered the eunuchs to let go her arms and ordered the woman to remove the niqab.

I could see her eyes now, long and dark, intelligent. She was both terrified and infuriated and when my eyes met hers she turned her head away sharply. Yasmin ordered her again to remove the niqab. She shook her head. Yasmin barked. The eunuchs grabbed hold again and this time the woman fought them, trying to escape and she did for a moment. She dashed for the door behind us. Still, Prince Rashid might have been watching a breeze flutter a leaf. The eunuchs caught her and, at Yasmin's command, delivered her in front of me. Her struggling became frantic. Now the Prince seemed hypnotized by her fury.

"Remove her niqab," he said. But the eunuchs could not let go long enough to achieve that so Yasmin stepped forward and tore it off. The woman turned her head away from me with frantic urgency as if I would turn her to stone. Yasmin grabbed her with two hands and forced her face my way. The woman looked at me in shame, and anger, and a lifetime of pain.

I saw her face and it was my turn to be paralyzed.

It was Leda.

CHAPTER TWENTY ONE: The Undiscovered Country, or The Man Who Did Not Know He Died.

There lived once an Englishman who thought he adored only adventure but he fell into a love which consumed him and made all other adventures mere larks and then his love was most brutally murdered and so the Englishman retreated from all he knew and hid in a strange place, among strangers who also had lost themselves, pouting and drowning in anger and self-pity. There came to him an Emissary of the Queen and he offered the Englishman a chance to adventure once again, to travel to Arabia in disguise and invade a harem to steal from it a concubine. The Emissary flattered the Englishman for his bravery and cunning and ingenuity and the Englishman indulged the flattery and believed that he alone could achieve this and in doing so might erase the thrill of love along with its pain and become the man he was before he knew love.

So the Englishman took his disguise and deceived many and fought those who doubted him and made friends and administered to the sick and endured betrayal and the greatest travails in a pit and was rewarded. And at the moment of his triumph, when he was accomplishing his mission, he was struck by lightning. He came face to face with his love. His dead love.

The Englishman turned to the Emissary who appeared before him wearing a horrible grin and the Englishman said to him, "I am dead and did not know I had died. Why didn't you tell me? When did I die?"

The Emissary did not answer him. The Englishman insisted: surely I am dead if I can see the dead, but when did I die? No answer came and so he revisited his past. Was it when I fought my love's brothers, when I attacked her father, when my comrades stopped me, when I fled to Herat, when the Emissary first came, in Cairo in the wakaleh, when I fought Gamil? Did I die on the ship the night I found Faris?

The Emissary snickered at him. "Why are you so certain you died after you fell in love? Your life overflowed with danger and conflict. Perhaps you died in India. Perhaps you died even before entering the Army."

"No!" The Englishman knew without thinking that he could not have been dead before he met his love. "Not unless I've never been alive!"

"Which woman will you choose?" the Emissary said.

He knew he would choose his love over the concubine he had been sent to rescue. No decision was made, no reasoning done, no consequences considered. He knew he would satisfy his longing. Alive that was always his way. Why would he change now that he was dead? Logic, obligation, duty, and his oath were concepts as insubstantial as the breeze.

"Might I die again?" he asked the Emissary. And again he received no answer. Dread spilled over the Englishman, dread of a world in which he could not die, a world without fear, a meaningless world. Fear permeated all that he knew to be good in life: love, danger, adventure. That was the secret he carried with him and that carried him along. But why venture without fear? You can lie down in the desert and face the beast or the vulture or the villain and mock his weapons and his desires, but to what end? Without fear, what matter if they bite or peck or stab you?

The Englishman wanted to know when he died, when his last fear was real. Was Arabia a mirage?

The Emissary said, "Which will you choose?" And the Emissary was waiting for the answer and his breath was short with eagerness.

"I choose the dead woman because I am dead. But tell me, please. Might I die again?"

No one answered. No one told him that he asked the wrong question.

CHAPTER TWENTY TWO: The Choice is made. The Prince extends his generosity, along with constraints.

Prince Rashid said, "Can you keep a woman in this way in England?"

"If you have enough money you can do anything you want to in England."

"Do you have enough money?"

"No. But I shall find a way nevertheless."

The Prince shrugged. "Have her learn to cook and clean and she will pay for herself when she is older."

Leda stood between us, eyes averted, as still as she was on the slab at her parent's house. I could smell the soap and perfume and her presence vibrated through me. If the Prince noticed me shaking, he was too polite to mention it. He had delivered her personally, though two servants stood just outside the door in case of another outburst from her.

"Still, I am surprised by your choice," Prince Rashid said. "I hoped you might prefer one of the blondes, Richard Francis Burton, or the Ethiope. I looked forward to the pleasure of conquering this one myself."

"How many will you trade for her?"

Prince Rashid didn't laugh at that. I turned my attention toward Leda who still hadn't looked at me and offered her my hand. She refused it with a slight shake of her head. I reached around and placed my forefinger gently on her chin and turned her face toward mine.

How little it takes to know you are alive. In fact! A finger on a thin cloth of the niqab and feeling the chin beneath it, the slow movement of her head, the acquiescence, the complicity. The cloth shielded me; the naked touch of her skin might have jolted me off my feet.

"Look into my eyes. Please look into my eyes."

Leda's eyes slowly rose to meet mine. They were stern, severe, and flashed a covenant: show nothing, not yet.

To cover my emotion, I said to Prince Rashid, "Her eyes are even more beautiful by daylight."

Prince Rashid said, "By daylight, by candlelight, or by the moon alone, this woman or that, each is more beautiful until the next moment and the next woman. That is the story of heaven and hell… as I understand it."

I called him a poet, knowing he said it to impress on Leda some of what she would be leaving behind, and remembering when I would have taken it for wisdom.

When he left, Leda tore off her niqab. We kissed and held onto each other like young lovers alone for the first time and not knowing what comes next.

"I didn't sleep," Leda said.

"Me neither."

I searched her eyes for signs of her ordeal, for suspicion, for cageyness, for the contempt that sprouts in captivity. I saw only perfection. But that gave me no relief. Invisible wounds are slowest to heal.

"Just let me look at you," she said. I raised an eyebrow as if to mock the solemnity, she said, "Don't," and I stopped. "Tell me what you see."

"I see Leda. I see the only woman I'll ever love."

"We'll see."

"No words could make me happier."

She laughed. No sound could make me happier. That she hadn't gone mad was proof that this was still the Leda I loved. What terrors had she muted? What agonies outwitted?

She took my hand and led me to the bed. She lay with her back to me and I put my arms around her. When I began to nibble her neck she said, "Not now, not yet."

And I said, "Not now, not yet."

At last she spoke again. "Richard, we can tell our feelings and our stories in time. But now… now where are we going?"

I fumbled for words. Everything had been so light and clear between us. We threw words back and forth and the sounds were joy itself. Not now, not yet. Each word had to be dredged up, heavy, slippery and loaded with the duel threats of the past and the future.

"We can go to Egypt. We can go to England…"

Her silence told her opinion. Soon her breathing settled and she slept for a couple of hours without moving in my arms.

She woke with a jolt, but stayed put and I clung to her.

"Richard, why are you here?"

Did she want me to say I had come to rescue her? She would detect the lie before I finished with it. I tried to deflect the question but she asked again. I told her about Hodgson, and about my mission.

She said, "You made the wrong choice."

I laughed. "Should I have left you behind? And done what? My duty? You know me better than that. You used to."

She turned toward me. Her eyes were clear and plain and matter of fact. "Don't say that. Don't say I used to… I'm the same no matter what. Understand that."

"I wanted to make sure you've been thinking about me."

"You used to know the answer to that." She smiled but she shook her head at her thoughts. "You made the wrong choice. Your English are going to kill you. They tried once and having failed they'll try harder. Anouka, that's her name, the Moldavian girl. Anouka would guarantee your life."

Past midday, preparing our departure, we stood in the forecourt dowsed by the post noon sun thick as any drenching rain. Even the sounds were soaked. After my pleasant recuperation in the luxury of the palace, and finding Leda, I had not prepared myself for the hardships of the trip. The sun didn't care. Ali had finished packing the animals with supplies. Prince Rashid's retinue turned the courtyard into a loud, jubilant, chaotic mess. They were riding north for a hunting trip, falcons as the pampered weapons. We were traveling west to meet a caravan on the other side of Medinah.

Bashir stood near the gate with his whip in hand, uncurling it intermittently like a snake's tongue. As Ali led our animals to us, two mounted men, fully armed, appeared outside the gate. They had accompanied us on our outing to witness Barzouki's death. Both were named Gassim – at least that's how I remembered it. The Prince told me that for safety's sake they would be escorting us to Jiddah.

I made the safest assumption: that I had misjudged the Prince and this was how he meant to assassinate me; and therefore I would have to kill these men first. There was no use arguing. I turned away.

"They are instructed to protect you, Richard Francis Burton. I keep my word. The worst mistake you could make would be doubting that."

I turned to him and smiled. "Would we be friends if I had not wondered?"

"We are friends, Richard Francis Burton. And I hope this is not the last time we meet."

I liked him sincerely, but it is easy to like a naïve man and foolish to trust him. We said our goodbyes and Ali, Leda and I followed the Gassims past Bashir and through the gate.

The caravan had not arrived at the crossroads and the Gassims suggested we tackle the *Mudarraj*, the basalt steps, while the light was good so we rode west into the sun. A good thing it was as the steps were uneven, slanting and loose. Going down was much more treacherous that ascending had been.

A thickening darkness billowed over the valley floor as if emanating from the depths. The Gassims raised their glasses to search for trouble ahead and I did, too. Did they see the same faint ripples I saw? Three of them. They conferred and decided we would be safest hugging the cliff that formed a semi circle on the west side of the valley and finding a spot to camp for a few hours while waiting for the caravan.

"We'll hear them coming in the dark. People falling. Camels honking. Shouts. They'll camp near here to fix up all the injuries," the shorter Gassim said.

Ali cooked. The Gassims had not brought servants along.

There was little talk. Leda looked down or at me and the Gassims dare not address her directly. But I didn't like the way they stole glances. The farther we got from Medinah, the thinner their vows to protect us would stretch. Lying to Prince Rashid about our fates would be easy. Also, I was bothered by the truth that Leda had spoken: Anouka was a safe passage back to England for us. Going to Jiddah made little sense without the Moldavian as barter. But that was where we were going nonetheless.

The caravan arrived – just the way the Gassims had described – and amidst the tumult of pain and accusation and threats, the Gassims and I found the caravan leaders and introduced ourselves. When we returned to our tents, three figures stood before Ali and Leda.

Both Gassims drew their swords but I stopped them and Abdullah stopped the ever hot headed Hossein from responding in kind. I greeted Abdullah and his brothers and introduced the Gassims. Constrained from fighting, they were eager to show their scorn for these lowly Bedawin. After all, the Gassims were guards to a respected Prince and these three men were wanderers.

That worked out well because Abdullah asked to speak with me and the haughty, preening Gassims would not sit with him. They moved off to demonstrate their superiority and I invited Abdullah, Hossein and Danesh to sit beside my tent. Abdullah did not start speaking until I told him that Leda and Ali should hear what he had to say. I was more concerned about others hearing his voice bounce off the canyon walls.

"We know now, Darwaysh, that you did not kill our brother, Faris, and we want to apologize for suspecting you. We know that it was Barzouki who killed him and that you exposed Barzouki to Prince Rashid. We want to explain, if you'll let us, why Faris was making the Hajj. He was a slave trader. And something happened to him in Persia that made him want to change, to make amends and return to the righteous path.

"Faris was the eldest among us. Our father died soon after Danesh was born and Faris took responsibility to provide for the rest of us. I was sent to work for an uncle in Asamilyah, but I was kidnapped and sold to a man of wealth in Damascus, to be a house servant. Faris searched for months until he found me and he then rescued me. But to do so he had to ask the help of certain evildoers who bought and sold people and in associating with them he learned their business which was lucrative. He rescued me, but he lost himself along the path.

"It happened in Persia that a young woman was found – through the betrayal of a house servant – to be sneaking from her family's house to tryst with an infidel. The family mourned for their daughter. They knew her to be headstrong and they pleaded with her to renounce the forbidden romance, but to no avail. And her father and her brothers determined she must die. They planned to poison her. But her mother could not bear the thought of killing her only daughter who she loved so dearly so she switched the poison for a potion which sent her daughter into a deep sleep that would fool the men in her family into thinking she was dead.

"The mother made arrangements with Faris. Paid him to spirit the girl away and supply another body for the funeral pyre, with only the promise that he would not kill her or cause her death. The mother's tears would not stop flowing as she listened to Faris's promise. No matter how often he swore to keep the girl safe, the mother demanded he repeat himself and reassure her once more.

"The girl was defiant from the start. Faris held her back from the market, trying to tame her with promises of an easy life. After a long journey, Faris sold the girl to Prince Rashid and profited mightily. But his greed shamed him and ate at him and the mother's voice haunted Faris, as well..."

Leda's cry rent the night. Searing, sharp and desperate. Piercing as a thousand cries from a thousand people. She fell into me. In the moment before I lifted her I caught the faces of the brothers and Ali.

They knew. They all knew.

CHAPTER TWENTY THREE: Leda's travels

Leda removed her niqab the moment we entered the tent. Tears wet her cheeks but she had stopped crying.

"Move them away. I don't want them to hear what I'm going to tell you."

"You don't have to."

"You have to hear it."

I went out. The brothers had already moved off. I asked Ali to join them. When I returned to the tent Leda was sitting cross legged, like a market square storyteller, her back to the entrance. When I settled across from her, she began.

"I woke up in a wagon. My hands and feet were bound. I was terribly thirsty. I called out and the wagon stopped. A little man with bulging eyes opened the rear curtain of the wagon and climbed in and knelt beside me. An old woman stood outside, his servant. The man introduced himself as Faris. His Farsi was weak, so we spoke Arabic. He wasn't mean or vicious or demanding, but I would learn that he knew his own mind and didn't care much what I asked for. On the other hand, the servant woman, Safiyah, was nasty and cruel.

"Twenty days I counted. He put a burka on me. I never wore one before. It was awful and if he came to the back of the wagon and I had shaken it off, he screamed at me. Once a day, most days, he would allow me outside to walk, always with my hands tied behind me and when I hadn't been fed for many hours, so I was too weak to run far. I tried to run the first few times but he always caught me easily. He was clever that way, stopping off the road where there were no easy paths.

"We were traveling west. Twenty days and he never told me anything about how I came to be in his wagon or where we were going. Twenty days. I thought: Richard will miss me. Richard will search. Richard will find me. And when you didn't find me, I cursed you. And now I know that the mistake was in counting the days… you have found me and saved me."

She paused. Her eyes flickered down, leaving mine for a few seconds, but there were no sobs. I was tempted to say something but what words could match the darkness she endured? Every thought was only a dream. How had she held onto herself?

"I counted days in an abyss that would not relent. I longed for my family and longed for you. No matter how I begged, Faris would not explain. My family would pay for my return, I said, but he just shook his head.

"We arrived in a city – Baghdad, I would learn later – and Faris put me in a house bound and gagged. He went off for hours and left me with Safiyah who seemed to delight in denying me any comfort. It was hot in there and I fell asleep. When Faris woke me he was quite excited and very solicitous. He ordered Safiyah to bathe me. Bathe me! Twenty days it had been. Until then I thought Faris had stolen me for himself, but then I was more afraid. As I dressed I heard voices. Faris came in and looked me over and said nice things and took me into the main room where a small pudgy man waited.

"The man circled me. He complained to Faris that I was pale."

"'You requested pale,' Faris said.

"The man made further complaints: I was too tall, my hair was too thick, my feet too big. Faris said he had other offers. The pudgy man told me to remove my abaya. I didn't move. He yelled. Faris asked me nicely to remove the abaya. Still, I refused. The pudgy man came close and before I could spit in his face, he slapped me. I staggered backward. He caught me by the collar and tore downward. I clutched at the abaya to cover myself.

"Suddenly, the pudgy man stopped moving. Faris held a knife in his side. Faris ordered him out.

"When he was gone, Faris looked at me and shook his head. He was unhappy, the worst I had seen him. He shook his head and it seemed his disgust was as much with himself as it was with me. They moved me into the wagon, bound me again and we traveled.

"Faris's manner changed. He became kinder, more gentle and patient, asking if I was hungry or thirsty, even allowing me to ride beside him a few times. Still, he never told me anything about how I came to be with him. I asked about my family and he said nothing. I couldn't ask him about you.

"I took advantage of his kindness and one night, after passing a small village, I managed to untie my bonds and ran into the dark while he and Safiyah slept. From a spot on the hillside, I kept an eye on the road. Faris returned to the village to look for me. Along came an open wagon with three women in back and one up front. I ran down and hailed them. I begged for a ride. This was a terrible mistake.

The women were drugged. I was taken to a house in the hills. I was beaten. I was....

"You don't have to..."

Her back straightened and she stared into my eyes. Here was the steel I loved and now it terrified me. I dared not look away. "I listen to it everyday. You have to listen to it. I was...

used. Used. We moved on. Stopped in towns all the way to Aleppo. You understand, Richard?"

"I do."

"The beatings came fast with any defiance and the men did not mind my bruises. Our bruises. Then, one day in Aleppo I was hauled out of a sleep and pushed out of the wagon. There was Faris. He acted as if he didn't know me. I played along, of course. Much like the pudgy man in Baghdad, he looked me over, complained about my condition and bargained. In the end, he bought me.

"We traveled to the coast, along with another servant. We spent five days there waiting for a ship. Faris scolded me for running away but was more concerned with my health and recovery. Then, before we got on board the ship, he had the servant paint boils and pocks on my face. "This way no one will take you," he said. We sailed to Alexandria."

"Alexandria! To think I might have passed you by. The timing must have been close."

"Were you shopping for a woman there?"

"No."

"Then we wouldn't have met." She paused, as if to consider the possibilities. "Again, as in Baghdad, I was cleaned up and presented. This time, the buyer was polite, neither critical nor complimentary. I was removed from the room and I heard Faris haggling with the man. A deal was struck. A moment later, Faris entered the room and shooed away the servant.

"At first, he didn't look me as he spoke. He said, 'I have sold you to a Prince in Arabia. The Prince is a good man and you'll be well taken care of. You will be well taken care. If... I beg you to submit. I beg you. I made a promise...'

"Who? Who did you promise. Please. Tell me only that much and I'll do whatever you ask. Who did you promise?"

"Tears formed in those bulging eyes, and thick they were. He wouldn't answer me. Couldn't answer me. Claimed he was protecting me. I cursed him for it. He took my hand and said, 'I've done terrible things. Terrible things in my life. But I am not a bad man. You've made me see that I can not go on this way. I can not go on this way. I would set you free, but that would destroy you. I can not set you free and I can not tell you why. This is the last time for me. I'm sorry and I hope someday you'll forgive me. I am sorry for you."

"He wouldn't explain any more no matter how I implored. I asked if my family were dead and he wouldn't answer. He dried his tears, kissed me on the cheek and left.

"And that was the last I saw of him. And I never knew what had happened until tonight."

She leaned forward onto her knees and then into my arms. "Say something."

Could I say I was sorry for her ordeal? How paltry. How angry that would make her, even if she didn't show it immediately. Leda did not tell me her story to gain sympathy, though maybe she wanted to check for lack of it. I talked about our future. How I longed for it.

I told her she was right to say that we needed Anouka, the Moldavian, to bargain with, and I told her my plan and that we had to act now before we got too far away. She chuckled and said it would never work. Then she said, "But we have to try it."

CHAPTER TWENTY FOUR: An invasion. A rescue. An escape.

At 4:00 a.m., an hour before we were to leave, the caravan was waking up in pieces, servants re-packing camels. The Gassims were brewing their morning tea. I joined them and we talked about the day ahead – south, then west, the caravan was taking the coastal route to Jiddah. One of them said, "It's the easiest one for a woman."

"Let that be my concern," I said, intending to stop any insinuations early.

The brothers had packed their tents and finished their meal. I rose and knowing the Gassims would be watching, wandered over to the brothers, intent on talking them out of leaving. That was not necessary.

Abdullah said, "We've decided to stay with you to Jiddah. To make sure you're safe. You and the woman. For Faris."

I praised my good luck and I thanked him. "There's something I'd like to ask of you. There's great risk involved. But if you join in, it would help us. Help us for the future."

No one spoke a word. They waited. I turned my back on the Gassims and began to explain the rough plan Leda and I had worked out in the night.

The brothers rode off, ahead of the caravan, hugging the canyon wall and they soon disappeared from sight. Leda came out of the tent and while she drank tea and ate and Ali finished the packing, I told the Gassims that I was returning to the palace. They laughed at first.

"With or without you, I'm going back."

"The Prince is not at the palace."

"Do you suggest he would refuse me the hospitality?"

"We were ordered to deliver you to Jiddah."

"You were ordered to protect me."

They had no choice but to come along, despite their suspicions. They couldn't risk a bad report to the Prince, and if I rode toward the palace, where would the Gassims go anyway? When the caravan started south, we retraced our route toward Medinah.

The shots came at us just before we reached the basalt steps. Two, from the cliff on our left. The shots hit in front of the Gassims. They reacted quickly, guiding us toward the protection of the rock face. They were sure it was the brothers shooting at us. Had seen their faces. I acted shocked.

"We parted friends," I said. "Impossible."

"I'll prove it to you when I bring back their heads." The taller Gassim made sure his rifle and pistol were loaded and took off up the canyon path.

"Let's go," I said and gestured to Leda to join me in following.

The shorter Gassim cut us off. "Wait here. It's not safe. The woman can not go into a fight." He crowded us against the wall.

Our plan called for both Gassims to chase the shooter and allow us to ride off. I called to Ali to ride up the path to help.

"Ali! Go with Gassim and help him."

Ali hid his surprise and started toward the path. Gassim ordered him to stop and return. Ali stopped but stayed still. Gassim yelled again. He looked back at Leda and I. Leda lost control of her camel who started to circle away from the protection of the wall. The animal suddenly nahked. Gassim rode toward Ali to force him back with us. Ali looked past him to me. I held up my hand to indicate he should stay still. Gassim grabbed Ali's camel by the reins. He turned quickly to check on me just as I was pointing my rifle at him. He pointed his at me. Ali was unarmed.

"I will shoot you, Darwaysh. Will you shoot me?"

"And I will shoot you in the back, Gassim." It was Leda.

We took his camel and left Gassim with water and food enough to last until his partner returned after his futile pursuit of Hossein.

We cut south of Medinah toward the palace and followed the low outer wall around the rear, opposite the harem. The world was stillness itself and we advanced like burglars feeling our way in the sun's blinding radiance. Not a sound came from the other side of the wall. No people were in sight. Without warning, Abdullah and Danesh rode up out of a swale and joined us. No one spoke. Abdullah held a string of three dead hares.

Danesh's eyes were saucers of fear, and rightly so. His part was to go over the wall and distract the leopards. He could only hope they preferred the three dead hares to a live boy. I held up five fingers to indicate the time, then Ali joined Leda and I as we rode to the front gate.

Just before the last curve in the wall, Leda and I dismounted. We peeked around, though we didn't need to; the snoring of the lone guard at the front gate was the only sound. I pushed open the gate and kicked the guard and told him I was returning Leda. "I've chosen the wrong woman. Don't worry. She's untouched."

We barged past him. He shouted at us to halt. I turned and told him to alert Bashir if he had any doubts. We carried on.

As soon as we got inside, we rushed. No one stopped us. Two servants washing floors just kept working. We passed through the next courtyard, into a corridor, and moved swiftly toward the harem. The leopards smashed their noses against the grate of the cages. We strode between them and I placed a knife in the belly of the sole guard. He opened the door. I pushed him back outside. Before I slammed the door, I caught a glimpse of Bashir coming into the courtyard. I locked the door and now Leda guided us. We had the advantage, and I wanted Bashir on the inside – eventually. He'd be alone, because he wouldn't be bringing guards into the harem and the unarmed eunuchs would be little help. And, he wouldn't know what or who we were after.

We passed the first two large and empty rooms. Leda peeked through the curtains into the atrium with the pools. Five women were bathing or lounging beside the pools. One was a blonde. I looked at Leda to ask if she was the one.

Leda whispered, "Only if that's the one you prefer."

She led me through the labyrinthine corridors stopping periodically to open doors. We saw women napping. We saw one woman reading. We found Anouka, lying on her back, her robes pulled high, her legs spread wide, and the face of one of the other blondes firmly planted there. Further proof that the Prince was indeed a naïve man.

The women jumped up when they saw us. Leda simply said, "This one." I ordered the other woman to remain where she was. Leda grabbed Anouka and returned to the corridor. Anouka was not compliant. She complained loudly. I handed Leda my second dagger and told her to use it if Anouka made another sound.

We retraced our steps slowly and quietly, hesitating at each turn. Before we reached the atrium, we heard Bashir ordering Fatima to help him search for us. Leda gestured at a route away from Bashir's voice. I didn't want that. We went toward the atrium. Bashir was in there yelling at the women to get out of the pools and at the servant women. The corridor before the atrium was low ceilinged but at the entrance to the next structure the curtains rose high. We backed up into the corridor to an intersection with another passageway.

I whispered to Anouka, "Scream now. Now, scream."

She was too terrified, even after Leda moved the knife from her back. Leda solved that by stamping on her foot. Anouka screamed. I ducked into the side corridor. A moment later, Bashir blasted through the curtain toward them. Leda backed up with Anouka and I planned for Bashir to rush forward so I could ambush him. He didn't rush forward. I had to step out and face him. Bashir raised his arm to crack his whip at me. The whip hit the low ceiling. I stepped in and hit Bashir full in the face. I picked him up, pushed the knife hard against his rib and ordered him to undress. Looking into the eyes of the viper in the pit was a delight compared to the darts Bashir shot at me. I slashed his robe with the knife and tore it down. He thought he was finished. He was mistaken. I cut his underclothes and ordered him to step out of them. His shame was my delight.

"If you resist me, Bashir, I'll finish the job. Now turn and march." I kept my sword to his back. Leda and Anouka followed. When we reached the atrium I regretted only that I couldn't see Bashir's humiliation when the concubines witnessed his nakedness. Their wracked expressions of wonder and stupefaction – and no embarrassment – would have to do.

The guards were waiting for us outside. To a man, they lowered their swords and pistols when they saw Bashir. I ordered them to drop the weapons. They stood there stupidly torn between stealing once in a lifetime glances at the atrocity before them or lowering their eyes to protect their futures. I prodded Bashir and he reiterated my command. The weapons clattered onto the dust. Leda took Anouka around the side of the harem to the rear wall where Danesh and his brothers were waiting.

Now, I had to hope Danesh was doing his part. I lifted the door to the leopard cage on my right, then the one on my left. They bounded out and after the guards. The guards fled back across the courtyard into the corridors, slamming the doors. I dragged Bashir back toward the wall. The leopards hadn't come around the corner after us yet. Anouka had already gone over the wall and Danesh was helping Leda up and over. He had laid the hares on the ground. As soon as Leda was over the wall, Danesh threw the hares back toward the door and just then the leopards came round. I boosted Danesh. It all worked. Bashir ordered the leopards to attack me but they stopped, grateful for the free meal. A last humiliation for the eunuch. I let him go and he ran away, hands covering his shame.

CHAPTER TWENTY FIVE: In which Ali and Danesh become rivals. We race toward Jiddah. A hunting trip. And an old friend brings bad news.

Anouka was tired. Anouka was hot. Anouka was thirsty. The brothers were amused by her complaints. Leda was not.

"The food will be better when you get back home to your family," I said.

"The food was better in the harem. I could use a bath around now," Anouka said.

"Maybe she could bathe in the well," Leda said.

That brought a chuckle from Abdullah and Danesh. Hossein had ridden onto the cliffs above us to scout. We were climbing sand ridges, and descending, as we traveled east into the darkness. Later we would turn south to pick up a trail cutting diagonally north of Mecca. Jiddah lay just beyond. Abdullah explained they had explored this route many times with hunting parties and when they had fought the Turks in a rebellion six years ago.

Anouka addressed Leda without ever looking her way: "You can make jokes about me all you want, but where are you going? You're stolen property and the Darwaysh is the thief. The Prince has a long reach. Where will you be safe? You think the English want you? A Persian girl with him? Laugh now."

Trying to dilute the sting, I said quietly, "She was your idea."

"I don't like all my ideas," Leda said and laughed and rode ahead at a trot.

I wanted to join her but Anouka called for me. She wanted to tell me about her father: fat, drunk, dishonest, cruel; forced her to attend a school! With each whining sentence Leda moved farther away, just out of reach. I signaled Ali to come closer, and said, "Ali, Anouka has the most fascinating story to tell." Ali was wide eyed with wonder. He had never seen anyone with blonde hair before and rarely got to see a beautiful woman's face – she and Leda wore only *keffiyahs* on their heads now, secured with a wound black *agal,* it was dashing and daring – and now to speak with her was like sailing into the horizon for him. I stayed with them long enough for Anouka to resume her grievances. When I glanced back, Danesh had joined in on Anouka's other side. Their attentions could keep her moving along.

Leda had disappeared around the bending path of the wadi. I followed, without rushing, assuming she would slow down or stop at some point. The channel narrowed as it wound between cliffs jutting forward like ship's prows, a fleet of them moored and straining against their anchors, altering the course below them.

I began to fear for Leda. Anyone could sit above, spot a rider and then set an ambush. With each turning I expected to see her; the nightmare I hadn't allowed myself now unfolded in this desert. I resisted the impulse to speed up – not for fear I would pass her by – rather because the slower I went the easier I could believe she waited for me just beyond. Why rush toward the end of a nightmare and its final pain. That's only for those who believe in miracles. In spite of being reunited with Leda, I held off believing in those until I could be sure the end wasn't near. Miracles and nightmares are best taken slowly.

At last I reached the end of the implacable armada and the path forked and the wadi ran down into a widening plain, green in patches. The sight of three lean oryx munching on a few paltry bushes brought relief. I scanned the rumpled hills close by for Leda and not spotting her, took the higher path so I might come behind her. I was certain she was hunting those deer.

First I spotted the barrel of her rifle, pointed at me, but when I said I'd rather eat the deer than be eaten, Leda came out of her hiding place. We settled in next to each other and kept a watch on the munching animals.

"This is all I ever wanted. This. Right now. Next to you. With you. We can go on like this forever."

"If the game is scarce we can start preying on caravans."

"Plenty of those."

That glib remark brought a skeptical look. She didn't want to play at being pirates. "If we'd never met until you came into the harem, and you saw me there for the first time, would you have chosen me?"

"Yes."

"Liar."

"Would you have wanted to come with me? Or would you be like Anouka, preferring to stay put?"

"You avoid the question."

"I can't answer because I can't imagine ever preferring another woman to you. I can't imagine the man you ask about."

I turned her head toward me and kissed her. I could have gone on, but she pushed me away and turned back to her prey.

"Together we can search for the source of the Nile."

"You'll need money. Who will give you money?"

"I can find money."

"When you find money, the world will find you."

"Us."

"Yes. Us."

"I don't care what the world thinks and neither do you."

Leda set the rifle down and turned her back on the plain below. Her voice stayed low, but the effort was obvious. "Do you think you want this more than I do? We're back where we were. Back in Isfahan and talking about going to England or exploring the Nejd. There it is, just the other side of the mountain. We can explore there until we die in a few weeks. I want to talk about how we'll live. This isn't a story to read. This is not a story."

"This is the story of our second chance."

"We don't belong in either world, yours or mine, so we're going to live on the run for the rest of our lives and I don't mind. Not at all. But I just..."

"What she said means nothing."

"I want to get out of here, that's all. Promise me we'll leave here no matter. Promise!"

"I do promise."

She kissed me, this time with surrender, but she soon pushed me away and reached for her rifle. She took aim. Before she could shoot, a voice came from just above us.

"Wait. Don't shoot. Please. Someone is following us." It was Hossein.

Leda looked past him – not for the danger, but to see where he must have been spying on us. But Hossein kept his eyes down, as if to show that anything he saw would remain private.

We reunited and rode hard as we could with Anouka in tow well past dark. The plan was simple: set up camp on the plain and hide nearby, on all sides. Leda and I took the west entry to the canyon. We huddled on a crag about half way up to the ridge. The air was cool and we could smell the moisture as it wafted from the valley floor.

Leda said, "It won't be Prince Rashid, will it?"

"He won't come alone."

"He doesn't want to kill you."

"It could be one of his scouts. The Prince won't go anywhere alone. Except the harem."

"That isn't what I meant. I watched him in the harem, when we were being… presented. He admires you." She studied me as she said it, looking for something in my face, as if she thought I might be pleased.

"He'll sacrifice his admiration and kill me anyway."

"He'll want to negotiate with you. Speak man to man. Friend to friend. He wants to be your friend. I watched him."

What terror she must have felt when she saw me seated before her in the harem, wondering if I would perform the final betrayal by choosing someone else. For me the decision was obvious from the moment I saw her, but she couldn't know for sure. How well I knew what treasons a man is capable of. How well she knew the same. She hadn't even known what betrayals had delivered her there. She turned away.

"I'm not with him. I'm with you. I'm with you," I said.

"I know you are. I just sometimes… don't understand..."

She'd been taught to doubt love, even mine, and I would spend the rest of my life chiseling away at that doubt. Happily. What more pleasurable task could I be sentenced to than the exquisite torture of perpetual seduction? But for Leda it would be something else; for her it would be perpetual terror. I'd always have a face. Would she see her father or her brothers or Faris or the Prince in some expression of mine, some movement? I would always have a mood, encounter others, turn away, rage with desire only for it to wane. It would be easier for her to have faith in my love if I were faceless and writing longing letters, or an invisible man in the sky, betraying her daily.

Not long after, the signal came: the intruder was captured. We rode down to our camp to find Sa'ad tied by three ropes attached to stakes driven into the desert floor. He was calm despite Hossein standing over him with his sword ready and the other brothers nearby with rifles.

"You can see, Darwaysh, that I came in peace, as I let them capture me. How easily I could have tossed them from the cliff. Explain this to them. Otherwise I will have to pull these ropes off me and tear them from the ground myself."

"I'm very happy to see you again, Sa'ad. Much sooner than I dared hope for. And I thank you for allowing yourself to be captured. And silently, too. But, please, for my other friends, explain why are you here."

"Release me first."

I looked at Abdullah – no sense checking with Hossein – and he shook his head. I shook my head. Sa'ad shrugged. As usual it didn't take much to get him talking.

"I was traveling north, not far, only up to al Lahien, just a village where I rested. When you have no destination, you have no reason to hurry there. The Prince's hunting party came through without slowing down. A few hours later, a rider stopped in town asking about the Prince. He was excited and in a big rush. No one would give him information about Prince Rashid, but he recognized me. I traded information with him. He told me of your raid on the harem and escape. In return, I told him a lie about where to find the hunting party. And now I have warned you: my trick will only have delayed them a few extra hours. They are coming.

I looked to Abdullah. He nodded to Hossein. He signaled Danesh and Danesh untied Sa'ad. We packed up and rode.

CHAPTER TWENTY SIX: Ali learns a lesson on love. An invitation is extended to me and I accept.

Abdullah, Hossein and I rode atop the ridges, ahead and behind our group, scouting for trouble. That left Danesh, Ali and Sa'ad to figure ways to push Anouka onward. She seemed fascinated by Sa'ad's stories and he never needed much encouragement. That attention made Ali and Danesh jealous, but Sa'ad was oblivious to their longing. Sa'ad, in the meantime, irritated Anouka by being solicitous of Leda, wanting to protect her for my sake. We did not move quickly. Sleep was not a possibility, though we had to give the camels occasional rests, no more than we figured the Prince and his hunting party would have to. By the second night we were all exhausted so our apprehension was diluted by relief when Abdullah rode back and informed us that bandits were coming our way from the south. He guided us to a sheltered spot on top of the ridge, a spot we could defend.

The plan was to lay low and hope the bandits passed us as they rode through along the lowland. And, even though Hossein catching up from behind, reported no sighting of the Prince's party, we hoped the bandits might run into them, allowing us free passage.

Anouka immediately began demanding a cooked meal. Abdullah forbade any fires. We slept in turns, two hours at a time. Fortunately, Prince Rashid had stocked us well and we still had plenty of dates, bread and onions – despite Anouka's hearty appetite – to hold us over. Leda slept first, or feigned it. Ali and I ate in silence. In this windless night, the only sound was Anouka's snoring, which Ali took for music. He couldn't detach his eyes from her. Danesh watched her with equal fervor from across the camp.

Ali slid closer to me and said, "Darwaysh, how do you know you're in love with Leda?"

"I feel love for her."

"But why? What is it about her that makes you feel that way?"

Anouka snorted violently and turned over. Ali looked like he was going to cry.

I stood. "Stand up, Ali, and I'll show you how to know if you're in love and if the love is real." Ali stood and we faced the cliff edge. "Anouka is shaped beautifully, yes?"

"Yes."

"Take one step. She has beautiful hair, yes?"

"Yes."

We took another step. Another step for her delicate white skin. One for the arch of her foot. One for the way her eyes show her feelings. Her beautiful, longing heart; her sharp wit; her delicate hands. Step, step, step until we reached the edge of the cliff.

"All those things brought you here and now you have to decide if you want to jump. If the answer is yes, then you're in love. But remember, all those things you love about her can disappear. Surely, she will grow fat, her hair will become grey, her wit will become tiresome when it is directed at you. You can back up, take back each step. And no matter how many fine qualities you count, they'll never take you farther than the edge of the cliff. They won't send you off the cliff. Unless you want to love her forever, no matter those things. You have to decide if you want to jump, knowing you can never come back."

"How do you know, though, if you want to jump?"

"The urge is irresistible, despite knowing what it might mean. One second you're standing here and the next you're falling. And hoping you never hit the ground."

Ali nodded. He leaned forward and looked over the cliff, though it was too dark to see anything. "You jumped off the cliff?"

"I did. All the rest doesn't matter."

"Thank you, Darwaysh."

He turned and walked past his sleeping beauty and stopped beside Danesh. Danesh jumped up. For a moment I thought they might fight. Ali said, "You may have her." Danesh squealed with glee and his brothers admonished him in strong whispers to keep quiet.

The second sleep shift was just beginning when a shout echoed across the mesas: "Richard Francis Burton! I know you're there! Richard Francis Burton! I know you're there. Talk to me. No one has to die. My word you won't be harmed."

CHAPTER TWENTY SEVEN: A meeting. A threat. Stalwart friends. And a gift.

No one thought I should go, but no one thought the argument could be won. At last, Abdullah said, "Take Ali with you. That way, when you're held hostage, he can ride back and inform us."

And so, as morning broke, Ali and I rode south along the ridge as far as it would take us, then we followed the path down to a narrow passage between the cliffs. It felt like the pit again; the sun would only creep down there a few hours a day. The formations took on the visage of unformed faces: sharp uneven chins, heavy chiseled brows, wide crooked noses: gods gestating for a few more centuries, or put in storage if that is your preference. We were easy targets and even in the shade I could see the fear in Ali's eyes. I sang '*The Farmer's Boy*' as boldly as I could, pretending to myself that I meant to give Ali courage.

The sun had set behind yon hills,
Across yon dreary moor,
Weary and lame, a boy there came
Up to a farmer's door
'Can you tell me if any there be
That will give me employ,
To plough and sow, and reap and mow,
And be a farmer's boy?

It didn't seem to be working. My voice echoing became a jumbled, terrifying choir. I slowed down and told Ali to join me in his first English lesson. He tried. I paused after each couplet. By the second time through he was paying more attention to the sound of his voice than to his thoughts.

'My father is dead, and mother is left
With five children, great and small;
And what is worse for mother still,
I'm the oldest of them all.
Though little, I'll work as hard as a Turk,
If you'll give me employ,
To plough and sow, and reap and mow,
And be a farmer's boy.

We rounded two more jutting, unformed slabs before we faced a lone rider. He waited until the last of our duet disappeared before leading us toward a steep incline lined by the Prince's guards. Prince Rashid, hawk on his wrist, waited for us at the top. There was a fire and a servant to tend the stew. Ali was allowed to fill his bowl which he took aside. I was not hungry.

Prince Rashid greeted me warmly, but then shook his head at me. "You should have told me, Richard Francis Burton, of your dilemma. Love is something I understand."

"Would you have let me take both women?"

"Of course not." He petted his hawk for a moment while I stared at our elongated shadows running off the edge of the cliff. "Here is what I would have said and I'll say it now as if nothing had ever happened. You owe the English nothing. Simply return Anouka. Stay here. Stay in Arabia. You may be my guest as long as you please. I will employ you to help me with all the complications of trading with the Russians and English and everyone else. It's clear that I need the help."

"Live at your palace with Leda?"

That remark pierced his protective naïveté. What expert on love could expect that plan to work? He shrugged and pulled his lips back in a half hearted grimace. "Be a Darwaysh. Everyone else is convinced, you need only to convince yourself."

"I will always know."

"You can't expect me to give in."

I wouldn't allow him to pretend I was naïve. "No."

"For both of us, then, it is a matter of pride."

"For you it's a matter of freedom," I said, knowing it would startle him.

"Freedom!"

"Freedom from your followers. Freedom to do as you please. Freedom to prove you do understand love, and friendship. Freedom from pride."

"You push too hard."

"For me, having saved your life, it is now my chance to save my own."

"Even if means your death?"

"Exactly."

He laughed at that and clapped me on the back. "I am here and bandits are on your other side. Go back now, Richard Francis Burton. You will die and I will remain in my velvet chains. But, I'll miss you."

We were boxed in. The bandits lurked between us and Jiddah. The Prince behind. I asked Abdullah if we could split the two forces and sneak through. He shook his head. "Not with her." Anouka.

Anouka said, "The Prince demanded my return, didn't he? Don't be a fool. If he gets me back he'll be a happy man and leave you alone."

"He didn't demand you. He wanted Leda."

She cried and Danesh consoled her while Ali looked on, regretting his magnanimous withdrawal from that rivalry. I expected a smile from Leda but she shook her head to reprimand me. As if to close off any hope, a shot was fired from just below us where Sa'ad was on duty as look out against the bandits.

He called up to us. "Worry not. They retreated once they saw who they were dealing with. They'll pay if they try again."

Hossein rolled his eyes. I told the brothers I had something to say to them. They summoned Danesh from Anouka's side.

"You've been true friends. Faris was lucky to have you on his side. You've helped me and I can never thank you enough. You're free to go now, though. You've done enough."

Abdullah shrugged. "Maybe we should just leave."

"There's only one problem," Hossein said.

"Who will go on the Hajj to redeem our souls?"

"I thought he liked us," Danesh said.

The brothers laughed. I respected them as much as any men I had ever met in England or India or Arabia. Having taken an oath, the matter was settled and no circumstance could dent their resolve. Even the thought brought laughter. I envied them, too.

I pointed east at the endless, barren plain – the Nejd. No one had ever crossed it, vague stories were told of bandits and cats and poisoned water. No hills, no shrubs, no place for a fly to find shade. "They won't follow us into the Nejd."

"They won't even retrieve our bodies," Hossein said.

Abdullah was milder. "They won't follow, that's the reason not to try it. I don't know where the wells are. I don't know if there are wells."

But the sight held us captive. For a moment we all dreamt together; the impossible pulling with a mysterious magnetism.

"What's that?" Anouka said.

She was pointing southeast across the desert and saw what none of us had noticed. A brown cloud gathered far across the plain, low, as if its buoyancy was lost. It was coming our way.

Hossein said, "*Sammun*!"

"*Haboob*," said Abdullah.

We had experienced the bad winds, the *Sammun*, but a sand storm was new to me.

"We can huddle below," Abdullah said. "Where Sa'ad waits."

"Wait." They turned toward me. I shouted, "*Haboob*! *Haboob*!" The others opened their mouths in shock while the word bounced on itself through the canyon. "I want to warn the Prince and the bandits. I want them to huddle down. Better if they don't see us.

"They know where we are," Hossein said.

"I mean we're going to ride the storm. Maybe all the way to Jiddah."

"We can fight the bandits and the Prince. We can't fight the storm."

"We don't have to fight it. We can ride it. They won't follow. You know that. It's a gift. Isn't it said, 'when danger approaches, sing to it?'"

CHAPTER TWENTY EIGHT: Riding into a storm. A fall and a rescue. And out the other side.

Though he made a big target, Sa'ad insisted that he lead the way down the trail. He was betting the bandits had retreated to wait out the storm, though his silence proved he wasn't sure of his bet.

The wind greeted us as we left the canyon and we turned our backs to it. The dusty desert floor widened for miles before us. Far off on the left, a clump of hills stood out as hardened blemishes. Abdullah pointed to them and directed us to aim for them if we got separated. The three brothers and Ali lined up and spread a rope across their saddles to help them stay together. Sa'ad and I flanked Leda and Anouka. We spread another rope and our line moved in front. We all pulled down our keffiyehs and set them tight around our ears. We pulled up our scarves to cover as much of our faces as we could.

And then Anouka's camel turned around to face the wind. Sa'ad grabbed the reins roughly. Danesh took offense at this and Anouka saw the opportunity to take sides. She preferred to have Danesh ride beside her. The storm refused to wait for her to extend her complaint, chanting its one fearsome note with ever increasing intensity. The switch was made. It was decided that our line would go behind, in the hope that Anouka's mount would keep moving if the animal in front of him moved.

A little army, we rode at a trot ahead of the pursuing force. Our animals were eager for once to obey. Was there a moment we dreamed we could outrun the *haboob*? Inevitable as time itself, the wind bellowed and the storm swept over us and dominated all our senses. There was little to see and we hardly dared look. Soon our eyes ceased to matter. It was dark but it wasn't darkness; we were inside a whale or a tree or beneath the sea. Another world. I stole a glance toward Leda but could not see her just two feet to my right. The sand assaulted us from behind and swirled hungrily to get us in front, too. In this torture chamber of wind, sand and gloom we tramped on, hopeful without reason that it would soon end and fearful that it would never end.

Leda grabbed me. I could barely hear her. "She fell. Fell." And with that a camel without a rider bumped me. Holding tight to the rope and Leda, I hurried forward to tell the others. They caught on quickly. We all turned into the wind.

The sand formed into a scalpel, peeling back the skin on my hands. Raising my eyes was out of the question. I pulled tight to keep Leda close and I didn't have to keep the camel from running off; it was plodding now, step by step. I hoped we didn't crush anyone. As much as I dared, I called out, but the reward was a mouthful of sand.

The murk lifted slightly and maybe the wind abated a bit. I saw no one. We crept our way back. Now I could see Sa'ad riding nearby and beyond him Abdullah and Hossein spread out to the south. I looked frantically for Ali. He was directly behind me. I found everyone but Anouka. And Danesh.

We walked our animals over the ground we had already covered but the slight thinning of the fury made it clear that neither Anouka nor Danesh were before us. They had vanished.

It was dusky then and still loud as we gathered and put our backs, again, to the wind. Hossein glared at me. Who else could he blame? "We've come too far. We passed him by in the haze," he said. He waited for me to argue but I didn't oblige him. This was not the moment to open a philosophical argument. We spread out and marched our camels over the ground just covered.

I held tight to the rope to Leda and moved slower than the others. Sa'ad sensed something but I signaled him to move on. When the others were safely ahead, I pulled on the rope. Leda understood. We turned into the wind again and rode as fast as the camels would allow. I was grateful they didn't rebel.

The brothers might think Danesh brave for trying to save Anouka, and that he was foolish, but they would never accept that he was fool enough to flee with her. Danesh wasn't my little brother so I could see him more clearly.

Leda and I rode farther back toward the cliffs and soon the shape formed in the few glances I dared: One shape, of a struggling beast and two people on board. They were still fighting the storm; with Anouka clinging on to Danesh they hadn't made much progress. I tried to check if we were close enough to the cliff for the Prince or his men to spot us but the cliffs were invisible. We managed to get in front of Danesh, blocking his way. Anouka shouted at him to go around. I only said, "Your brothers are looking for you." Danesh hung his head as he turned around. He was relieved.

We lagged behind him for a way, grateful not to be able to hear Anouka's goading. When we drew closer, I pulled up next to Danesh and told him to ride ahead of us and greet his brothers with joy, as if he had been looking for them all along. "They'll never know," I said.

"I'll tell them!" Anouka said.

Leda grabbed her arm and squeezed. "No you won't," she said.

Ghosts, proud ghosts, triumphant ghosts, we entered Jiddah from the north at the Al-Medinah gate carrying so much sand and dust that my Darwaysh robe had lost its color. Trouble had been evaded, not escaped, but that was enough for the moment. Two tall black minarets guided us through the city toward al-Mazloum, the District of the Wronged, where friends of the brothers would be our hosts. In the harbor, near the souk, just as tall as the minarets, rose the masts of H.M.S. Cyclops, anchored in the bay.

The large flat where the brothers led us lay high up in the back area of the souk along lanes more twisting and confounding than the corridors of the Prince Rashid's palace. And these lanes were more dangerous. Outsiders entered at their own peril and only the status of our hosts and their love for the brothers guaranteed our safety. We all agreed Anouka must never be allowed out of the apartments.

After bathing, we dined on *saleeg*, made with chicken and sweet milk and I pitied our hosts because Danesh and Ali seemed to be competing again, this time over the food. The hosts told us their stories. They were thieves who prospered at their trade, and deciding their good luck must run out one day, invested in a business in Jiddah: they provided protection to importers, watching their goods as they were unloaded, taking only a small portion for themselves and selling whatever that portion might consist of from a shop in the souk. They knew every rascal and villain in the city. Their connection to the brothers remained a mystery and I saw no reason to pry.

I wrote out a note for Hodgson – 'I have the woman Anouka. Come to see her. B' – and gave it to Ali with instructions to deliver it only into Hodgson's hand on board the ship in the harbor.

"Tell him nothing, Ali. He'll try to pry information from you. Nothing. *Mafish.*"

Sa'ad said, "Danger lurks in every corner, even as it does in the Casbah in Tangier where I traveled as a young man and made many friends amid adventures too plentiful to tell. Young Ali must beware and be armed. I insist."

I interrupted. "You want to accompany him, Sa'ad?"

"I have never before been on an English warship and I'm very interested."

"Very well," I said. "Only this is a peaceful mission. Conflict, even if you win, will not help me."

So Sa'ad promised his best behavior and off they went.

Sa'ad returned a few minutes later. "Ali is off to the ship. I returned to let you know the Prince's men guard all the entrances to the souk. I even saw Bashir. They saw me. They saw Ali."

29.

That was it. The last page.

First, I cursed Hodgson for the manipulating devil that he was. Next, I rechecked the envelope for pages that might have been left behind. Then I cursed Hodgson some more. He would know I'd be yanked out of the dream of that adventure. He would know that I wasn't hanging on the cliff's edge, I had jumped off. Willingly. He would know I'd be desperate to find him and find the ending.

The hazy sky was just lightening. I packed quickly and stuffed the manuscript inside my coat. Outside in the mist, I faced yet another sleepy, clip-clopping milk cart nag and his sleepier driver. Maybe it was the same one but this time the sight of the old horse and its old master infuriated me. The horse and carriage turned up the hill, squeezing into a narrow alley without caution or care. There was life in all its somnolent, rote blandness. I wanted to return to the pit, the palace, the harem, the desert storm. My mind was in Jiddah, waiting for Hodgson, waiting to ambush him, waiting for revenge. But the only way to find out was to find another cart to clip clop me to the mountain.

Below, in the harbor, three sailors from the U.S.S. Atlanta rowed to the pier and climbed up. I didn't see any available carriages but kept going, figuring I could dodge the sailors if they came close. I heard a voice, "There he is." In English, from behind me. It was those three U.S. sailors I had seen at the funeral. "Mr. Reynolds. Please wait. We've been looking for you."

The other three continued their march up toward me. To my left ran a narrow side street and into it came a horse and carriage. The same milk rig. I ran toward it, squeezed past the nag's nose and hopped on next to the driver. I grabbed the reins. He woke up at that.

"Don't worry. Go back to sleep if you like. I'll buy the remainder of your milk."

There was no whip, no stick, nothing to prod the animal. I tried to whip the reins but that had no effect. Clip-clop. Clip-clop. The driver shrugged and closed his eyes. The nag was a genius, defying gravity: how do you go that slowly downhill? Within seconds, the three sailors appeared in front of us, blocking the way. That gave me hope: the horse would not stop, it would trample them. But this clever animal turned out to respect the uniform.

The other three sailors came up and greeted their colleagues. "We found him." "Out here on the street?" "What luck." "I was hoping he'd wait another day or two. Want to see more of Trieste."

And when at last I arrived before them… "Lieutenant Reynolds, we've been scouring the city for you."

"I've been resting up for the trip ahead of me."

"The trip? It's only a couple of hours."

"Hours?"

"Mr. Hodgson requested that we deliver you to a place called Opcina."

"He's quite eager to see you."

I checked in at the lodge and after freshening up in my room, met Hodgson on the terrace. His breakfast had hardly been touched. The waiter came and I ordered a pastry and coffee. Hodgson asked for more hot tea. He wore a blanket across his lap. His rigid posture was enforced with effort.

When the waiter left, Hodgson said, "I should have thought you'd finish the manuscript sooner, Reynolds. Did you read it twice?"

No mention, of course, of the set up in Mrs. Burton's library. "I haven't finished."

"No. No one has." He chuckled and that led to a coughing fit, which sounded rougher than usual. A breeze slid off the mountain and I pulled my coat tighter and rubbed my hands. Hodgson coughed again. Neither that nor the breeze brought any ruddiness to Hodgson's cheeks.

"Would you rather go inside?"

"If you're cold just say so, Reynolds."

The waiter delivered the coffee, tea and pastry. Hodgson busied himself with his tea. Ali came onto the terrace. He nodded his hello to me and gave the slightest shake of his head to Hodgson, the changing motion of his head giving the impression that he couldn't make up his mind.

Hodgson said, "So, Ali has searched your bag, Reynolds, and did not find the manuscript. I assume it's tucked there inside your coat."

"Why did it end there? With you on the ship?" I said.

"Don't skip ahead, Reynolds. You'll find out now. First, how did you get it out of the villa? Ali is quite sure you weren't carrying it."

I explained.

"Well, Ali. He certainly had you. Good work, Reynolds. Give him the envelope, Ali." Ali placed a thick white envelope on the table and pushed it toward me. "Everything you asked for, Reynolds. You've won. Now, hand over the manuscript, please."

I pulled the papers out of the white envelope and scanned the first few. Indeed, everything I had asked for was there, and more. I placed the envelope in my pocket. Our transition was complete; Hodgson was my agent now. We each knew our parts though this would be the first time we played them: he would talk and I would listen. Whatever lies he told would be in the service of truths. I didn't expect many lies this time. He wanted to tell the whole truth.

I handed over the manuscript and he slid it out of the envelope. I expected him to leaf through it as he had the Arabian Nights, but he only glanced briefly at the last page before returning it with elaborate care into the envelope.

He placed the envelope on the table between us, like a bible.

30.

"Would you like to tell this part, Ali?"

"You do it, please."

"Well, Reynolds will want to know if I miss anything so interrupt as you see fit. He's become quite the stickler. Jiddah… bustling city at the time, crowded with shops and street merchants, all the released energy of Arabia. Foreigners come to do business. To remind me of the purpose of the whole mission, we had to wait to enter the harbor because a Russian ship was leaving. Three days after we arrived, this young boy, Ali it turned out, delivered the note, the note telling me that the mission was a success. B for Barzouki, mind you. Success! Should I complain that Burton tricked me there? I brought along a guard of four but Ali insisted they stand outside the Souk. Too dangerous for them to enter.

"Ali proceeded to lead me a fandango through the souk which might as well have been Buckingham Palace at tea time for the reception I received. Maybe it's better to say I was being measured but none of them intended to pay for my coffin. No matter how often I asked Ali if he knew where he was going, he just kept going. I kept my right arm bent and hand close to my pistol.

"A tall man came out of a doorway and brushed me harshly and intentionally as he went past. I turned to look him over and when I turned back, Ali was gone and I faced a huge black man. My introduction to Sa'ad the Demon. And next to him stood three fierce looking Bedouin. I turned back. The tall man faced me. Without warning he grabbed my pistol and with his other hand he grabbed my collar. I was inches from his face.

"'Do you wish I were dead now, Major? Or are you glad to see me? Will I kill you or save you?'

"Burton?"

"'Alive.'

"And no wonder," I said. "Your disguise fooled even me."

"I was escorted by Sa'ad, the three Bedawin and Burton to an apartment somewhere in that jumble of buildings and put into a small room. Eventually, I was brought into a larger room where Burton sat in a large chair and a very beautiful young woman sat beside him. I don't have to tell you who she was. But I did not know, could not know who she was. I only knew she wasn't the woman I had sent him for. I only knew that Burton had come to Arabia and found himself an extraordinarily beautiful woman. I only knew that there was no chair for me. And I did not like that, Reynolds. Burton, being alive, remained a junior officer, a junior officer whose eyes shot bullets of hatred at me, hatred too overwhelming to include delight at his superior position. He had outsmarted me and now he held the upper hand and in return I hated him for it."

"You claim you have the Moldavian woman, Burton. This is not her. If that's true, you've done good work. Hand her over and we'll be done with it."

"I did not expect we would be done with anything so easily but I had to keep myself from asking him how he survived. As you know, Reynolds, better to allow others to open their own faucets. Gloat without prompting. Yields more. Only ask when they're too reticent.

"'"I have her,' Burton said. '"But why should I hand her over to you?'

"I saw just the slightest flicker of concern at his remark from the woman by his side."

"Come now, Burton, soldiers are sent to the front on excursions of little hope all the time. I gave the orders I had to give."

"'They don't expect to get shot in the back!'

"I am ordering you to give me the girl."

"Burton laughed and said, 'You won't get ten yards from here. Better to order me not to kill you.'

"The woman said, 'Richard, we do owe something to Major Hodgson…' She looked at me plainly, as if to say 'I've done this for you; now it's your turn.' She knew that Burton would follow her lead. That's what impressed me. She knew her power over him. No one had power over him. She had power over him.

"Burton ordered a chair for me, though there was no one in the room to hear him. Ali delivered a chair. Another boy brought in tea. Burton said, 'Pour three cups and allow Major Hodgson to choose which he prefers.' I saw that the woman understood the reference.

"I waited, watching Burton gather his thoughts. At last he said, 'Major Hodgson, meet Leda.'

"I was too dense, Reynolds! Too dense at first. How Burton must have enjoyed my confusion. He went on and told me where he had found her, but little else. Nothing about how he had survived, or how she had survived. His hatred seemed to be put aside. He said he would give me the girl but wanted things in return."

"Of course you do," I said and I immediately regretted my tone. The cynical arrogance seemed out of place in front of her.

'"British passport for Leda. The top one. Citizen of England.'

"Fine."

'"And, the Nile exploration which you already promised.'

"Of course."

'"There will be more. For my friends...'

"Let's get on with this, shall we?"

'"It's not that easy, Major. Prince Rashid is upset. He wants one of the women back.'

"Only one? You are good."

'"It's a matter of honor for him.'

"It's a matter of honor to me, too. And you, I assume."

'"He won't let us leave the souk. Every entrance is covered. You'll have to make some sort of arrangement with him.'

"But Burton had no suggestions on what type of arrangement that might be. We sat in silence until Leda spoke up. She asked if I had ever met Prince Rashid. I asked why that would matter and Burton said, 'He has.'

"Leda said, 'You wanted to kill the Prince because he wouldn't choose sides between you and the Russians. He cares only for profit.'

"That was the cause of the problem between us."

'"And so let that be the solution. You have money. Pay him. Give him an easy way to trade more with the Russians, within limits, and in return he will spy on them for you. And he will let us go.'

"I wanted to make some remark about how I now understood, at that moment, the agony of Burton's loss. Difficult to make sure that's taken as a compliment, though What their reunion meant to him was beyond my imagination. I didn't want to imagine it. Understand that! I didn't want to marvel at the twists in his fortunes."

Hodgson's watery eyes seemed to be melting but the tears would not form. I said, "You were jealous."

"As you are, even third hand. Don't accuse me. You didn't see her. You didn't hear her. What are we, Reynolds? We don't send these men out to be heroes. They're wretches who we have to prop up and manipulate. Not heroes. Not heroes."

31.

"Burton wrote a note and escorted me, along with Ali and the Sa'ad, out of the Souk. Prince Rashid's guards were easy to spot. They jumped when they saw Burton and my soldiers jumped when they saw me. Burton ignored them all and walked up to Bashir, the Prince's creature. Bashir tensed up and pulled his sword. Burton held out the letter to him, introduced me and instructed Bashir to take me to see the Prince.

"'Don't tarry,' Burton said as if Bashir were his servant. Bashir did not move. The guards circled us. 'If you harm me now the Prince will not get either woman back and he'll cut up what's left of you and feed it those leopards. Now be off.' Burton turned to me and smiled. 'I think you'll be quite safe, Major.'

"Prince Rashid occupied a large house in the al-Yemen district, the southern part of the city. The two Gassims (I was informed of their role later) escorted me through the streets followed by jeers and threats for my British uniform from citizens at every turn. The house was teeming with the Prince's guards, both outside and in, who snickered in welcome and bantered with my followers.

Prince Rashid and I had a dance to do and I knew the steps: wait, be admitted, listen to him rail about my plot, discuss Burton and our mutual admiration for him. What struck me throughout was the contrast with Burton. I was once more in the presence of an ordinary man, a man I could predict, a man I could manipulate.

"Prince Rashid wondered how Burton could bear to deal with me, wondered if my crime against Burton was greater than my crime against him. I agreed that it was, but the letter was proof that Burton was, indeed, dealing with me.

"'You tried to kill me and now you offer me the opportunity to be your spy.'

"I offer you a chance at peace and prosperity."

"'But I am doubly injured. Making a deal with you is one thing, but Burton stole from my harem. That can not be ignored. You understand? This is more than politics or trade. This is a matter of honor and pride.'

"My understanding is that you encouraged the theft so that you could force the British to grant you more favorable trading terms and opportunities – along with a pile of gold sovereigns, I might add. A clever ploy by you. Great riches in exchange for just one harem girl. Thus adding to your reputation for such shrewd maneuvers."

"As Leda predicted, Prince Rashid found the deal to his liking. We made arrangements for the handover of the booty, at which point he would withdraw his men from guarding the souk, allowing us to leave with both women. I then asked him to confirm the terms and he did so accurately and I felt that I had a promising partnership in Arabia.

"Prince Rashid saw me out. Before I left, he said, '"Major, you could have come to me and made this deal without sacrificing so extraordinary a man as Richard Francis Burton.'

"Do you believe that?"

He looked perplexed. I knew it would be a fool's errand trying to enlighten him and that I was more likely to sprout wings than to pierce his protective shell with words, but I was still young enough to indulge the occasional fool's errand. I wanted my disregard for his ingenuous remarks to be acknowledged.

"In fact, I couldn't have. If you had proposed it to me in writing, I still would have gone ahead with the plot. In fact, I would have rushed it. I tell you this so we can begin our partnership without any more secrets than we need keep from each other." I waited for him to reaffirm that. He seemed stunned by my statement. "I am done, now, betraying Burton. May I assume you will not begin?"

"You may be certain of it," he said.

"I was not certain of anything. The most difficult people to deal with are the ones who think they're innocents. Prince Rashid could have me shot in the back and consoled himself with half dozen cozy lies.

"Ali fetched a package waiting for me at the dock while Sa'ad guided me safely to the apartment. Burton and Leda had just returned from shopping in the souk for gifts. He marveled at the variety available. Leda wanted to hear what I had to report about my meeting with the Prince. We were all apprehensive. For Burton, though, apprehension and joy went hand in hand. And with Leda beside him the joy was multiplied. I was not joyous.

"We reviewed the arrangements for the next day. I wanted a stronger British force on shore for the exchange. Burton wanted less. He trusted Prince Rashid. I asked whether the eunuch could be trusted to obey the Prince's orders. Burton was certain he would. Ali arrived with the packages. The largest was a captain's uniform for Burton and the sight of it sent Burton into a hole. He set it down amongst the gifts and stared as if it were incriminating evidence to be disposed of. I had worn a uniform every day for over twenty years at that point and never questioned the need or the responsibility. For a moment I pitied Burton, realizing how far he had come and how long and difficult the road back would be for him.

"It was time I met Anouka. Burton asked for the payment and the passports, which I handed over. Leda disappeared for a moment. Before Anouka entered the small room, I heard, 'I haven't even finished my dinner. Are you saying my father's here?' When she was escorted in, she sat down in Leda's seat next to Burton.

"I'm a friend of your father's," I said. "I'm going to return you to him."

"'It's hard to imagine him having any friends. Can't I return to Prince Rashid? Have you ever been to Moldova? I can hardly breathe there.'

"You've been well treated?"

"'By some.' She looked darts at Leda.

"The door opened and Abdullah came in with apologies and the request for Burton to minister to a sick relative. Burton excused himself. That left Leda, Anouka and me. I got lost in the contrast between the two women and let the silence linger too long. Leda assumed she was in the way, and moved out to the balcony. Anouka answered a few more questions and when I was sure I had the correct woman she returned to her dinner. I went outside and stood beside Leda, close to her, close enough, Reynolds.

"From the balcony we could see the harbor and H.M.S Cyclops with the Union Jack lifeless in the dead air. Want to guess what was on my mind, Reynolds? Standing next to her, alone with her. I doubt you have to at this point. Leda did not have to guess either."

"He won't stay long in that uniform," I said.

"'"But once he puts it on he has to obey you.'

"It's a formality."

"'"Yes, a formality until he puts it on, then it's a manacle. But he must know that and he'll wear it anyway.' Another ship was entering the harbor, this one with a Greek flag. 'You're very confident, you English,' she said. 'A more insecure ruler would insist that some sailors on every ship in harbor fan the flag to keep it from hanging limp.'

"I'll bring it up."

"She kept leaning on the wall and barely turned her head my way. It was oddly intimate, as if she were an old friend, completely at ease. 'He thinks he can trust you now. He takes your word. Why? As… an English gentleman?'

"Her scorn was as casual as her posture. If any of my hopes breathed, her question suffocated them. It was the last completely foolish thought I ever had and it haunted me… Haunts me."

Hodgson seemed to sink into himself. I was reminded of his description of the miserable, piteous inmates of the opium den in Herat. I thought he might end the story right there but he straightened himself, stifled a cough and went on.

"Do you think Burton is a fool?" I said to her. "No, but you fear that I am. He's a great man and a very, very lucky one. I won't betray him again, or you."

"Leda turned to me. Her eyes, usually so calm, tightened with pleading. 'Why? Why does he believe you?'

"Perhaps because he knows I'm not an English gentleman."

"I wished I could give her more, but I did not know why he could trust me, only that he could. We hold that over women, don't we. Like a threat. Our little mystery."

Hodgson fell silent. With much effort he turned his shoulders and head toward the mountains, as if checking that they were still there. He shrugged. "Burton insisted that he escort me through the souk himself this time and back to the ship. The eunuch jumped when he saw us, but Burton told me to ignore him. 'He won't dare go against the Prince,' Burton said. But Bashir did follow us with two others – the Gassims, I was told – who seemed to particularly hate Burton. Burton's mind was elsewhere: the Nile expedition.

"'Leda will come along. She'll be a help. She can learn languages as well as I can.'

"You'll have to be constantly protecting her."

"'Well, it would be worse in England. I want her with me, Hodgson. I need her with me. And this way I won't be longing to come back.'

"I should have thought longing to come back an important part of making it back."

"'Happiness isn't fragile, Hodgson. It wants to be used.'

"Who was I to tell him I understood, but that it would never work? Burton could do things I could never imagine. He was happy. Happiness has always made me skeptical. At the time I thought only fools took it seriously. Now I know that only fools don't."

Hodgson mused on that and Ali stepped into the breach. "It was time to say our goodbyes. We would be leaving in the morning. Mr. Burton thanked our hosts and gave them an English tea set because they were curious about English habits regarding tea. Goat's milk did not go well with it, though. He gave Abdullah and Hossein each a sword. For Abdullah he also had a rifle, called a Sharps rifle, very good for long distance, he said. And for Hossein he had a pistol, an American Colt revolver. Abdullah made a joke about Hossein, the hothead, being better off having to reload – and maybe reconsider – between each shot.

"Danesh was waiting. He had been sulking, knowing that he had to say goodbye to Anouka. She, seeing that he could no longer help her, had been shunning him brazenly. Mr. Burton handed Danesh a package wrapped in paper tied with a string.

"His Darwaysh robe!

"I was consumed with jealousy. Danesh was the anointed one. Mr. Burton did not so much as glance my way.

"'You'll grow into it, Danesh,' he said. 'You've taken the first steps. Let your heart heal, but remember the pain.'

"Danesh cried and hugged Mr. Burton while I fumed. Leda noticed, of course, and took my hand.

"The brothers acceded this time to Mr. Burton's request that they get away before he left in the morning. Once he was gone, they would be in danger, there was no telling how the Prince or the Gassims would react. Mr. Burton told them again that they had redeemed Faris's soul and they all swore their eternal brotherhood and their prayers for each other's well being.

"Mr. Burton turned to Sa'ad. 'You have courage and wisdom and true strength. You have love in your heart. You, too, are my brother.'

"He handed over a sheet of thick paper filled with writing. Sa'ad was puzzled. Mr. Burton gently took it back from him and read. It was a passport. It described Sa'ad – Sa'ad al Djinn – as a black man over six feet tall, and entitled him to be treated as a subject of Queen Victoria. 'With this you can travel the world, with me or without. You have an open invitation for as long as you live.'

"Sa'ad lifted Mr. Burton off the floor in joy and bellowed his gratitude and praise for the great Darwaysh. I'm sure the entire souk heard him. He hugged each brother in turn. They were small men and disappeared in his arms. He hugged our hosts. He boasted of the adventures he was going to partake. India! China! Places I never heard of. He looked at Leda and wanted to hug her. He looked to Mr. Burton for permission. Mr. Burton said to ask her. Sa'ad did and she accepted and he embraced her as delicately as a man that big could.

"Next, Mr. Burton turned to me. He spoke in English – my first lesson beside the singing. I couldn't understand anything he said. I looked from face to face and they were all smiling but I knew they couldn't understand. I knew that. Mr. Burton then handed me a passport like the one he gave to Sa'ad. At last, through his actions and everyone's expressions I understood: I was to come with him and Leda. Wherever they went. I cried terribly and, embarrassed, ran into another room."

Tears formed in Ali's eyes as he told it all these years later. He didn't try to hide them but I looked away at Hodgson: sallow, weak and small. Weak beyond the hope of exertion, suddenly not the fearsome, cunning spy I'd come to know. This was not the time for rest, though. I was not going to allow him out of his seat until he took me through the end of the story. He nodded as if he read my thoughts – as he so often did.

32.

"We left the ship and arrived in the square just at the Muezzin's call. Before the stalls were set up, before the trading began. A troop of eight and me. All that Burton would allow. The Prince's creature, Bashir, had already stationed himself opposite the souk and four other guards loitered between the souk and the harbor. None of them left for prayers. I deployed two men flanking the exit from the souk where Burton would arrive. Four stood to the west, backs to the ship – they had the Prince's booty which I put into an impressive looking chest and ordered two men to carry it so it looked heavy. Two to the north, on either side of Bashir, because Prince Rashid would be arriving from the south."

Ali interrupted. "I came out first. Remember?"

"Yes. You were there." Hodgson seemed thankful for the correction.

"I was worried about Bashir. I'd seen his cruelty in action."

Hodgson said, "Prince Rashid rode in with about twenty others. About ten dismounted and took defensive positions around the Prince. Five others moved close to Bashir. We waited for Burton."

"Mr. Burton had gone to prayers. In his British uniform," Ali said.

"Others began filtering through the square, but I gestured to Prince Rashid and he ordered his men to shoo the intruders away.

Then, at last, Sa'ad showed himself. He checked in each direction and, satisfied, reached back and brought out Anouka. Burton, in uniform, followed next with Leda. I was ready to deliver..."

Ali interrupted again. "Bashir aimed his rifle at Mr. Burton the moment he came out. Mr. Burton let go of Leda and moved a few steps away and stared openly, defiantly, at Bashir."

"Yes, and I stepped between them with two soldiers behind me toting the loot over to Prince Rashid. He dismounted. I asked him if he wanted to see the money or count it but he said it was in my interest to pay him the correct amount. He had other things on his mind: Burton. His men took the chest of loot. I stepped aside. Burton came forward."

"And Bashir tracked him all the way like a hunter. But Prince Rashid saw him and shouted, 'Do not harm him.' Bashir lowered his rifle."

Hodgson said, "Prince Rashid and Burton embraced. The Prince admired his uniform. Burton said, 'Lucky for you not to wear one.'

"The Prince answered him, 'Well, we each have our constraints. I wish this could have been different...'

"Burton began quoting, '*Perhaps... out beyond ideas of wrongdoing and rightdoing...*

"'*...there is a field. I will meet you there.*' A poem of some kind that they shared. They stared into each other's eyes for a long moment. Then the Prince turned abruptly and mounted. Before he rode away he admonished Bashir again. 'Do not harm him.'"

Ali took over. "And all the while Sa'ad was watching Bashir. Ready to pounce on him. I thought it a miracle that he stayed silent."

"We only had to get back to the ship then, with Anouka. But Bashir remained and with him the Gassims and others," Hodgson said.

Now Ali and Hodgson became a chanting chorus. Not rehearsed, but in harmony with each other, as if they were there outside the souk. As if they were watching it all unfold once again.

Ali: "And Anouka was not silent. She whined. She wanted to go with the Prince. To Leda she said, 'I don't really want to go home. I never liked it there. I couldn't have anything and it's cold, which I detest. Surely, you can understand not wanting to return to your parents.'

"The cruelty of it startled Sa'ad, and though Leda remained still, he let go of Anouka thinking Leda might need his support."

Hodgson: "Anouka ran shouting after Prince Rashid. But he was too far away to hear her, or he pretended he didn't. Anouka shifted and ran toward one of the Prince's men standing near Bashir. Sa'ad lumbered that way, intent on dragging her back."

Ali: "Mr. Burton yelled out for Sa'ad to stop. He was still at the spot where he'd met the Prince. Leda stepped forward but she stopped, too, next to Sa'ad."

Hodgson: "Burton walked calmly toward Anouka. Bashir turned the rifle on him. Burton kept walking."

Ali: "Bashir was shaking. You could see it. I think the Prince's command was all that was stopping him."

Hodgson: "Burton kept coming forward. The others turned their weapons on him. He kept coming."

Ali: "And then Leda rushed toward Mr. Burton to stop him. I don't think he saw her."

Hodgson: "She looked back at Bashir. Maybe to see if she had time to reach Burton."

Ali: "Bashir, I could see him stop shaking. See him, like time stopped. His eyes met Leda's."

Hodgson: "Just the slightest swing of his rifle. One shot. One shot."

They stopped. Hodgson's breathing became shallow and thin. Ali put a reassuring hand on his arm. Neither of them would meet my eyes. Hodgson reached out for his tea, sipped and made an effort to straighten up.

"The entire square fell silent except for the boots of my soldiers pounding the stones as they rushed forward. Without an order they stopped and faced Bashir and the others. Then Anouka began screaming. Just screaming. I went forward and grabbed her away from the guard. He didn't resist.

"Burton knelt beside Leda and lifted her head. She tried to speak, but couldn't make any sounds. Think of it. Think of it. He looked into her eyes and watched her die. A second time. She died twice and so did he. How much of anyone is there? Twice! Gently, he put her down. He rose and marched toward Bashir who was furiously trying to reload. One of the Gassims, the tall one, shot at Burton but only nicked his shoulder. I shouted out to my troops, "Kill anyone who tries to stop him!"

Ali said, "Prince Rashid and his retinue rode back then. The Prince shouted to his men to hold their fire. He was horrified. I could see it. The Gassims lowered their weapons."

"Burton advanced. Bashir had not reloaded. He swung the rifle at Burton but Burton caught it with one hand and ripped it away from him and tossed it aside. He grabbed Bashir's throat. He squeezed. He lifted Bashir and slammed him on the ground and pounced. Over and over, he slammed the eunuch's head onto the stones. No one dared step in. No one took so much as a step forward. We stood in awe, with dumb respect for the savagery. For the merciless, feral purity. Burton was something else, something I'd never seen. He tore Bashir's throat out. Blood coated Burton. I'd been on battlefields. I'd seen things, but… Burton's mouth opened and a sound came out, a cry, but it was… inhuman. It was agony itself. And just as suddenly he stopped as if the fire had gone out or some beast inside him died. He just stopped and sat in the blood beside the corpse. His head down.

"Sa'ad came forward then and lifted Burton and carried him to the ship."

33.

Hodgson was not well. Even his cough was weak. Food was brought up to him but he hardly touched it. I sat near his bed wondering how to ask the all the questions I still had. I was encouraged that he was back to changing the subject, avoiding giving answers and generally being difficult.

"Do you think it would be too sentimental of me to return to England to die?" he said.

"Entirely."

"I do like you, Reynolds. Are you sure you're American?"

He asked me to send down to the harbor for passage on the next ship leaving for England. "You were right, Reynolds. They don't want me there, except to make certain I'm dead. Pins in the corpse. That's why I have to go. Last official mission."

Ali and I took a morning hike toward the mountains and he filled me in on some details. H.M.S. Cyclops had dropped them at Suez and they traveled overland to Alexandria. Burton was not well so they rested there for days. During that time Burton told Hodgson everything, every detail of his adventure, beginning with Isfahan and all the way through Jiddah. That is how Hodgson knew so much. Once Burton was well enough, they caught a ship to Naples. Hodgson took Anouka with him to Budapest where she was delivered to her father. Burton went on to Boulogne where Isabel was staying. That's where Ali first met her, before the marriage.

"She was kind to me from the start," Ali said. "Very kind. And so much in love with Mr. Burton and he needed that, though he would never admit it. I could see it. I prayed that he would marry her. He never referred again to what happened in Arabia, to what really happened and I knew not to bring it up. Sometimes, though, I would catch him looking at me and I knew where his thoughts were. Maybe that was why he kept me around."

"It sounds like he cared deeply for you, Ali."

"I know." He nodded and regained his composure. We finished our lunch and rose to start back. Ali's mood lightened. "Sa'ad left us in Naples. Some Garibaldi-ist militia group asked him to join the fight alongside them. Sa'ad couldn't resist. None of us ever saw him again. But when Mr. Burton was consul in Damascus he traveled the countryside, stopping in the smaller villages, as he liked to do, and one storyteller told of a huge black man who fell in love with a European woman and when her parents discovered their love, killed her, or so he thought..."

The lobby of the hotel held a surprise: Daisy Letchford. And more surprising than her presence was her cordiality. As false as that was – and it was obviously false – so true and honest was my skepticism. She claimed it was all a coincidence. She wanted a brief respite before sailing for England. She was traveling on the same ship Hodgson was booked on. What were my plans?

"Wide open. I was thinking of going to England, as well. What a delightful coincidence this is."

Coyness set in. I excused myself, telling her I hoped we could take a hike together tomorrow. She gave me a meek 'perhaps.'

I mentioned her presence to Hodgson. He smiled and his eyes twinkled with mischief. "Somehow she got the impression that you possess the much coveted *Scented Garden* manuscript. Weep for me openly, Reynolds. It will make her think she can take advantage of you."

He asked me not to leave. "They're going to bring my dinner. I hate ignoring it alone." He paused, then said, "Go ahead with your questions."

I decided to loosen him up with an easy one. "Did Anouka's father provide the information he said he would?"

"He did. Elaborately."

"Did it make the difference you hoped for in the war?"

"The war office failed to pass the information along to the Generals involved. I knew better than to ask why."

"On the ship coming back, after he recovered, before you parted…"

"Come now, Reynolds, are you trying to kill me now that you have the manuscript? I hardly have the strength to go through all that again."

I didn't answer him, knowing there was more to come. He didn't take long. "Burton said, 'my wishes killed her.' That's what he said. Will that do? I took it to mean she was the djinn, after all. And his wishes killed her. If you feel better for knowing it, you'll be the only one."

"How did you come to know of the manuscript?" I tried to make it sound like a casual inquiry, like I only wanted to change the subject.

"How could a man like Burton, who wrote so much, wrote three volumes on the Hajj alone, not write an account like that?"

"I wonder why he didn't publish it. Burton was not a man to be afraid of consequences."

"Burton was a wreck and Isabel saved him. Far more than I did. She understood him, understood his needs. It was Isabel who brought him back to life. And, Burton had no gift for betrayal. Not like you or me, Reynolds. Sort of an extra limb we have. Publication would have hurt her. Burton couldn't do that."

That was a classic Hodgson answer: every word true and yet, not the truth, not the truth I asked for. "But how did you come to see it?"

He picked at his food. Looked at me. Dropped his fork. I ignored the fork and so did he. At last I said, "You wrote it."

"I should have thought you could tell from its paltriness," he said.

"No. Only because it isn't finished. You wanted to send it to him but you couldn't send him the whole story. You couldn't bear that. You couldn't bear hurting him. Just for the same reason you didn't betray him a second time in Jiddah. The reason Leda worried over."

"And just what is that?"

"You're a romantic, Colonel. Burton gambled that you could feel some of what existed between him and Leda and that you would go to the greatest lengths not to damage it. Betray him? Burton knew it was one of the few great moments of your life just being near it."

"Do shut up, Reynolds."

"Did he read it? Did he tell you he read it?"

"No." Then, "Of course he did. Destroy that manuscript, Reynolds. I can't do it but I… why hurt the merry widow now? I've lost track of whether she deserves it or not. I only know he didn't want the story told."

I wondered when he went from wanting to keep Mrs. Burton from destroying the manuscript, to wanting to insure she never saw it.

Hodgson died that night. Ali and I found him in the morning and before notifying anyone we went through his belongings, removing his correspondence and code books. In the inside pocket of his jacket, I found a small, snakeskin wallet – white squares lined in black – and inside that a single sheet of paper. On it, in Burton's hand, was written *'So you do, after all, understand something of Friendship. And of Love. B.'*

I kept the paper and Ali kept the wallet as a keepsake. We made the arrangements to send the body to a family plot in Warwickshire.

As Hodgson suggested, I wept for him in front of Daisy Letchford and it had the desired effect. My heartache was real enough and she faked her sympathy well. But when she made noise about accompanying me back to Washington, I got cold feet. Undoubtedly, she would have searched my cabin and I couldn't risk her finding Hodgson's manuscript. That was my excuse to myself, anyway.

Before sailing I called on Mrs. Burton. It was a brief meeting. Her arrangements for Burton's burial in England were accelerating and keeping her in motion. The news of Hodgson's death elicited little more than a shrug. I reassured her that I never had any intentions of finding *The Scented Garden*.

"Also, if I may, I want to tell you that Mr. Hodgson, just before he died asked me to tell you that he regretted his role in Burton's Arabian adventure and more than that, regretted the stories he told afterward. They weren't true and that haunted him."

Mrs. Burton's mouth dropped open and her eyes squinted with doubt. Maybe she couldn't believe Hodgson apologized, but I didn't take it that way. I think she was shocked that he lied to me. That she knew it was all true.

She said, "Love always tells the truth, Mr. Reynolds."

Mrs. Burton was not a woman given to irony.

When I arrived in Washington I handed over the material I had extorted from Hodgson, telling my superiors that I'd stolen it all from the British consulate in Trieste – thus my delinquent return – by tricking a clerk there named Jenkins.

Not long after the turn of the century and a few promotions, I retired a Colonel. Ali and I started a business importing foods and wine from Italy to the U.S. I saw him often. He died six years ago. No one is left alive who could be hurt by this story so I decided to publish it. We're in the Great War now and England is our ally. Hodgson is long forgotten.

I thought when I left the Army I was done with my spying but I found that I missed it. So on my many trips to Europe I made it my business to build a web of informants. I missed the lies and the liars. I missed the intrigue and the dangers. I missed the stories. I didn't want to lose all that Hodgson had taught me.

And, I realized over time that I, too, am a romantic.

Glossary

Aakal – a twisted bit of rope or yarn to keep one's kerchief in place

Aba - long skirted and short sleeved cloak of camel's hair

Akit - dried sour milk dissolved in water

album graecum - dung of dogs or hyenas that has become white through exposure to air. It is used in dressing leather

Al-Eddeh – the costume donned by pilgrims before entering Mecca

Alhamdulillah – praise be to God

Al-Hijaz – the western region of Arabia in which Burton traveled

Al-Ihram – the ceremony in which pilgrims bathe and dress themselves before entering Mecca

Assafoetida – a herb used for flavoring

Bab al-Ziyadah – one of nineteen gates to the Grand Mosque in Mecca, this one close to the Ka'aba

Badawin – Bedouin

Bakhshish – a tip, or a charitable gift, or a bribe depending on the circumstance

Calcutta Khitmugar – a butler or man-servant

Catafalque – framework upon which a coffin is laid

Charay – a short, curved and pointed sword from Persia

chevaux de fries – a bulwark fortified with pikes or swords. Burton uses the phrase metaphorically here

Darwaysh – a Sufi holy man. In English, a dervish

Dhoti – type of sarong that outwardly resembles trousers, it is a lower garment forming part of the national or ethnic costume for men in the Indian subcontinent.

Fleam – a blade used for bloodletting

Halaled - referring to food that has been prepared according to religious law

Harim – Burton uses Harim to refer to the Kaabah, the center of prayer in Mecca

Ifrit – a winged demon from hell

Iirjae – return (a command)

Isha – an evening prayer

Izar – Burton uses this to refer to a cloth donned as part of the ritual before entering Mecca. It wraps around the waist and down to the knee. More commonly it refers to a sarong like gown worn by women in parts of the Arab world

Jambiyah – a dagger with a short, curved blade

Jammu – a city in (then) northern India territory Jammu and Kashmir

Jubbah – a long sleeved, ankle length robe worn by men

Kaabah – the square building in the center of the Great Mosque of Mecca. The most sacred site in Islam

Kahk – a sweet bread

Kamis – a long outer robe for men

Kefiyah – Kufiyah – a large square kerchief of silk and cotton mixed

Labbayk – a prayer of submission recited by pilgrims before entering Mecca

Lancet- a small surgical knife

Lisam – the part of the head scarf which covers the mouth and chin

mafish – nothing

Maghrabi – Arabs from northwestern Africa

Mas'hab – stick used for guiding camels

Mikat – the point at which pilgrims must stop and prepare themselves for entering Mecca

Misyals – stony ramps, like passes, between hills

Muezzin – a man who calls Muslims to prayer from the minaret of a mosque

Nabbut – a long, thick stick used as a weapon, sometimes four feet long

Nizam – Burton uses this term for Turkish soldiers. More often it refers to Mughal royalty from Hyderabad

Pathan – Muslims from the area where India (now Pakistan) met Afghanistan

Petrale – a type of sole

Rais – ship's captain

Sakkas – the traditional water carriers at the Great Mosque in charge of the well of Zemzem

Salam – peace, as a greeting

Sambuk – a sailing ship, a dhow

Sammun – a dry, harsh, hot wind

Sar – blood revenge

Shugduf – a litter placed on the camel's back in which a rider (or two) can be comfortable

Suk – the bazaar in Jiddah

Sulaymanian – Soloman-like

Tahlil – a prayer meaning 'there is no deity but God'

Takbir – The phrase 'Allahu akbar' – Allah is great

Talbiyat – a prayer promising to perform the Hajj for the glory of Allah

Tawaf – the circling of the Kaabah seven times

Wadi – a dry riverbed or gully

Wahabbis – followers of a conservative sect in Sunni Islam

Wakaleh – a section of Cairo where Burton found lodging. It forms a neighborhood

Wishah - scarf

za'abut – the Darwaysh robe

Zemzemiya – a goat skin water bag

Afterword

My thanks to Bill Spiro, Sue Schoenfeld, Rick Wilkof, and Howard Blum for reading the manuscript and for their helpful advice and criticism. Also to Alan Holleb for his research and consultations on harems.

Richard Francis Burton's adventures had fascinated me for many years and I'd tinkered with different stories about him until I read a letter his niece, Georgiana Stisted, wrote which mentioned that Burton had fallen deeply in love with a Persian woman whose parents had killed her when they discovered the affair. That woman became Leda. I found no record of her true name.

Reynolds, Hodgson, and Ali are fictions. Isabel Burton did burn many of Burton's papers after his death. She also arranged to have a generator attached to the corpse in the hope of rehabilitating it.

The sections which Reynolds reads and which appear in italics are taken directly from Burton's journal "Personal Narrative of a Pilgrimage to Al-Madinah and Meccah." I left Burton's spelling intact. And when Burton speaks in other parts of the book, I kept his spelling there, too.

The found manuscript is fictional.

For those interested in learning more about Burton I recommend “The Devil Drives” by Fawn M. Brodie, and “Captain Sir Richard Francis Burton” by Edward Rice.

Thank you
David Rich

About the Author

David Rich is the author of two previous novels, "*Caravan of Thieves*" and "*Middle Man.*" Much of his writing life has been spent in the film and television business in the U.S. and Europe. He lives in Connecticut where he teaches in a graduate writing program.

Printed in Great Britain
by Amazon

87194298R00174